Blood on the Marsh

Blood on the Marsh

Peter Tickler

ROBERT HALE · LONDON

© Peter Tickler 2012
First published in Great Britain 2012

ISBN 978-0-7090-9907-9

Robert Hale Limited
Clerkenwell House
Clerkenwell Green
London EC1R 0HT

www.halebooks.com

2 4 6 8 10 9 7 5 3 1

Typeset in 11/14.75pt New Century Schoolbook
Printed and bound in Great Britain by MPG Books Ltd

ACKNOWLEDGEMENTS

This is my third crime novel, and yet the first time I have acknowledged anyone, so perhaps first I should apologize to and thank the various people who have helped and supported me practically and emotionally over the past two novels. My wife, Fiona, has put up with and encouraged my writing habits, even at the most inconvenient of times, and for that I thank her with all my heart. Not to mention Aenaone, Oswin, Ben, Hugo, Simon and Penny. I could go on, but I am reminded of an anecdote when some notable said to Churchill something along the lines of 'Winston, I don't think I've told you about my grandson' and he replied, quick as a flash, 'And don't think I'm not grateful!'

As for this book, I have received technical advice from Martin Brodetsky, Simon Lubin of the British Transport Police, and Dr Aenaone Wearn. If I have – deliberately or otherwise – misused their advice and information, the fault is entirely mine.

As for the geography of Oxford, I try very hard to be authentic, but occasionally I do just make buildings and streets up. And my human characters are all pure fiction (though not the dogs).

PROLOGUE

'Stupid! Stupid! Stupid!'

Nanette Wright was teetering on the edge. If there had been a Richter scale for temper, hers would have been right up there at the top end – 9.5 pushing 10. Not that a close observer of her behaviour would have been surprised – and there had been several of those recently. For the truth of the matter was that ever since she had arrived at the Sunnymede Care Home some six months previously, the tectonic plates which kept her nature under control had come under increasing pressure. And today they were on the verge of collapsing altogether.

'Stupid! Stupid! Stupid!'

She clasped her hands to her head, and screamed inside. God! First there had been that wretched nurse, Bella. She thought she was the bee's knees, that one did, but she was nothing more than a jumped-up skivvy, an auxiliary. It was common knowledge that she'd only got the job because of her sister. Half the time she flounced around pretending she was Florence Nightingale reincarnated. That was bad enough. But recently she had become a complete cow, slagging her off something terrible just because she'd had the slightest accident. Well, wasn't that what she was paid to do? To clear up after accidents?

As for Bella's sister, Fran, she was no better, lecturing her about not leaving her food. Well, she'd eat it if it wasn't so inedible half the time! Maybe the disgusting dyke should sort out the kitchen staff, and leave old ladies like herself alone.

Nanette leant over to her side table, pulled open the middle drawer and fumbled around until she found what she was looking for. She pulled it out, leant back against her pillows, and grimaced. She didn't feel too good. She hadn't done so for a while. Not that anyone here seemed that bothered. They all pretended, of course, but she could see through that. Only Dr Featherstone seemed genuinely concerned. But then he was no spring chicken himself, and he could appreciate that old age is no fun. Still, life had its compensations, and she was holding one of them in her hands – a hip flask. Her husband Ronnie had bought it in Brighton years ago, but he was dead so now it was hers. And what a lifeline it had become, stuck as she was in this miserable nursing home, with her aching bones and decaying flesh. Old age! What she'd give to be young again! But at least she could have a drink to keep her spirits up. She unscrewed the cap, and took a swig. It stung the back of her throat, and she instantly felt better. She took another, and then another.

Well, she'd show them. She'd show them all. She'd put in a formal complaint. That'd serve them right.

And she took another swig.

'Stupid! Stupid! Stupid!'

They were the last words of Nanette Wright. Or rather, they weren't, because words are either written or spoken, and these were neither.

Admittedly, they appeared as thoughts in her raddled brain, but only milliseconds before a tsunami of nausea engulfed her body. They rose nevertheless to her lips which pursed and twitched and contorted in a vain attempt to bring them into uttered life. But they never became words. And even if they had, and even if someone had been at her bedside to hear them, to whom would they have referred? To Bella the negligent nurse? Or Fran? Or maybe to a member of her family (her son,

if the truth be told, was a front runner in the stupidity stakes)?
Or even, perhaps, to herself?

'Stupid! Stupid! Stupid!'

The last words she never spoke.

CHAPTER 1

It is Tuesday 1 December in the year 2009, about 8.50 in the evening. Oxford United are losing at Crawley, and our main rivals Stevenage Borough are beating Ebbsfleet, and my world is falling apart.

And my mobile is ringing. S H I T!

I ignore it at first, turning up the radio in the hope that this will somehow shut the caller up, and that whoever it is will get the idea and go away. But it refuses to stop. So I pick it up to see who it is. It's Mum! What is she doing ringing me now, today, at this time? She knows I'll be listening to the football. I saw her on Sunday, and I'll see her tomorrow, like I always do on Wednesdays. So why the hell is she ringing me now?

The phone stops eventually. After eight rings. That's how I've set it, to switch to the answering system after eight rings. Not that I am counting the rings, because I am too busy listening to the commentary, and ... 'Yes!' I begin to yell and scream. Max, who lives in the flat below me, won't like it, but who cares? Ebbsfleet have equalized against Stevenage. The tide is turning. 'Come on you Yellows!' I go to the fridge, pull out another can and sit down again. I can feel the adrenalin fizzing round my system like cherryade.

Then, wonder of wonders, Ebbsfleet score again, so Stevenage are losing. 'Yes!' I shout and swig and jump up and down all at pretty much the same time. Some of my drink ends up on the floor, but who the hell cares?

The commentator on Radio Oxford is getting excited. Oxford are applying the pressure, but time is slip-sliding past. We've got to get the ball into the net. And fast. And then, unbelievably, we score. Goal! Get in there! Oxford 1, Crawley 1. The commentator is screaming, and he, I and every Yellows fan worthy of the name unite in celebration. Take that, you Crawley bastards!

But the mobile is ringing again. Would you believe it? There are only ten minutes to go and it's Mum again. Should I or shouldn't I? What on earth is she ringing again for? I am tempted to press the red button, but I can't do that, not to her. So I answer it. I'll keep it short, and then I'll be able to listen to the rest of the game in peace.

'David Wright here,' I say. I always say that when I answer my phone. Even when it's my mum ringing.

'David.' Her voice is faint and somehow odd. 'Something has happened.'

'What?'

'Something very sad has happened.'

Christ, can't she get to the point? 'What has happened?'

'It's Nan.' Mum is having trouble saying whatever it is she wants to say. And I'm having trouble hearing her because the guy on the radio is going nuts again. We've got a penalty. 'She's dead,' she says finally.

'What do you mean?' I say.

'Nan Nan has died.'

I say nothing at first. It's hard to think with the radio blaring like that. And then, shit! Would you fucking believe it? Beano has missed the penalty. Oh my God!

'Shall I come round?' I say eventually.

'Oh, yes please.'

'OK.' I terminate the call, and then power off the phone. I take a final swig from my can, drop it on the floor, and jump on it with both feet. Once, twice, three times. Not that there's any need because it was pancake flat after the first jump. I pick it up, and take it to the blue recycling box. Then I sit down, and turn up

the volume one more notch. How the hell can Beano have missed a penalty? We are into injury time. And now the guy on the radio is screaming. He is going absolutely sodding bonkers. We've scored again. A header by Beano. Genius! Brilliant! 2–1. We've only gone and won the game! We're still top. Five points clear and a game in hand. Promotion here we come! And I shout as loudly as I possibly can so that everyone else in the flats will know my joy.

I go to the loo, have a piss, and then I turn my mobile back on. I key in a message – 'On my way' – and I send it to my favourite.

The stalker had stamina, that was for sure. He had parked his car – a T-Reg Peugeot – in Lytton Road at 7.00 p.m. that Wednesday evening. His quarry might be in the house, or might not. The curtains were drawn, so it was impossible to know. He would just have to wait and hope. At 9.30 p.m. he was still there, patiently waiting, but an increasingly noisy part of his mind – not to mention his bladder – was telling him he might as well give up for the night and try again another time. He looked at his watch. He'd give it until 10.00 p.m. That would be his limit. It would leave him time to go and get a well-deserved pint. But as it was, he had only two more minutes to wait, before the front door opened and his quarry emerged.

He recognized him instantly from the photos: tall and angular, black hair cropped short, circular glasses, and a loping gait that made him stand out from the crowd. Not that there was a crowd. Lytton Road was never a place for crowds, and certainly not on a damp winter night. He slipped out of the car, locked it, and lit a cigarette. The cigarette wasn't just the result of a craving. He had had one inside the car only ten minutes earlier, but he needed to look busy, just in case his quarry turned round. But the man was walking enthusiastically away from him, arms swinging like a pair of pendulums, towards Rymers Lane, on his way home, or so the stalker hoped. It had been easy to find out where his parents lived, but where he lived himself, that was what he wanted to find out now. He started to pad in pursuit, at first very steadily, and then accelerating as his quarry disappeared to the right, up Rymers Lane towards the car park. The pursuit lasted some ten minutes, threading its way across Between Towns Road, up the hill of Beauchamp Lane, and into Littlemore Road before turning sharp left into Bartholomew Road, and right along to its end. Here the stalker hurried again, as his quarry jogged across Barns Road before turning right past the deserted children's playground and along the damp pavement for some fifty metres. Finally he veered off to the left, taking a diagonal path that led to a compact three-storey block of flats. Here he stopped, keyed in a number and pushed open the main door. His pursuer, who had chosen not to cross the road, but instead to track along the opposite pavement, cursed, aware that he couldn't possibly, at that distance, see the combination entered. Nevertheless he stood and waited, and was rewarded thirty seconds later by a light being switched on in one of the top floor rooms. He watched a figure come to the window and pull first one curtain and then the other. He nodded with satisfaction. Just one more thing to do. Now it was his turn to jog across the road and walk up to the main door. There he stopped, pulled a torch out of his pocket, and checked through the name tags against each number. There, near the bottom, was the one he was looking for: D. Wright. He turned and began to walk back whence he had come, pulling his mobile out of his pocket. He must tell her what he had discovered. She'd be pleased. Maybe she'd be so pleased that she'd let him stay.

Bella Sinclair's body moved. For the previous seven and a half hours it had lain as still as death, a warm corpse in a dishev- elled sea of bedding. Occasionally the violent shock of ginger hair would twitch, as if to demonstrate proof of life, but other- wise nothing. It was Wednesday, and it was Bella's day off, and deep within her subconsciousness she knew that today she could lie in.

Outside, the sun suddenly emerged low and cool from behind the grey wintry cloud. Its light lanced through the gap in the curtains of Bella's bedroom and homed in on the flash of her hair, ruthlessly exposing the cheapness of the dye she had used. Not that there was anyone there to notice, for Bella had slept alone. For a second time her body stirred. This time it also uttered a low grunt, followed by a loud fart. Bella's lips adjusted themselves into a smile, and she wriggled down further into the bedding, unwilling to engage with the day. But her bladder had other ideas. It was demanding attention. She groaned, wrenched back the duvet cover, and rolled out of bed, stumbling with eyes half closed along the short, familiar route to the loo. And once there, she sat, thinking of nothing, until there was no need to continue sitting. She tore some paper from the roll, wiped herself, and staggered back towards her bed, in the hope of recreating the blissful refuge of sleep.

But sleep wouldn't come, for her brain had kicked into gear and was revisiting and reprocessing the phone call she had received from Roy Hillerby. Poor Roy. She should have asked him round after all he had done for her, at least given him some company. But he would have ended up staying, she knew that, and he would have wanted more than company, and that wasn't what she wanted. She should never have slept with him in the first place. It was a potent and dangerous combination feeling sorry for someone and feeling sorry for yourself. It led you down avenues that turned into dead ends, and then how the hell did you get out? She tried to close her mind to him, to everything. She pulled the duvet tighter round her, and screwed her eyes shut, but her peace had gone.

It was then that her mobile rang, shrill and insistent, its sound magnified by the silence of the room. She swore and rolled over, stretching her right arm towards the side table. She pressed the green button on her handset as it rang for the fourth time, registering as she did so that it was 9.43 a.m. and that the caller was not a familiar one.

'Is that Arabella Sinclair?' It was an unfamiliar voice too, and no one, but no one, called her Arabella.

'Are you selling something, because the answer is no.'

'This is not a sales call.' The woman spoke firmly, with an edge to her voice. 'This is Margaret Laistor. I'm the human resources manager at head office.'

Bella shivered. Margaret Laistor. She knew her. At least she knew the name, from the letter she had received when she had been hired, and from the occasional pedantic email that would appear in her inbox, with policies and codes of practice attached. What the hell did she want?

'It's my day off.'

'I do know,' the woman said.

An image of Ms Laistor materialized in Bella's brain – horse face, hair tied back tightly in a bun, and a nose that matched her stuck-up voice – and a flash of anger ran through her. What right had the cow to ring her at home on her day off? 'Can't it wait until tomorrow?' she demanded.

There was no immediate reply, merely the distant sound of breath being sucked in. 'I'm calling to inform you that you've been suspended.'

'You what?'

'With immediate effect,' the woman continued, toneless and emotionless – a female robot auditioning for the role of GPS voice. 'You will not go into work until allegations against you have been investigated.'

Bella was fully awake by now. With a single kick of her legs, she freed herself from the duvet and raised herself so that she was sitting upright on the edge of the bed. 'What allegations?' she demanded.

'All I can say for now is that, if proven, they would amount to gross misconduct.'

'What are you talking about?'

But Ms Laistor had said all she was going to say. 'I shall be posting a letter confirming our conversation later today. By special delivery. In the meantime, goodbye.'

Less than fifteen minutes later, Fran Sinclair stormed along the short stretch of corridor that separated her tiny office from the much less tiny office of Paul Greenleaf. He was the manager of the Sunnymede Care Home; she was the assistant manager, and she was steaming. She banged loudly on his door and pushed it wide open without waiting for a response.

Greenleaf was sitting at his desk, and his head resolutely refused to lift. He knew instinctively who it was, and he was pretty sure he knew exactly why she was there. He tensed himself for the onslaught.

'What the hell is going on?' She had advanced to the desk, placed both hands on its surface, and was leaning forward so as to get as close to him as her 158 centimetres would allow. Her body was stocky, her hair was short, dark and more than tinged with grey, and she was nobody's fool. 'Well?' she demanded, when there was no instant response.

Greenleaf lifted his head. His hair was longer than hers, falling almost to his shoulders. It framed a strikingly round face, but if his chin failed to jut aggressively, his eyes were hard and uncompromising. 'Ah!' he said, 'I can only assume from your manner that you have just heard the news about Bella.'

'Too right I have. She's just rung me and told me she's been suspended because of you.'

'Actually, she's been suspended because of herself.'

'You complained about her, you bastard! And now head office has gone and suspended her indefinitely.'

'We have to run a professional service. The fact that she is your sister does not put her outside the rules.'

Fran Sinclair's eyes had been locked on to his throughout this exchange, but now she dropped her gaze to the desk, as if unable to tolerate looking at him any more. It was then that she noticed the paperweight. She didn't recall having seen it before – a semi-globe of glass with some twisting greens and reds inside – but then she didn't make a habit of visiting Paul Greenleaf in his lair, not if she could avoid it. Her left hand shot forward and grabbed it, and almost in the same movement she stepped backwards, well out of his reach.

'Hey!' he said. 'Put it down.'

'When you've answered my questions.' She smiled at him, tossed the paperweight casually in the air and caught it, and then repeated the action, again and again. The feel of the object, satisfyingly heavy and smooth and so full of possibility, calmed her down. Raw anger gave way to something more calculating. 'What exactly has Bella done?' She spoke slowly and precisely. 'What did you say to head office? And why the hell didn't you discuss it with me first?'

'I didn't discuss it with you, firstly because you, as Bella's sister, have a clear conflict of interest, and secondly because I am the manager of Sunnymede and therefore the buck stops with me.'

'So what is Bella supposed to have done?'

'Some money has gone missing from Mrs Wright's room.'

'You mean Nanette Wright, who died?'

'Her son and daughter-in-law have complained that the fifty pounds that they gave her the day before her death was missing from her effects.'

'Are you saying Bella stole it? And what proof have you got anyway?'

'No absolute proof. But I have to take complaints seriously. Furthermore Mr Day's family are also unhappy about some bruising on his arms, and they too have complained to me and threatened to take it further. As you know, Bella cares for both these persons.'

'That doesn't mean she's responsible. There are plenty of others who go in and out of their rooms. Hell,' she sneered, 'even you visit patients occasionally!'

But Greenleaf was not to be distracted. 'Obviously, there will be an investigation, and that will determine Bella's guilt or otherwise, but for now she remains suspended from work, on full pay. However you, Fran, as my assistant manager, should be concerning yourself with this.' He pushed across the desk a ring-bound A4 booklet. 'It's the report on Sunnymede. As you will see, it's not entirely favourable, and—'

She cut across him as anger began to rise like an erupting geyser again. 'When did this come in?'

'Last week.'

'So why have you waited until now to let me see it?'

'I needed to read it, and reflect on it myself. And consider what steps we might take.'

'Ah! Of course. I see.' It was as if a light bulb had been turned on in Fran's brain. 'And the reporting of Bella is one of those steps, is it? She's the scapegoat to get you off the hook?'

'I'm not the only one in danger of dangling from a hook.' There was a note of menace in his voice, and he thrust his forefinger towards her. 'May I draw your attention to the criticism of our drugs regime and the quality of our food in the report. These are both areas that come specifically within your remit.'

He stopped talking and waited for her reaction. Initially there was none, for she too had fallen silent as she considered what he had said. Then she again tossed the paperweight in the air with her left hand and caught it with her right, before lobbing it suddenly at his head. Taken by surprise, he ducked and held up his hands to catch it at the same time. It hit his right hand, and then thudded onto the desk. 'Butterfingers!' she said scornfully, before picking up the report and marching out of his office.

Bella woke at 6.30 a.m. the following day. That was the time she always woke in order to get to work for 8.00, but there was, of course, no need today. Nevertheless, she swung herself out of bed, padded barefoot through to the kitchen, and turned on the kettle. She had plans for the day, plans to make the most of her enforced rest. In fact, her suspension could just turn out to be the best thing that had happened to her for a long time. And so it was that Bella Sinclair showered, dressed, breakfasted, brushed her teeth, and put on her make-up in just forty minutes, and left her flat even earlier than usual. And she did all of this with a feeling of expectation so powerful that it blotted from her consciousness the distress of the previous day. Look'forward, not back. That was her motto. She had been given an extraordinary opportunity, a second opportunity, and she had no intention of letting it slip. Paul Greenleaf could wait till later.

Detective Inspector Susan Holden paused in front of the door, took a deep breath, and knocked. She heard a muffled voice from inside, assumed it was an invitation to come in, and opened the door.

'Ah, Susan! How nice to see you.' Detective Superintendent Collins stood up. The tension inside Holden eased a fraction. First names and manners; it couldn't be a dressing down, then. 'Do be seated.' He waved towards the chair opposite his desk. She sat down, but her mind was slipping into panic mode. Maybe he was being nice because what he had to tell her was nasty. Ever since she had returned to work, she had had the feeling she was on probation, that after her six-month leave of absence, no one was quite sure if she could cut it any more. And now here she was, being summoned by the big cheese, with his big Cheshire cat grin and an unseen agenda.

'So, how are things?' the flashing teeth said.

'Things are fine, thank you, Sir.'

'You're sure about that?'

Holden looked at him. She could give him a load of flannel or she could be straight. And flannel wasn't her style.

'Well, actually, since you ask, things aren't really fine.'

'Oh?' There was sudden interest in his voice. 'You mean

you're finding it difficult to slot back in after your ...' He paused, struggling to find the words. She waited, unwilling to give him any help. 'After your misfortune,' he concluded finally.

'Absolutely not,' she snapped back. 'I don't know what gave you that idea! I'm fully recovered.' The words came out automatically. She had rehearsed what she might say in such a circumstance, but she had failed to allow for the anger that · arose in her like an avenging fury. Misfortune! What sort of word was that for describing the death of Karen, the woman she had loved above all others? Misfortune? The patronizing git! She tried hard to rein in her emotions. She was aware that his eyes had narrowed. He was watching her, sizing her up. She needed to be careful. 'With respect, Sir, the fact is that I'm bored. I want to get back onto real detective work, not the Mickey Mouse stuff you've been funnelling my way. I didn't sign up for that. I want to solve real crimes.'

His eyebrows twitched – or appeared to do so. Holden wondered if she'd said too much, but there was no taking it back now, and besides, she didn't want to. He had summoned her, and this was her chance to say what she felt. She might not get another.

He leant back, steepled his fingers under his chin, and smiled. 'That's a very good sign, Susan, being bored. Just what I'd expect of a good officer. What you went through was make or break stuff. And the fact that you're bored, well I'm not a psychologist, but I'm pretty sure it's a damned good sign.'

'Thank you, Sir.' Holden wasn't quite sure what she was thanking him for. It had only been words so far. Nice words, but even so.

Collins picked up an A4 folder in front of him and passed it across the desk. 'This is for you. It's a suspicious death. An old lady dies in a nursing home. On first appearance, it all looks very straightforward. The only problem is that the pathology guys have found something unexpected inside her. Looks like it could be an accidental overdose or even murder.'

'Thank you, Sir.' This time she really meant it. The file in her hand was light, but her fingers were grasped tightly around it. This was her chance to get her career back on track.

'You're reporting directly to me on this, Inspector.' He switched from first name to rank with chilling swiftness. 'And Sergeant Fox will be working with you.'

'Thank you, Sir.' Now that she'd started thanking him, she couldn't stop.

'If you feel you need more help, whether it's more people on the ground or....' He paused again, apparently uncertain of the words to choose. 'Or if you need any other sort of help for yourself, then you ring me. Right?'

'Sir.'

'You do understand what I'm saying, Inspector?'

'I think do, Sir.'

'It's just that, if you take any more sick leave or special leave, it wouldn't be good for your prospects.'

'I understand.'

'I do hope so.'

For the second time that morning DI Holden found herself poised outside a rather unprepossessing wooden door. This time, at least, she had the comforting presence of Detective Sergeant Fox at her shoulder. Fox would never be the life and soul of any party, but as he had driven them over from Cowley station, he had been – for him – remarkably chatty. He had told her how pleased he was to be working with her again, and had waffled happily on about his sister's new house in Portsmouth. He had even started to recite the plot of the film *2010*. Holden could certainly have lived without that, but she had been content to let it run.

The pseudo-brass plate in front of her bore the name of Dr Charles Speight. She took a deep breath. Speight was Karen's successor, and it was impossible to be here without memories coming back. She knocked, and pushed open the door. Dr

Speight was a tall man, as quickly became apparent as he unfolded himself from his chair and rose in greeting. 'Detective Inspector Holden, I presume,' he purred, as he made his way round the desk and extended a hand. Holden took the handshake, firm and somewhat clammy.

'This is Detective Sergeant Fox,' she responded.

The two men locked hands. Fox himself was fractionally the shorter, but he carried more weight, and for a moment Holden had visions of them engaging in a trial of strength, each refusing to let go until the other was on his knees. But the handshake was brief, nothing more than the most perfunctory touching of flesh, the minimum the situation required.

At Speight's suggestion they sat down, but Holden was not a person to waste unnecessary time on formalities. 'I understand,' she said, plunging in, 'that there were irregularities in the death of Mrs Nanette Wright.'

'Irregularities?' Speight's voice was soft, sardonic and public school. 'I suppose that's one way of putting it.'

'If you want to put it another way, Doctor, that's your choice, but I'll stick to calling it irregularities.' Holden spoke assertively, thrusting her face forward as she did so. 'And you can stick to telling me what those irregularities are.' There was a short, impatient pause. 'If you don't mind.'

'Of course!' Speight had heard about Holden, about her relationship with his predecessor Karen Pickering, and about her extended period of sick leave following Karen's death, so he was prepared for her to be a bit prickly, but not this combative. 'At first sight, it looked like heart failure. Mrs Wright fell asleep early evening, or so it appeared, but when the nurse went in to tidy her up, she realized she was dead. The doctor who attended knew she had heart problems, but when he examined her he wasn't entirely happy about her symptoms, and so he asked for an autopsy. So, we conducted one and found a high concentration of morphine in her bloodstream.'

'And that killed her?'

'Yes.'

'You're sure?'

'Of course I am!' It was Speight's turn to get assertive now. Doubting his medical prowess was akin to questioning his manhood. 'If I wasn't certain, I would say so.'

'Point taken,' Holden said quickly. It was the closest thing to an apology he was going to get. 'So how much morphine does it take to kill someone?'

'That depends.' He paused. It was an annoying reply. At least he hoped it was annoying for the detective inspector; he still felt riled by her. But the fact was she needed his medical knowledge, so she'd have to blooming well be a bit nicer to him.

Holden didn't rise, though she sure as hell felt like it. In fact, she felt like giving him a bloody good slapping, or even better, doing something irreversible to his testicles with a large pair of pliers, but instead she buttoned her metaphorical lip and waited for him to continue in his own self-important time.

'Morphine provides pain relief, as I am sure you know. For example, one might give it to persons suffering from terminal cancers. As time goes on, the pain may increase and the body may get used to the morphine, so the dosage level has to be increased to be effective. However, in the case of an opiate-naive patient, that same level of dosage could be fatal.'

He paused, or rather stopped. He wanted a response, prob-ably a question about what opiate-naive meant, Holden reckoned, but she wasn't going to give him the satisfaction. 'So Mrs Wright wasn't on morphine?'

'I rang and spoke to a Ms Fran Sinclair at Sunnymede. She says not.'

'So how might this morphine have got into her system?'

'Well, injection is the most direct, but there's no sign of any puncture marks. I've checked for that. Otherwise, morphine comes in tablet and liquid form.'

'And how many tablets, for instance, would she have had to take to end up dead?'

'Maybe half a dozen.'

'And liquid?'

'Maybe thirty millilitres. Ten milligrams in a tablet is the equivalent of five millilitres.'

'And does morphine have a strong taste? I mean, if someone had slipped it into her tea or cocoa, would she have noticed?'

'That depends on her sense of taste.'

'Because either she administered it herself, to commit suicide. Or somebody else did, and in that case we're talking homicide or murder.'

Dr Speight shrugged dismissively. 'Well I guess that's your call, Inspector.'

CHAPTER 2

Yesterday was a strange day. Very strange. This woman came to my shop. Well, not my shop, Jaz's shop. She runs it, and I work there. It's called 'Frame It'. Because we frame pictures. We also sell frames, and pictures, and posters and display cases, but my job is to do the framing. I'm good at it.

Jaz is a friend of Mum's. I like her. She has blonde hair, and a thin oval face, and perfect teeth, and she calls me her left-handed right-hand man. She's funny too.

Jaz had popped out to Tesco. She always uses that expression. 'I'm going to pop out for a few minutes, David,' she says. 'You're in charge. I've got my mobile. If there are any problems, just ring me. OK?'

I don't like her to pop out for too long, in case things happen. So I am glad she always takes her phone. It makes me feel safe.

So, she had gone to Tesco, and I was sitting behind the desk in case anyone came in and wanted something. I can't make frames and look after customers at the same time. It's too much. Jaz agrees it's too much.

Anyway, almost as soon as Jaz has gone out, this woman walks in. She has long hair, longer than Jaz's, and it is bright ginger. I think it must be dyed. She is thin like Jaz, and is wearing jeans and a pink T-shirt, and a leather jacket, and she has a stud in her nose.

But what is odd is that she got on my bus that morning. I catch the Number 1 bus from Barns Road, opposite my flat, and I get off at the penultimate stop on the Cowley Road. I know it is the penultimate one because once I was so busy sending a text to Mum that I missed it, and I had to get off at the next one, just before the roundabout.

Anyway, the point is that the red-headed woman was at the bus stop that morning. There were five of us waiting. The other three were regulars, but I hadn't seen her before, so when we all got on the bus, I took out my notebook and I wrote down the date and time, and I drew a picture of her. It's a good picture. I'm good at drawing. I might show it to Mum later.

When I got off the bus, she got off too. I pretended not to notice, but it was hard not to stare at her red hair. And then, just after Jaz had gone to Tesco, she walked into the shop.

'Can I help you?' I said.

'Do you make frames here?'

It seemed a silly question to me. Wasn't it obvious we make frames? But Jaz says it is important to be polite to everyone, so I said 'Yes'.

'Good,' she said.

'Do you have the picture with you?' Now it was my turn to ask a silly question, because she wasn't carrying anything except a brown handbag that was slung over her shoulder. But maybe it was a very small picture.

'It's at home. I saw your shop, and I thought I'd drop in and ask.'

'I make the frames.' I couldn't think of anything else to say, but it is important to keep conversations with customers going. 'Whatever size you want.'

'Perhaps I can bring it in another day.'

I nodded. I really couldn't think of anything else to say.

She nodded too, and smiled. 'Do you have a business card?'

'No.' People didn't usually ask me for a business card. I wished Jaz would come back. I had three pictures I had to get framed, and I didn't want to be asked any more questions.

'What is your name?' she said.

'David Wright,' I said. That was an easy one to answer.

'And are you open on Monday?'

'Yes.'

'In that case, maybe I'll bring my picture in then, and you can frame it for me.'

Jim and Maureen Wright lived in an unprepossessing semi-detached house in Lytton Road. Built in the 1920s, it had been adapted more recently to the modern age: the front garden had been concreted over to provide a parking space for Jim's white van, and the windows were PVC and double-glazed. The only sign of nature was a pot of chrysanthemums by the front door. Holden pressed the bell, and heard from inside the eight-note call of the door chime. She winced. A few seconds later, the door was opened by a man barely an inch taller than she herself was. That was as far as the similarities went. He was considerably rounder than her in face and body, and he had a head from which every trace of hair had been ruthlessly removed.

Holden displayed her ID card. 'Detective Inspector Holden, and my colleague is Detective Sergeant Fox.'

He took the card, studied it as if it was a distinctly unconvincing fifty pound note, and then handed it back. 'I'm Jim Wright.'

'Can we come in?'

He led them along the short hall corridor, and through a door on the left that opened into the front room. 'Sit down if you want,' he said, without enthusiasm. 'I'll give the wife a call.'

But his wife needed no calling. She had materialized at the door behind them. 'God, you're quick, aren't you?'

Holden was thrown off balance by this greeting. As far as she was concerned, their visit ought to be a complete surprise, but it clearly wasn't.

'Are you Mrs Maureen Wright?'

'Yeah. That's me. And have you found the money?'

This time, the surprise showed on Holden's face. 'What money?'

'The money that was stolen from our Nan. Fifty pounds. We gave it to her on Sunday, but she died on Tuesday, and when we collected her possessions on Wednesday, there was no money. So we reported it. Isn't that what you've come about?'

'No, it isn't.' Holden sat down in the armchair, and waited for the others to follow suit. She didn't want anyone fainting on her.

'We have come about Nanette Wright, however. You are aware that the doctor asked for a post-mortem to be carried out on her body?'

'Yeah,' said Jim. If they had come about Nanette, then it was his business – she was his mother. 'He said to us it was just a precaution. He was ninety-five per cent certain it was a heart attack.'

'I am sorry to have to tell you this, but the post-mortem has revealed that Nanette had a significant amount of morphine in her system.'

'Morphine?' The surprise in Jim Wright's voice appeared genuine. 'What are you talking about? She wasn't on morphine.'

'So I have been told.' Holden had switched into robot mode. It was easier to deliver the information like that. 'But the fact is she died as a result of a high concentration of morphine in her body, and for that reason I have to tell you that we are treating her death as suspicious.'

'What do you mean?' This time it was Maureen speaking. 'Do you mean they were trying to keep her quiet by dosing her up with morphine? Are you saying that bloody woman Fran did that and killed her?'

'No, absolutely not!' Holden spoke firmly, conscious that this conversation was in danger of running out of control. 'We have, at this stage, no idea how the morphine got into her body. And we have no reason to believe that Sunnymede staff were using morphine to sedate her. However, clearly the morphine got into her body somehow, and that is going to be at the centre of our inquiries.'

'Just because they weren't meant to give her morphine doesn't mean they didn't.' Maureen Wright was leaning forward, and wagging her forefinger to reinforce her point. 'I wouldn't put anything past that dyke Fran Sinclair and that sleazeball Paul Greenleaf. Absolutely nothing!'

Holden could feel the woman's anger and prejudice. It flew from her mouth with every word, like spittle, and Holden felt only revulsion. And yet, of course, the same thought had already occurred to her, that someone in Sunnymede had resorted to morphine just to quieten down a difficult old lady. That had to be the most likely scenario, one in which an over-dose had led to death. But that thought wasn't something she was going to admit to in front of these two. Not until she had more evidence. Instead, she glanced at Fox and stood up. She had broken the news. She had done what she had come here to do. It was time to make their excuses and go.

Despite lying deep within the boundaries of the city of Oxford, Sunnymede Care Home occupies an almost rural location. It is tucked away discreetly at the end of a no-through road, between the Oxford Golf Club and the sports fields of the Oxford School. It is most easily accessed via the Cowley Road, yet unless you work there, live there, or know someone there who needs visiting, Sunnymede Care Home might as well not exist. That had been the case for DI Holden until that very morning. Fox, however – who had spent the whole of his life in Oxford – had had no difficulty in negotiating his way to it.

'This would be a nice place for your mother if she ever gets to that stage,' Fox said as he pulled up in the gravelled, tree-fringed car park.

'She'll have to be dead before she leaves her flat in Grandpont Grange.'

Fox chuckled. He had met Mrs Holden a couple of times. She was, like her daughter, a woman of spirit, a woman who would fight to the end to keep her independence.

A man emerged from the main entrance and strode across towards them. He was of medium height, with wide shoulders and tan-coloured hair that flopped down almost to his shoulders. He was, Holden judged, in his late forties, yet with an appearance that harked back to more youthful days, an ageing surfer perhaps, stranded now in a city that could barely be further from the sea.

'Good afternoon,' he said with an overzealous smile. 'I'm Paul Greenleaf.'

Holden displayed her ID, and Fox followed suit. Greenleaf had obviously been watching out for them. Holden doubted he rushed out to greet every visitor, but when you're being investigated because of the unexpected death of a patient, the last thing you'd want is the police wandering around unsupervised, asking awkward questions of all and sundry. Greenleaf ushered them inside, along a corridor, and into a small office in which a woman was already ensconced. Fran Sinclair made no attempt to rise from her chair, merely nodding as Greenleaf made the introductions. She thought maybe she had met the inspector somewhere, socially, but she had no intention of saying as much. Besides, the inspector had already started speaking.

'You are both aware of the results of the post-mortem.' It was a statement rather than a question. 'Can you confirm for me that morphine had not been prescribed for Mrs Nanette Wright?'

'I can confirm that.' It was Fran Sinclair who spoke. The medical side was her overall responsibility, and she knew she had no chance of help on this from Greenleaf.

'But you do keep morphine here?'

'Some.'

'I see.' Holden nodded slowly, apparently deep in thought as she pondered the implications of this response. Then she looked across at Fran again. 'Would you describe Mrs Wright as a difficult patient?'

This time it was Fran who paused. She had expected a grilling about procedures and practices. Were all medicines kept locked up? Who had access to them? How many keys were there? That sort of thing, but not this question. She tried to look Holden in the eye. 'No, I wouldn't. She had her moments, but then most old people do.'

'That's an interesting expression: "She had her moments". What do you mean? Was she cantankerous, and bad tempered? Did she swear at the nurses? Throw her food on the floor? Shit in the bed?'

Fran Sinclair's face was square and expressionless under the fringe of hair. 'I would say she was one of our better-behaved patients, actually.'

'Except when she had her moments.'

'I'm not sure what you're getting at.'

Holden smiled innocently. 'I have an elderly mother. Sometimes, I could strangle her. Not literally, but you know what I mean. And I've seen it on TV. You know, documentaries about old people being abused – sometimes by families at home, sometimes by staff in nursing homes.'

'What the hell are you insinuating?' Paul Greenleaf had risen to his feet.

Holden didn't flinch. She continued to look across at Fran Sinclair, as if Greenleaf didn't even exist. 'I am not suggesting that there has been any abuse in Sunnymede. But I just wanted to underline how old people sometimes drive their carers to distraction. If Mrs Wright drove someone here to distraction, then maybe that person might have been tempted to administer morphine to quieten her down, and maybe if that person wasn't too experienced, well I am sure you can see how an overdose might have occurred, with fatal results.'

Greenleaf reluctantly sat down, but his face was still flushed, and he thrust a finger at Holden. 'Shouldn't you concentrate on finding evidence rather than fabricating wild theories?'

Holden's face swivelled to face him. There was no smile on her lips now. 'Who was it who found Mrs Wright dead?'

Ania Gorski entered the staff room with her eyes on the ground. Holden and Fox had commandeered it for the remainder of their visit, and had had time to drink a slow cup of tea as they waited for her arrival. She was on nights, and hadn't been due in for another hour, but the joy of mobile phones means you can contact people at the most inconvenient times. Ania Gorski had picked up on the second ring and agreed to come straight in. She was Polish with a kind, rather than a pretty face, Fox reckoned. She had mousey brown hair that hung just short of her shoulders, and a slightly plump figure that he found rather appealing, but she glanced up only briefly at Holden when she introduced herself, and not at all at him.

'It's good of you to come in early, Ania.' Holden began.

'I am not used to this.'

'No, of course not.' Holden could be comforting and reassuring if she needed to be, though she hadn't had much practice recently. 'Please try not to worry. It is just that we have to ask you a few questions because it was you who found Mrs Nanette Wright dead.'

'Dead, yes!' she gasped, and her hand moved to her mouth. 'I have only worked a few months here, and I never found a person dead in bed.' It was, Holden reckoned, one of the inevitable parts of a job at a nursing home, that you would sooner or later find a patient dead in bed, but of course she wasn't going to say that now.

'I know you may find it distressing to think about Mrs Wright, but it is very important that I ask you some questions.' She paused, giving the woman time to prepare herself.

'Please, ask me.' Gorski was looking at Holden now, with unblinking green eyes.

'I want you to think back to when you found her. I want you to try and picture in your mind what you saw, and then tell me about it.' Holden smiled encouragingly. 'When you are ready,' she purred.

'It is about seven o'clock. After supper. I try to go around and say hello to all my ladies and gentlemen after supper to see if they are all right, but Mr Day has made a mess in his bed, and I have to clean him up and calm him down. So I am late when I get to Mrs Wright. She is in her chair. The TV is on, but her eyes are shut and I think she is asleep.'

'So what did you do?'

'I wish to turn the TV down. It is very loud, and she has the controller in her hand, but when I take it from her, her hand is cold.' Again her hand flew to her mouth. 'I feel her pulse. But I cannot feel it. So I ring for help.' There was distress in her voice, and Gorski began to cry.

'Here.' Holden passed a tissue to her, and waited for her to recover herself. She could do sympathy up to a point – say comforting things, behave patiently, show concern – but she was more interested in getting answers. So she asked another question. 'Did you notice anything else?'

'Anything else?' Gorski looked at her as if she hadn't understood the question. 'She is dead. I call Miss Sinclair for help. What do you mean?'

'Did you notice anything unusual?'

Gorski made a face. The British policewoman was very odd. Why so many questions about an old lady who has died? She tried to focus her mind back to the time she realized Mrs Wright was dead. 'No. Nothing unusual. I tidy Mrs Wright up while I wait for Miss Sinclair to come. I try to make her look peaceful. And I take the flask from her.'

If eyes had stalks, both Holden's and Fox's would have been fully extended on them.

'What flask?' Holden tried to keep the excitement out of her voice.

'Mrs Wright has a flask. It is naughty, no? She thinks it is her secret, but we know. She likes a nip of whisky. That is what she called it. A nip. And the flask is in her other hand. So I take it and put it in her cupboard to be tidy. It is a matter of respect, I think. I did right?'

'Yes,' Holden replied. Of course it was right to give a dead woman a bit of decency in death. 'Was there any whisky left in the flask?'

Gorski made a face. 'I think not. I shake it, but it is empty. Mrs Wright has been drinking, I think.' And then she began to cry again.

'Where is Nanette Wright's flask?'

Ania Gorski had gone off to start her shift, and almost immediately Fran Sinclair stuck her nosy head round the door. 'Everything all right?' she had said.

She was worried. Holden could see that. It was a stressful situation, but even so, she seemed very on edge. Not that Holden had any interest in making her feel better. That wasn't what she was here for. So she had fired off the question without any preamble. 'Where is Nanette Wright's flask?'

'Her flask?' Fran looked puzzled.

'She had a hip flask. She was holding it when she died. Ania put it in her cupboard. But it isn't there now. So where is it?'

'I hadn't realized.' The look of incomprehension remained on her face.

Holden pressed on, her natural scepticism now fully activated. 'You hadn't realized what? That she had a hip flask and liked a tipple? Or that she was holding it when she died?'

'Well, I knew she liked a drink occasionally.'

'Don't you have rules about that sort of thing?'

Fran's look of innocent amazement receded, and was replaced by an altogether tougher expression. 'We aren't running a concentration camp here. It's a place for old people to live the last of their days peacefully. And as pleasantly as possible. If they like an occasional drink, and it doesn't conflict with their medication, then what harm is there in that?'

'So you knew she liked a drink?'

'Yes.'

'And that she had a hip flask?'

'Yes.'

'And that she died with it in her hand?'

'No, I didn't know that.' The answers were quick and decisive.

'So where did she get her whisky from?'

Fran Sinclair shrugged. This was beyond her knowledge, she was implying, but she'd make an intelligent guess. 'Nan would go home for lunch most Sundays. So presumably she got the flask filled up there. Why don't you ask her son?'

'We will,' Holden replied, though her mind was already moving on, or rather picking up an earlier thought she hadn't pursued. 'When was Nanette last seen by a doctor?'

'I'd have to check.'

'You don't know?' Holden said this as if she couldn't believe that someone in Fran Sinclair's position wouldn't have this information immediately to hand.

'Actually, I do,' came the curt reply. 'When she was dead! Dr Featherstone certified her dead for us. But I'm presuming you want to know when he last saw her alive, and that is a question I'd need to check her records for.'

'I see,' Holden said, but in a manner that indicated beyond all possible doubt that she didn't see.

'Look!' Fran Sinclair was irritated. If there was one way to get her roused, it was to doubt her professionalism. 'The doctor comes in every Monday and Thursday as a matter of course. Obviously, if medical problems occur, he comes out when we call him. But when he's here, I don't monitor his every move. Dr Featherstone is popular with the residents. He's an old-school GP, and a lot closer to their ages than he'd probably care to admit, so he likes to go round and say hello, not just dole out prescriptions for those who have obvious problems. So I can't for sure say when he last saw Nanette. If he had prescribed any medicines for her, then that would be recorded. But I don't have a photographic memory. So that's why I'd need to check her file.'

'So he'll be here on Monday, will he?'

'God willing.'

Holden nodded, apparently unperturbed by the forcefulness of the woman in front of her. 'Well,' she said, suddenly standing up. 'I'll look forward to seeing him then. Perhaps you can arrange it?' And she smiled her best, synthetic smile.

Ten minutes later, Holden and Fox were outside again. It was dark, and cold, and there was a drizzle in the air, but neither of them showed any sign of getting into the car. Fox was on his mobile phone, and Holden was smoking. She had started again big-time during her six-month period of leave, but now she had managed to get it back under some sort of control. She always carried a packet with her, but there were never more than two cigarettes in it at a time. It was her insurance against binge smoking. When she got up in the morning, she put two cigarettes in the packet. She didn't want to get hooked again, not that hooked anyway. She was hooked in a small way, she knew that, but this way she maintained control. Sort of. She took a final drag, then stamped it out in the gravel. She ought to pick it up and dispose of it tidily, but her mind had better things to worry about.

Fox clicked his mobile shut. 'There's only the daughter, Vickie, at home. Her parents are both out. She doesn't know when they'll be back, so I said to tell them we'd call round tomorrow morning about 8.30 a.m.'

Holden knew most of what he was telling her. Listening to one side of a phone call often tells you more than half the story. She'd like to have called round now, but tomorrow would have to do. At least it would give her time to think. Mind you, she wasn't sure she wanted too much time to think. Since Karen's death, she had found that thinking often led into dangerous areas.

'Can you drop me off at my mother's, Sergeant?'

'Sure.'

They got in the car, and Fox started up. Holden got out her mobile, and then lay back in the seat with her eyes shut as it rang. It was late notice, but her mother could knock up supper at the drop of a hat. That was something she had always been good at.

CHAPTER 3

Mum is upset. She keeps bursting into tears. I feel sorry that Nan Nan is dead too, but I don't feel like crying. I never do. I mean, what is the point? It won't change anything. Nan Nan is dead. She died after supper in Sunnymede. But she was old. Life wasn't much fun for her any more. So what's wrong with her being dead?

She was my grandmother. Everyone called her Nan because her name was Nanette. That's interesting, isn't it? But she was my Nan Nan and Vickie's Nan Nan and nobody else's, and if I don't feel the need to cry, why should Mum? The fact is Nan Nan is better off dead at her age.

She was nice to me most of the time. When I was little, she'd give me sweets every Sunday. She'd come over for lunch, and afterwards, when she was drinking a cup of tea in front of the TV, she'd call me over and open her handbag and pull out a tube of fruit pastilles, or a packet of Skittles. And Mum and Dad would tell her she was spoiling me, but she'd wink at me and say: 'That's Nan Nan's prerogative, to spoil little David.'

She would come and babysit me every Wednesday. But there were no sweets then. She'd read me a story at bedtime, but only one, and then she'd put my light off. And that was it. I had to stay there. Once, I felt hungry, so I went downstairs and asked her if I could have a bowl of cereal. She was watching the TV and she was furious. She grabbed me by the arm, and slapped me really hard. I wanted to cry, but I didn't because I was afraid she'd slap me again. 'Go to bed, you wicked boy!' she shouted, and I smelt this stinky smell coming from her mouth, and I ran as fast as I could upstairs again, and I slammed my door shut behind me and hid myself right under my duvet in case she chased after me. But she never did.

That was the way it was with Nan Nan. Nice if you behaved yourself; nasty if you didn't. But I was her favourite – until Vickie was born.

'So what is it you want? I like to have a lie in on Saturdays.' Maureen Wright had been dressed when she answered the door just after 8.30 that morning, but she had already made it crystal clear that it was only because her daughter had warned her.

Holden slipped into appeasement mode: 'We'll try to keep this very brief. We are truly sorry to spoil your Saturday morning.'

'Yeah, right!' came the truculent response.

'Is your husband in?'

'He's out all morning.' There was no further explanation.

'No matter. I'm sure you'll do just as well.'

'Why don't you say what's on your mind, and then let me be?' Maureen Wright was growing more confident and stroppy with every passing moment. Not that Holden cared.

'Where's your mother-in-law's hip flask?'

The sneer on Maureen's lips vanished, and there was – for a flickeringly brief moment – a pause. 'Her hip flask?' She was playing for time. Holden had absolutely no doubt about it. Maureen Wright was trying to work out what to say.

But Fox had already had enough. If he was giving up even part of his Saturday, it wasn't so that this woman could piss them about. 'It was amongst the bag of your mother-in-law's possessions that you took from Sunnymede following her death. We want it now. It's evidence.'

'What do you mean – evidence?'

Fox stepped forward, so that he was just in front of Holden. He raised his voice. 'Where is it?'

Maureen licked her lips. She felt a familiar fear, the fear of male aggression, fear of a sudden fist in the stomach. Not that the hulking detective would do that to her, here. But that's what Jim had done, plenty of times, and fear was hard-wired into her gut. She bowed her head in auto-submission. 'I'll get it.'

She brought it to them in a large carrier bag, which she placed on the round pine coffee table as if it was an explosive device. 'It's all there. All her stuff. I couldn't face going through it.'

Fox put plastic gloves on, and looked into the bag. He fished into it and pulled out the hip flask. He shook it, unscrewed the top and then sniffed it. He offered it to Holden. She too sniffed. Then they both looked at Maureen Wright.

At 8.05 on the following Monday morning Fox picked up Holden from Chilswell Road, in South Oxford. Some fifteen minutes later they pulled into the car park of the Cowley police station. Holden had been tempted to go straight to Sunnymede, but there were things that had to be done first. Inevitably, emails had to be checked, before they built up to a ridiculous degree. But even as her computer was kicking itself into life, the phone rang. It was Detective Superintendent Collins.

'How are things going, Inspector?'

The very sound of his voice caused a ripple of anxiety down her spine. 'I'm fine, thank you, Sir.'

'I meant what's the progress on the Nanette Wright case?'

'Oh!' She was momentarily flustered, an unusual sensation for her.

'It's just that I've had the press on the phone.'

'There's nothing new for them.'

There was a snort from the other end of the phone. 'And is there anything new for me?'

'She was killed by a large dose of morphine. Possibly medical negligence, possibly murder.' She spoke briskly, and with a

scarcely concealed impatience at having to waste time humouring her boss. 'Mrs Wright was holding a hip flask when she
died. We've been waiting for forensics to come back to us over
that.'

'Was she now?' There was a pause. 'Well, I suggest you keep
behind them, because I'd like to put out a statement a.s.a.p.'

She fought the temptation to be bloody rude. Of course she'd
keep behind them, but not so that he could keep the press
happy. 'Actually, Sir,' she said with a huge effort, 'that was
going to be my first job. I've literally just sat down at my desk.'

'Ah, I'm delaying you, Inspector, am I?'

Holden had the sense not to be as blunt as she felt. 'Sir, I
assure you that I'll keep you informed of any significant developments, and as soon as they happen.' That wasn't entirely
true, but it was close enough.

'Good,' he replied.

Holden put the phone down. The logon screen had appeared
on her monitor, and she entered her username and password
and hit the 'Enter' key. Then she got up and wandered down
the corridor, got herself a black coffee and returned to her desk.
Only then did she pick up the phone to ring forensics. The
delaying of the call by a couple of minutes was, she knew, a
pathetically pointless act of defiance, but it made her feel
better. A woman called Doreen answered, listened, talked to
someone in the background, and assured her that the hip flask
was receiving their top priority. Holden thanked her and rang
off, both pleased and irritated that the phone call had achieved
nothing.

Another two phone calls, nearly thirty deleted emails and
some fifty minutes later, Holden and Fox entered the staff room
of Sunnymede Care Home. Almost immediately Paul Greenleaf
appeared, obsequiousness personified. Holden ignored his offer
of coffee: 'We need to speak to Ania Gorski again.'

The smile that had been plastered across his face faded.
'She's not in trouble is she? She's a very good worker.'

'Where is she?' Holden was giving no ground, and no information either.

'You're in luck, actually.' He tried another futile smile. 'She's working days this week. I'll go and find her, shall I?'

'Just a minute.' Holden held up a hand. 'If last week Ania was on nights looking after Mrs Wright, who was on the day shift before her?'

Something flashed across Greenleaf's face, a look of surprise, maybe even alarm. At least, that's what Holden thought she saw. 'It's not quite like that. In the daytime patients tend to move around. They aren't confined to their rooms.'

'But let's suppose Mrs Wright chose to stay in her room last Tuesday.' She spoke briskly, and with irritation in her voice. She hated being patronized, and she hated it when people didn't answer her questions. 'Wasn't there a nurse allocated to look in on her, make sure she got a meal?'

'Well, yes.'

'So who was it?'

'It would have been Bella Sinclair.'

'Well I'd like to see her after Ania, in that case.'

There was a noticeable hesitation. 'I'm afraid she's off work.'

'Off work? Why's that?'

Again Greenleaf hesitated. 'Actually, she's been suspended.'

'Suspended?' Holden's head jerked up as if it had been yanked by a puppeteer. 'When did this happen?'

'Last Thursday.'

'And why has she been suspended?'

Holden felt she could smell Greenleaf's anxiety. He was still standing, near the door, his body half turned towards it, as if desperate to be allowed to leave. 'She was accused of stealing some money from Mrs Wright.'

Holden nodded, remembering the conversation with Maureen and Jim Wright. But she continued as if it had never occurred. 'From Mrs Wright? How much? Why haven't you already told me about this?' She could feel her pulse hammering in her neck. She tried to slow herself down. 'And when did this occur?'

'Fifty pounds. Mrs Wright's son, Jim, gave her fifty pounds on the Sunday when he visited her. But there was no sign of it when they collected her possessions on Wednesday. So they made a complaint.'

'Why do you think it was Bella who stole it? Couldn't it have been someone else?'

'There have been other issues with Bella. Another of our patients, a Mr Day, had bruising on his upper arms that we weren't happy with. So we took the decision to suspend her until we could investigate both matters fully.'

'Who is "we"?' Holden was letting nothing pass. Fox felt a burst of pleasure. This, he realized, was what he had missed most of all, seeing his guv doing her impression of a terrier with behavioural problems.

'I was required to report it to head office.' There were globules of sweat on Greenleaf's forehead, and very little conviction in his voice. 'Ultimately it was they who implemented the action.'

Holden felt the bitter taste of bile in her throat. She knew what it was like to be suspended and she knew too where her sympathy lay. What the hell did he mean by 'ultimately'? It sounded like a cop-out to her. He had reported the woman, knowing what it would mean, but he didn't have the balls to accept responsibility. Still, right now, she had other priorities.

'When you've found Ania,' she said, signalling the end of the session, 'I'd like you to go and get me Bella's contact details. In fact, while you're about it, print me off a list of contact details of all your staff. My sergeant will come with you. Also, he needs to know which of those staff were in the building for any reason on Monday and Tuesday of last week.'

'As you wish.' Greenleaf turned quickly away and left with Fox, chuckling, in his wake.

Ania appeared two minutes later. Holden had placed a chair in the centre of the room, and she waited for her to sit down on it.

'Thank you for coming.' Holden smiled, hoping to set the woman at ease. 'I just have one or two details to clarify. On Friday, you told us that after you found Mrs Nanette Wright dead in her chair, you put her flask in her cupboard. Is that correct?'

'Yes.'

'Did you at that time or later wash out the flask?'

A frown crossed the nurse's face. 'No.'

'You are sure about that?'

'Yes. But I do not understand. Should I have washed it out? It was a great shock to me, and I had other patients to look after and—'

Holden cut across her. 'I understand that the following morning, Mrs Wright's son and daughter-in-law came here and collected Mrs Wright's possessions, including her hip flask. Did you help with this?'

She shook her head firmly. 'No. I am on nights last week. They come in the daytime.'

Holden nodded. She was inclined to believe the Polish woman. There was no doubt that she was nervous, but who wouldn't be, being interviewed by the police in a foreign country far from home? That Ania might now consider Oxford home did not occur to Holden. 'Thank you,' she said, her tone softening. 'You can go now.'

Dr Alexander Featherstone was busy with a patient. That was what Fran Sinclair had told Holden when she had appeared at the door and offered her another coffee. Holden had thanked her, not because she needed or even wanted another coffee, but because it was either that or have a cigarette, and it really was too early to be smoking the first of her two. She stood up and waited, looking through the window at the cars parked out the front. What was it Yeats had written in his poem about the lake isle of Innisfree? 'I shall have some peace there, for peace comes dropping slow.' At school Mr Malone had insisted they all learn it, and now she had forgotten it all except that bit. Peace comes dropping slow. Not in her life it didn't! Peace had always been elusive for her, and it felt like it always would be.

'Excuse me,' a voice said behind her. 'I'm looking for Inspector Holden. You don't happen to know where he is?'

'Jesus!' she said out loud, and immediately felt guilty. Her mother would be horrified if she heard her, especially with her renewed zeal for church. But it was anger she felt more than guilt. 'I'm Inspector Holden, and in case you've not noticed I'm a she.'

'Ah!' he said, covering his error with a grin. 'It's an easy mistake to make.'

Holden did not grin back. 'I expect you make it all the time.'

The smile disappeared deep within a choleric-looking face. 'I'm Dr Featherstone,' he said, his voice now stripped bare of bonhomie. 'I understand you want to see me.'

'I do,' she said, surveying the man in front of her. He was short, with a flourishing moustache, largely bald pate, and a lazy left eye. He was dressed in a dull grey suit, white shirt, heavily patterned tie and black shoes. And he couldn't, she thought, be far off retirement age.

'Please, sit down,' she said, though it wasn't politeness that made her say it. Fran Sinclair was hovering at the door with coffee. Holden moved towards her, heading her off and ushering her out as she took control of the tray. She put it down, poured coffee into a cup, added milk, and then thrust it in front of the doctor. 'Here you are,' she said brusquely. She hoped he hated milk and liked three spoons of sugar.

She remained there, standing over him, so that he was forced to crane his neck upwards to look at her. 'When did you last see Nanette Sinclair alive?' she demanded.

'Monday, the day before she died. I think.' His furrowed brow furrowed even more. 'Yes, definitely, it was Monday. It's just that when you're seeing so many people …'

'Quite,' Holden said sharply. She turned, went and poured herself a coffee, and sat on the sofa opposite. She had made her point. Besides, she wanted to be sure she could see his face.

'So why did you go and see her?'

'I was doing my rounds. I'm a doctor. That's what I do. I go round and check on my patients.' There was irritation in his voice.

'Did she have a lot wrong with her apart from being old and feeble?'

He took a sip of coffee, made a face, put it down on the table, and leant forward as if finally getting down to business. 'Old and feeble. That covers a lot. Do you not have a mother?'

'I do indeed,' she replied. 'I always have had a mother, as a matter of fact, and she is still alive.'

'Well, ask her what it's like being old and feeble. She'll tell you better than I can.'

'She does, regularly.'

'Well, good for her.' He picked up his cup again and drained it. 'Delicious,' he said.

Holden felt herself warming to him despite her innate suspicion of anyone who reminded her of her father. 'Why don't you tell me about Nanette?'

'She was a nice old lady.'

'I'm more interested in her health.'

'Are you?' The smile flickered briefly again across his face and then was gone. 'I take a broader view. Anyway, as I was saying, she was a nice old lady. She came here about six months ago. There was nothing that was immediately terminal with her, no tumours, no cancer, just the onset of heart failure that would have eventually ended in death.'

'Did you give her any morphine?'

'No.' His reply was emphatic. Perhaps too much so.

'A significant level of morphine was found in her system.'

'I do know that,' he said sharply. 'I've read the autopsy report, and I know the significance of the level found.'

'So how did it get there?'

'How on earth should I know?'

'So you didn't prescribe her any morphine?'

'There would be a record if I had.'

Holden changed tack. 'What was the quality of her life, would you say?'

'Not as good as it should have been.'

'What do you mean by that?'

'Quality of life isn't just about physical health. It's about emotional and mental health too. She wasn't loved, Inspector, not by her son and not by her daughter-in-law. If they had loved her ...' He paused, and scratched at his ear, from which, Holden had already noticed, there grew a substantial amount of hair. 'There was no real need for her to come here when she did. Not in my view. With the right level of support from her family, she would have been fine outside, but they couldn't be bothered.'

'Did she sometimes get pain?'

'I expect so, yes. Certainly discomfort. She had her good days and her bad days.'

Holden stood up, and walked over to the window, looking out again at the cars. The doctor's was an old Volvo estate, P-reg. She had seen him drive it in. She turned to face him.

'How often do you prescribe morphine for patients?'

'Only when they are in pain.'

'And you never prescribed it for Nanette?'

'I thought I had already made that clear.'

'But she got some, didn't she? That's a fact. That's why she's dead.'

It was Featherstone's turn to stand up now. He was barely taller than her, and they stood face to face, like two boxers sizing each other up. 'I do hope you're not accusing me of anything?' He almost hissed the words.

'Certainly not,' she replied.

*

It wasn't until 3 o'clock that afternoon that Fox and Holden stood at the main entrance to a block of flats in Blackbird Leys Road. It stood tall and graceless in the grey light, overlooking the much maligned Blackbird Leys estate, convenient for the buses into Oxford city centre, for the community centre across the road, and for the parade of shops at the end of Cuddesdon Way. Fox pressed the number 13 bell, and when a disembodied and almost indecipherable female voice answered, he pushed open the door. They took the lift, but said nothing as they rose to the fourth floor. There was graffiti on the walls and the light in the ceiling flickered erratically. Fox smiled. His Uncle Jim had lived here in the 1980s, a fat jovial man with serious body odour problems, and a passion for fish and chips, liberally sprinkled with vinegar. Fox could almost smell them, pungent and compulsive.

The lift juddered to a halt. Fox led the way out, and knocked on a tired green door immediately opposite them. Several seconds passed before there was a scrabbling sound from within. The door opened to reveal a woman of almost identical height to Holden. Her hair was thick and red, there was a stud in her right nostril, and she wore a black three-quarter-length coat. A striped red and grey scarf was draped around her neck.

'Sorry,' she gasped, as if in explanation, 'I only just got back.'

Holden presented her ID. 'I presume you're Bella Sinclair?'

'Yes.' She turned without any further comment, leaving them to make their own way in. She sat down on a black sofa – a DFS special, Fox reckoned, from at least ten New Year sales ago – still in her coat, and waited. The flat, Fox couldn't help noticing, smelt, not of smoke or food or burnt toast, but of an indecipherable flower smell. Was that what she had been doing while she kept them waiting, spraying air freshener in the hope of convincing them that the flat really wasn't that dirty?

Holden was already making a start. 'We need to ask you a few questions about Nanette Wright.'

'So you said on the phone. But why? She just died, didn't she, like old people do?'

Holden spread her hands. 'Technically, people don't just die. There's always a reason, and our job is to determine the reason for her death. It may well be quite innocent and straightforward or....' Holden didn't finish her sentence, but it provoked a laugh from the woman facing her.

'Or it could be murder most foul?'

Holden looked down at her hands, which she suddenly realized were clasped tightly together. She deliberately separated them, resting each hand on a knee, and looked up.

'Were you aware that Mrs Wright had a hip flask in her room?'

'Yes.' Her reply was instant, as if she had anticipated the question. 'It wasn't a secret.'

'Do you know what she drank from it?'

'Whisky, I think.'

'You think?'

'Yes, I think. That's what she told me.'

'Did you ever fill it up for her?'

'God, no! It's against the rules.'

'And you're a stickler for rules, are you? It's just that you don't look like it.'

'I wouldn't want to get in trouble.'

'But you've been suspended, haven't you?' It was below the belt. A cheap shot. Holden knew that before she made it, but it was something she had to explore. If Bella Sinclair was the sort of person who stole fifty pounds from a dead woman and physically abused an old man, then she was surely capable of overdosing an old woman who was causing her trouble.

'Christ, so that's it!' The earlier confidence had been replaced by something not so far from panic. 'Look, I've done nothing wrong. Absolutely nothing. That bastard Paul wants to get rid of me. He wants to use me as a scapegoat. You ask my sister.'

It was Holden's turn to be taken by surprise, though she tried to hide it. 'Your sister?'

'Fran Sinclair. She's my sister.' Bella grinned. 'You didn't know, did you? You call yourselves detectives, and you hadn't even worked that out?'

'You don't exactly look like sisters.'

Bella laughed out loud. 'Well, I got the beauty, and she got the brawn. She'll tell you that. But actually we reckon we've got different fathers, but Mum never admitted it.'

'Right.' Holden nodded and looked down. She noticed that her hands had twisted themselves together again, but she didn't try to untangle them this time. She just needed to keep on track. 'Why do you think you're being made a scapegoat?'

'That's Fran's theory. Sunnymede has had a bad report. She says Greenleaf is using me as a fall guy. If they can demonstrate that there's just one bad apple, it looks better for him.'

'You say that's Fran's theory. Do you have a different one?'

Bella Sinclair stood up abruptly, peeled off her coat and scarf, and tossed them down on the other end of the sofa. She walked over to the large double-glazed window and stood with her back to it. She was still an attractive-looking woman, ridiculously trim and with strikingly good legs. Holden felt a pang of jealousy. 'Paul Greenleaf is after revenge.' Bella spoke as if on stage, delivering a monologue to a packed audience as she explained the intricacies of the plot. 'He fancied me, you see. Fancied me like crazy. The only problem is, he repulses me. Creepy, he is. I knew on the day of my interview he'd be trouble.'

'When was this?' Holden realized she didn't know how long Bella had been at Sunnymede.

'Five, six months ago. I spent nearly ten years in New Zealand. Travelling at first, then working. I even got hitched to a Kiwi. But that all fell apart and I came back to England, and Fran got me an interview at Sunnymede. Last June, it was. Greenleaf was all over me. "How do you like your coffee? It isn't too hot, is it? I've got a special supply of chocolate biscuits. Have one, but don't tell your sister." God, he was pathetic. I should have walked out. I knew he'd be trouble, but I needed the job and I reckoned I could handle him.'

She paused, and turned to look outside. Somewhere, the grey cloud broke ranks, and a shaft of sunlight burst into the room, illuminating her profile. Holden swallowed. It was easy to see Bella inspiring lust in men. And not just men. 'So was there an incident?'

Bella continued to look out across Blackbird Leys. 'I managed to put him off at first. Whenever he tried to chat me up, I found something else to do. It wasn't difficult. There's always stuff to do at Sunnymede. But then one Wednesday, he turned up here. Wednesday is my day off, but at 10.30 that morning the bell rang and it was him. I was stupid enough to offer him a coffee, and well, you know how it happens, next thing was we were in my bed....'

'A moment ago you said he repulsed you.' Holden liked to think she could smell bullshit a mile off, and right now Bella stank something terrible.

'Jesus, Inspector, hold your horses. Sometimes in life you make mistakes. Sometimes you sleep with people you never should have.'

'And sometimes people lie to the police.'

Bella showed no sign of being affronted by Holden's accusation, but she rebutted it firmly. 'Look, I know I'm not perfect, but I can assure you that I'm not lying. Ask Mr Greenleaf.'

'I will.'

'Of course, he may try to deny it.'

'Oh?' Holden was puzzled by the 'of course'.

'Well it wasn't exactly his finest hour.'

'Not his finest hour?' Holden paused. 'What do you mean?'

Bella smirked. 'I'm sure you can work that out for yourself, Inspector.'

'So what happened after that?'

'He asked if he could come over again another day.'

'And what did you say?'

'The very worst thing.' She paused, milking the moment, and turned to look back again out through the window. The chill sun had disappeared as suddenly as it had arrived. 'I laughed at him,' she said.

CHAPTER 4

She came back. The woman with the red hair came back to the shop yesterday morning. I think she's mad.

She brought a picture with her this time. She said it came all the way from New Zealand. It wasn't very big. It was a painting of the sea, and there were very steep cliffs, and a rock with seals on. She said it was a place called Doubtful Sound. Doubtful Sound! What sort of name is that? I think she was kidding me. People do. They think I'm stupid, so they tease me.

We've got lots of different samples of frames on the wall, and she chose one, and I worked out how much it was going to cost. I wanted to check the price with Jaz, but she had popped out again, and the woman told me not to worry. She'd pay what-ever it cost when she collected it.

At lunchtime, I ate my sandwiches in the shop like I always do. Then I went for a walk, ending up at George and Delila's for an ice cream. I always eat it very slowly, and I never have the same ice cream two days running. Yesterday I had pistachio.

And then the woman with the red hair walked in. Her name is Bella. I didn't call her that, of course, because she is a cus-tomer, but it's easier than describing her as the woman with the red hair. She bought me a passion fruit and mango ice cream. I shouldn't have agreed to that, but I got flustered, what with her coming in and saying at the top of her voice what an amazing coincidence it was us meeting again, and maybe it was written in the stars. She started to sound really weird, so when she asked me if I wanted another ice cream, I said 'Yes' even though that broke all my rules. Only one ice cream at lunchtime. And then she sat down opposite me. She had got herself a choco-late ice cream, and as she ate she waved her spoon around and talked about how great it was to be in Oxford and how she loved shopping in the Cowley Road. I could smell her perfume, only it wasn't as nice as Mum's.

'Tell me about yourself,' she said eventually.

I looked at my phone. It was only 12.42. I couldn't go back to the shop yet. 'I'm David Wright. I live in a flat in Barns Road. It's what they call a studio flat. I like it.'

'Tell me about your family.'

'I have a mum and a dad, and a sister called Vickie. There used to be Nan Nan too, but she died.'

'How old is Vickie?'

'Twelve.' I stood up then. I didn't like her asking all these questions. 'I'm going to the toilet,' I said.

I took as long as I dared in the toilet, and then I went back over to the table, and looked at my phone and said I'd have to go because I had to be back at the shop. Actually, I could have stayed for five more minutes, but I didn't want to hear any more questions. 'Thank you for the ice cream, Ms Sinclair,' I said. It is important to be polite, even to people who are a bit mad.

'Call me Bella,' she said.

But I didn't.

'Goodbye.'

'I've got the results on the flask back from forensics.' Holden spoke without enthusiasm. It was Tuesday morning, shortly after 8.30 a.m., and DS Fox had just sat down opposite her, a coffee in his right hand, a pad and pen in his left. Despite the necessity for all detectives to grapple with the wonders of information technology, he remained at heart a pad-and-biro man. He took a sip and waited for Holden to speak.

'Not a trace of anything in the flask. It had been washed out very thoroughly.'

Fox wasn't surprised. There hadn't been the slightest whiff of anything when he had sniffed it. 'What about fingerprints?'

'None.'

'Not even the old woman's?'

'Not a single print.'

Fox grunted, and took another sip of coffee. He wasn't the sharpest knife in the drawer, but he recognized the importance of this. 'So the flask was washed and wiped clean. By the person who put the morphine in the flask, presumably.'

'Or maybe by someone who likes washing up in rubber gloves.'

Fox looked at Holden sharply. He didn't like being teased. Was she being serious? It was hardly a joking matter.

'If that was the case,' he replied, 'then they would admit it. And so far no one has.'

'No. But maybe we've just not asked the right person.'

'Is that what you think?'

Holden smiled bleakly at her sergeant. Sometimes she liked to wind him up a bit, but right now it was more a need to distance herself from the tension she felt inside her head. 'Not really. It's a possibility, that's all. But what this does indicate is that in all likelihood we're dealing with murder, or at the very least, homicide.'

'In which case, we're looking at someone who works at Sunnymede, or one of her family.'

'Or someone who visited her at Sunnymede.'

'Do you think her family could have got hold of morphine?'

'If they wanted to kill her, yes. But Sunnymede seems the most likely source.'

'So what's the next step?'

'I think I'll ring the super, and ask for some extra help. I bumped into DC Lawson when I arrived this morning. I know she's up for it. And from what she said, Wilson would be too.'

*

Vickie Wright half ran along Barracks Lane. She had twenty minutes before the next lesson, and she wanted them to herself. It was colder than she had thought. She'd left her coat in the classroom, but she wasn't going to go back and get it now. As she came to Fitzroy Close, she almost turned right into it, and then upbraided herself for being an idiot. That was force of habit, she knew. How many times had she gone up there at lunchtimes to pay her Nan a visit? But there would be no more of that. Even so, she was tempted to head up towards Sunnymede. It would be a way of remembering her Nan. But then she remembered her dad. He might be there. He was doing a few jobs for the care home. He had been talking about it the night before. The boss – Paul something – sometimes gave him jobs to do around the place, and the last person she wanted to run into was her dad. She continued walking along Barracks Lane, her pace now more regular. The wind was blowing from the northeast, down across the sports fields and straight through her. To make things worse, she could feel rain in the air. She stopped and pulled out her mobile. What was the point of rushing all the way to the framing shop, when she could much more easily ring David? Her fingers flickered across the key pad, and she put the phone to her ear. He answered immediately:

'David Wright speaking.'

She smiled. There was something very reassuring about his predictability.

'Hello, David Wright,' she replied. 'It's Vickie.'

'I know it is,' he said.

'How are things?'

'I'm working. Jaz doesn't like me stopping to answer my phone.'

Vickie made a face. Jaz wouldn't care at all. She knew that. Jaz was really nice, the nicest of all her mother's friends. 'Shall we meet up after you've finished work? I could come to your flat for a bit.'

There was silence at the other end of the phone. She

expected that. David didn't like sudden changes to his plans. He would need to think about it.

'Please!' she implored. 'Mum and Dad are both working late today.' That was a lie. But not an important one.

'All right,' came the reluctant reply. 'I finish at 4.30.'

'I'll meet you outside the shop.'

'Don't be late.'

'Don't worry, David Wright. I won't be.'

Whatever Detective Superintendent Collins' faults were – and in Holden's view he had a self-confidence and self-importance that were almost Blairite in their intensity – procrastination was not one of them. Barely half an hour after Holden called him, there was a knock on her door, and in came Detective Constables Lawson and Wilson. Holden looked up and returned their broad smiles.

'You look like you've just won the lottery.'

'Almost as good, Guv,' Lawson replied, still grinning. 'We've escaped Sergeant Johnson's community policing seminar.'

'Well, that is a shame!' Holden leant back her chair and surveyed them. She had always liked Jan Lawson, from that first day when the WPC, as she had been then, had buttonholed her in the station car park and had told her that her label was showing. She had short blonde hair, mischievous eyes, and a character to match. Wilson, she thought, looked older, more mature. His dark hair was longer than she remembered (slightly), and he stood there smiling languidly, apparently more at ease with himself than she ever remembered. It was the first time she had seen him since her extended break, and he seemed to have aged several years in those six months. Mind you, that was just as well. Half the time he had looked and felt like an awkward 16-year-old schoolboy, not a young detective making his way.

Holden picked up the phone. 'I'll get Sergeant Fox, and then we'll bring you up to speed.'

*

'It's good of you to see me at such short notice.' DC Wilson sat down opposite Charles Hargreaves. The solicitor had kept him waiting outside for ten minutes, but he hadn't minded because Hargreaves's PA, Miss Celia Johnson, had not only brought him a cup of tea, but had then engaged him in bright conversation. Her round face was framed by brown curly hair, and her laughter rose deep and rather coarse from within. Wilson had found himself wondering how she might react if he asked her out.

'Not at all.' Hargreaves waved a hand dismissively. 'When the police request an urgent interview, I always do my best to co-operate. I'm sorry to have kept you waiting, but I just wanted to run my eyes over Mrs Nanette Wright's papers so that I could answer your questions.'

'Well, we just need to check out her will. To see to whom she left her estate.'

'Of course.' Hargreaves nodded vigorously, and looked down at the open file in front of him, as if he needed to double check the details. 'In fact, it's all very straightforward. She left all her estate to her son, Mr James Wright, all except for some items of jewellery that she has specified be given to her granddaughter, Victoria.'

'What about her grandson, David?'

Hargreaves looked down again, adjusting his glasses as he did so. 'Nothing was left to anyone else.'

'Oh!' Wilson felt a spurt of sympathy for the forgotten boy. He hoped his own gran wouldn't ignore him just because he was male.

'I believe David was adopted,' Hargreaves said, looking up. 'Maybe that explains it.'

'Oh!' Wilson said again. He didn't remember being told that in the briefing. He'd check it out later, but right now there were other questions to ask. 'Do you know how large her estate is?'

Hargreaves leant back, and smiled at Wilson as if he was a

rather uncouth young nephew. 'That's a question to ask her accountant, I think.'

'Yes, of course.' Wilson flushed, but not – as might once have been the case – with embarrassment. It was anger he felt, anger at being so patronized by this man who felt a hand-made suit and a public-school accent put him above people like himself. 'I would imagine,' Wilson persisted, 'that you have some idea of your clients' financial affairs. After all you wouldn't want them defaulting on their bills.'

'Indeed.' The hand waved again, a tennis player's hand perhaps, acknowledging a good return of service. He leant forward. 'What I can tell you, Constable, is that about a year ago she took a quarter share in her son's house. I had to draw up the agreement.'

'Really?'

'Really! But as I say, if you want financial details, you'll need to speak her accountant. His name is William Kelly.'

'Do you have an address and phone number?'

Hargreaves leant back again, and pointed a single complacent finger towards the ceiling. 'Next floor up, young man.'

At much the same time as Wilson was being patronized by Charles Hargreaves, Holden, Fox and Lawson were undertaking the grunt work that a police investigation typically involves. From the list that Fox had compiled the previous day, it had become obvious to Holden that there were all too many people who could potentially have put morphine in Nanette Wright's hip flask and so caused her death. Quite apart from all the staff, there were visitors and business callers. 'And, of course,' Holden pointed out, 'we shouldn't ignore the possibility of other residents being involved. The question is where to start. We aren't necessarily looking for someone with an obvious motive to commit murder. If the morphine was put in the hip flask by someone merely hoping to quieten Nanette down, then we may be looking for someone with a petty grudge against the old woman, or someone whom she managed to rub up the wrong way. But if the intent was to kill, then well ...' Holden shrugged and opened her hands in apparent supplication to a higher being.

'There is another way of approaching the problem.' Despite her lack of experience, Lawson was not a person to hold back. Keeping quiet gets you nowhere. That had always been her motto. 'What I mean is that we could start with the people who could most easily have gained access to morphine. Which is presumably some of the more senior nursing staff.'

'I take your point, Lawson.' It was a guarded welcome. 'In fact,' Holden continued, 'my next move is to go and talk to Fran Sinclair about their drugs regime.' Lawson felt a flush of pleasure. There was a juvenile part of her that needed her boss's approval. 'But', Holden was saying – of course there had to be a 'but' – 'I don't want to make too many assumptions yet. What I want you and Fox to do, Lawson, is to try and build up a picture of Nanette Wright's life here, and in particular her last few days. Did she tend to wander around a lot, or stay in her room? Did she have particular friends? Was she popular or unpopular? Get people to talk about her, and try and find out who she related to. Did her family visit her much during the week? You don't need me to spell it out. Just find out as much as you can.'

William Kelly was the very antithesis of Wilson's idea of an accountant. For a start, he was dressed an in open-neck black shirt and black jeans. The top two shirt buttons were undone, revealing a small silver cross on a fine chain, and there was noticeable stubble on his face. His hair was jet black and short, and his eyes flickered with amusement.

'So you've been and seen Charles, I gather, and now it's me for the third degree.'

'Just a few questions, if you don't mind.'

'You want to know how much Nanette Wright was worth, I expect.'

'Yes.'

'So her death is suspicious?' The amusement in his eyes had dissolved.

Wilson pursed his lips. 'All I can say is that we are investigating her death, and we need to collect all the information about her we can. Mr Hargreaves told me that she became a part owner of her son's house about a year ago.'

'And I expect you've already worked out that six months later they were shunting her into a care home. It makes you think, doesn't it?'

'I assume she needed more care than her son and daughter-in-law could give.'

Kelly made a face. 'You can assume what you like, but I wouldn't treat my mother like that. Never!'

'Was her son short of money?'

'Is her son a bastard? The answer is yes to both questions. I never liked him. He came round here with her a couple of times and asked a lot of intrusive questions. So when they'd gone, I did some of my own investigations. He had his own building business, and it was quite successful for a while. He even bought property out in Spain, doing it up and selling it on, but when the property market there crashed in 2007, so did his business. Now he's just a jobbing builder, but my guess is that he's still skint. That's why his mother had to buy a stake in his house. He needed cash.'

'So Mrs Wright's death is a bit of a windfall for her son.'

'It's certainly damned convenient. Apart from her share in the house, she has maybe twenty grand left, which he'll now get. But, of course, she's been shelling out several hundred pounds a week for Sunnymede, and if she'd lived for a while longer, she'd have had to ask her son for her money back. And that would have made things difficult for him. So if you're looking for a motive for murder, then Jim Wright – not to mention his wife – has it in spades.'

*

Holden tracked down Fran Sinclair in her office. It was, she noted, much smaller than Greenleaf's, and with the desk, sideboard, and two wall cupboards it felt cramped and unwelcoming. The single small window in the back wall, which seemed to have escaped the attention of whoever it was who cleaned the windows, did nothing to change that impression.

Sinclair did not rise. She had a mug of something hot in one hand, and a chocolate biscuit in the other, which was poised in front of her mouth. Her eyes ran up and down her visitor, and then, without a word of welcome, she thrust the biscuit into her mouth.

'I'd like to talk to you about your drugs regime.'

Sinclair continued chewing. Holden sat down. Sinclair now took a sip from the mug, wiped her mouth with the back of her wrist, and sniffed.

'So, what do you want to know?'

'Where do you keep your drugs for your patients?'

'In the drugs trolley.' Sinclair sniffed again.

'I assume that it's lockable?'

'Of course it's lockable. And it's kept locked.'

'And do you have much morphine in it?'

'None.'

'None?' The surprise in Holden's voice was obvious, and it provoked an immediate smile in the woman opposite her. Fran Sinclair was more than happy to play silly buggers. 'Are you saying there's no one in Sunnymede who is taking morphine?'

'No!' The smile was even more smug now. 'Morphine is a controlled drug. And like all controlled drugs, it has to be kept in a locked and immovable container, like that cupboard on the wall.' She pointed high towards Holden's right. 'That way, no one can walk off with the whole lot.'

'So how much morphine have you got in there at the moment? Can I look inside?'

'No need.' Sinclair picked up a black A4 book sitting on top of a pile of papers. 'This is our register of controlled drugs. We log them in, we log them out. We keep a running total.'

'Can I see?' It was a polite request, but Fran Sinclair didn't immediately pass it over. Holden felt her patience running thin. She didn't like the woman sitting in front of her, and she certainly didn't like her attitude.

Sinclair opened the book and leafed slowly through several pages, before turning it round so that Holden could see it.

'That's a good example. One of our cancer patients. She needs morphine on a daily basis. As you can see, each dose is logged, signed for, and witnessed. And the balance of the drug in the cabinet is also recorded.'

Holden nodded. She had never seen one of these before. 'So you check the balance on the book against what is in the cupboard?'

'Yes.'

'And if there was a discrepancy, what then?'

'There never has been a discrepancy,' she replied icily. Sinclair's brief attempt at being human had apparently come to an end.

'But just suppose a discrepancy had occurred,' Holden pressed.

'Then that would be a serious matter. I'd have to report it.'

Holden turned a page in the book. Her eyes scanned the entry for a Mrs Diana Leigh, but her brain was already moving on: 'And when a patient on morphine dies, what happens to the rest of the morphine?'

'All unused drugs would be safely disposed of via a licensed waste management company. And before you ask, let me tell you we keep full records of that too.'

Holden nodded again, though not because she was satisfied. If there had been a discrepancy – if morphine had disappeared – would Fran Sinclair really be happy to report it?

CHAPTER 5

I don't know where to start. I can't stop thinking. My head is a whirlpool. My head is an unexploded bomb. I have not slept well. Every time that I closed my eyes, my brain went into over-drive. So let me tell it in order, the whole day, from the beginning to end, and maybe then I will feel better.

I got up when my alarm went off. I had a shower and I got dressed. I put on clean pants and clean socks, but the rest of my clothes I had worn the previous day. I had breakfast – a little packet of porridge with milk which I microwaved for two and a half minutes. I put soft brown sugar on top – just one level dessert spoon – and I ate it slowly, with a glass of orange juice. Then I brushed my teeth, put on my anorak and my Oxford United scarf, and went to catch the bus. I got to work a bit early, so I went and stood outside the music shop in the Cowley Road and looked at all the guitars. I wish I could be a pop star.

Then I went to the shop. Jaz was already there, and I had four frames to make, so I concentrated on that. She popped out to the bank at 11.30 a.m., so I sat at the front and waited for customers, and then in walked Bella. She had come for her painting of Doubtful Sound. Jaz had told me that it was a real place, in New Zealand, so I felt bad that I had thought she was teasing me.

She paid me, and I said 'Thank you' and she said 'Thank YOU' and that made me feel better.

Jaz came back from the bank a few minutes later, and since it was 12.01, I went and ate my sandwiches at the back of the shop, and then I went for a walk. When I got to George and Delilah's for my ice cream, Bella was already there, sitting at the same table as the day before.

'What are you doing here?' I said.

She smiled. She has a nice smile. 'I want to buy you an ice cream, and then I want to tell you a secret.'

All afternoon the secret she told me was whizzing round my head, so I found it really hard to concentrate. I left work at 4.30 p.m., and outside there was Vickie, waiting for me.

'Hello, what are you doing here?' I said.

'I rang you, you twerp,' she said. 'We arranged that I could come round to your flat.'

She was right. I had forgotten. 'Are you wanting supper?' I said.

'I've got some money,' she said. 'I'll buy us both fish and chips.'

So we went back to my flat, and we ate at the table, and afterwards I made us each a mug of tea. But when I turned round to give her hers, I saw she was crying.

'What's the matter?' I said. I'm no good when people cry. I went to the bathroom and got her some toilet paper. After a while she stopped crying. 'Are you all right now?' I said. What else could I say?

'It's Dad,' she said.

'What do you mean?' I said, though I thought I knew what she meant.

'I hate him,' she said.

'Has he been hitting her again?' I felt myself getting angry just thinking about it. I saw him hit her once, right in the stomach with his fist. Mum had said he didn't hurt her, but I knew he had. I knew the bastard had hurt her.

'No,' Vickie said quickly. 'At least, I don't think so.'

'Tell me if he does,' I said.

'I wish I could stay with you,' she said.

I was confused. I couldn't keep up with what she was saying.

My flat is tiny. She has a double-size bedroom at home. 'Don't be silly,' I said. 'I've only got one room.'

'I wish I could stay here forever.'

People are hard to understand. I didn't know what to say, so I changed the subject. 'Do you want to know a secret?' I said. I was bursting to tell someone, and she was the best person to tell. Except maybe Jaz. But Jaz was always too busy.

'What secret?' She looked at me with eyes wide open. They were red, but she had definitely stopped crying.

'I met my mother today.'

She really did look surprised. I was pleased. 'What are you talking about?'

'I met my real mother today. She bought me an ice cream. Her name is Bella.'

'What do you mean, your real mother? Mum is your mother.'

'Mum is my adopted mother, you know that. Bella is my real mother.'

Then Vickie said something terrible. Or rather she shouted something terrible, at the top of her voice. 'Mum is your real mother, you idiot! She is the one that has loved you since you were little.'

'Bella has always loved me,' I said. I knew that because she had told me so, while I was eating the ice cream.

But Vickie just shouted at me again, about how ungrateful I was. And then she picked up her rucksack and her coat and said she was going home to tell Mum.

That made me angry. Really, really angry. So I grabbed her. I am much bigger than her, so it was easy to grab her by the upper arms and shake her. 'It's a secret,' I shouted. 'You mustn't tell anyone. Bella said it had to remain a secret.'

She tried to break free, but I'm strong, and I held her tight until she stopped struggling.

'Let me go,' she whined.

'Not until you promise to keep it a secret.'

She looked up at me then and I could see that she was scared. 'I promise,' she said.

But I didn't believe her. I couldn't be sure she wouldn't tell her mum. Her mum. Not mine. Bella had told me I had to start thinking of her as my mother, and Vickie's mother as my adopted mother. But we had to keep it a secret for now.

'Say it again.'

'I promise,' she said. 'David, I really do promise.'

This time I believed her. Almost. I gripped her arms even harder, digging my fingers into her flesh, and she started to cry. I pushed my face close up to hers. 'If you ever tell anyone, I will kill you', I said, and I snarled as I spoke. I wanted to really, really frighten her. Then I let her go.

'What are you doing here?'

Bella Sinclair recognized the voice only too well, but she resisted the urge to turn round. She had known that by coming back to Sunnymede she risked the chance of bumping into him, but he held no fears for her. When Fran had helped her get the job, she had been broke and so very glad of it, but now things were different. As jobs went, it wasn't exactly the be-all and end-all of her life, and if she lost it because of that bastard, then so be it. As she had walked up Fitzroy Close that morning, it had been anger that fuelled her, not fear. She had found herself reciting the conversation she would have if she bumped into him, and she had graphically imagined the scene – her and him having a stand-up row in front of a crowd of fascinated onlookers. Of course, reality rarely lives up to fantasy, but when she heard his voice, she was ready for him.

'You're suspended,' Greenleaf bellowed. 'You have to leave now!'

She turned round. His face was flushed, but seeing this only strengthened her resolve. 'I'm so sorry, Mr Greenleaf.' Her voice was mocking. 'Have I done something wrong?'

'What the hell are you doing here?'

Her face and her voice hardened. 'What the hell does it look like? I've come to get some things from my locker.'

'You know you're not allowed on the premises!'

'As it happens, I didn't. I've never been suspended before. But I'll go as soon as I've collected my things.' She turned her back on him and pulled open the locker door. In fact she had already got what she needed, but that wasn't the point. She removed a copy of a Susan Shields novel that she had already read twice, and pushed it into the hessian bag she was carrying. She would go when she was ready and not before. Besides, she was aware that she had an audience of at least two. A man and woman were standing several metres away along the corridor beyond Greenleaf, and they were obviously fascinated.

'You'll go now, or it'll be all the worse for you.'

She slammed the door of her locker shut, turned the key in it, put it in her pocket, and turned round. Her audience, she couldn't help noticing, was still there. 'How can it be worse for me, you arsehole? You've got me suspended. If you're going to threaten me, you'll have to try a bit harder than that.'

'You'll be unemployable if I've anything to do with it.'

'Really?' she said, and then allowed her eyes to look past him. She saw alarm register on his face. He turned and saw what she saw.

'Can I help?' he snapped angrily, all the veneer of politeness stripped from his voice.

'So what was that all about?' Holden was sitting in the staff room, and Greenleaf was opposite her. She had already heard Lawson and Wilson's versions of the incident. They had been able to agree most of what was said, despite the fact that at the time neither of them had fully understood the potential importance of what they were hearing – because neither of them had encountered Bella Sinclair before. Right now the two of them stood as observers on either side of the room. Only Fox was absent, ensuring that Bella Sinclair stayed put until Holden had had a chance to speak to her too.

'As you know, Bella is suspended. She shouldn't have been here. We were just having a few words.'

'From what my colleagues say, it was more than a few words.'

'We were both a bit on edge. What do you expect?'

'You threatened her.'

'In what way?'

'To make her unemployable.'

'If she's found guilty of theft and mistreatment of patients, then she will be unemployable. That's pretty much a fact, not a threat.'

'It sounded more than that to my colleagues.'

'Look, we were both shouting. Sometimes it sounds worse than it is.'

Holden frowned, and worried at her bottom lip with her forefinger. She didn't believe him. 'I understand Bella turned down your advances.'

'What are you talking about?'

Holden worried a bit more with her forefinger. He knew damned well what she was talking about. He was playing the innocent, playing for time. 'I'm talking about the time you went round to her flat unannounced, and ended up in bed with her.'

For a moment, he looked bemused, and then his face creased into a smile. 'Is that what she told you?'

'Actually,' Holden continued quickly, 'she also said that when you suggested doing it again another day, she laughed at you.'

His smile turned rueful, and he himself gave his own brutal laugh. 'There are two things you need to know about Bella. First, she's a pathological liar; she wouldn't recognize the truth if it stood up and bit her on the nose. And second, it was she who hit on me. We slept together a couple of times, in her flat. When I went round there that day, it was to tell her it was over. End of story.'

*

Five minutes later, and it was Bella Sinclair who was sitting in the chair opposite Holden. Her red hair was tied back tight behind her head, exposing the whole of her face. This did not, Holden reckoned, do her any favours, for it accentuated the lines across her forehead, the darkness under her eyes, and the creases at either corner of her mouth. The anger that Lawson and Wilson had witnessed had disappeared. Bella seemed tired, as if the encounter with Greenleaf had drained her of her spirit.

'I'd like to ask you what was so important in your locker that you came in this morning to get it even though you're under suspension?'

Bella shrugged. 'There was a ring I wanted, and a book I hadn't finished reading, and I thought why shouldn't I come in and get what belonged to me.'

'Can I see the ring?'

'If you want to.' There was no resistance, no reluctance. She pulled it off the third finger of her right hand and passed it across to Holden. 'It belonged to my mother. It's not very valuable, but it's important to me. I always take it off when I'm working, and last week I forgot to put it on again at the end of the shift.'

'And the book?'

Bella dug into her bag, removed the copy of *Unless* from it, and passed it over.

'Is it any good?'

'So far, yes.'

Holden began to flick through the pages. 'Where have you got to?'

'I'm about half way through, I think.'

'Hmm.' Holden continued to flick through the pages. 'It's just that I can't find a bookmark. Don't you use one?'

There was the briefest of pauses before Bella replied. 'Not a bookmark as such. Usually just a scrap of paper.'

70

'There's no scrap of paper.'

'It must have fallen out.'

'That's awkward for you.'

'Not really. I know where I got to. I'm at "Yet".'

'Sorry?' Holden looked at her hard. 'What do you mean?'

'I mean that I've reached the chapter called "Yet".' She paused, enjoying the confusion in the detective's eyes. 'All the chapters have strange names, like "Wherein" and "Otherwise". I'm at "Yet".'

Holden ate at her mother's flat again that night. It was becoming one-way traffic. She couldn't remember when she had last cooked for her mother. She had taken her out to the new restaurant on Folly Bridge a couple of weekends previously, but she hadn't actually cooked for her for ages. Whereas her mother had fed her at the drop of a hat last Friday, and had then rung her up on Sunday and invited her round for Tuesday. It was strange how they had slipped back into the role of mother and daughter. Only to describe it as slipping back wasn't quite accurate. It had been with her father that she'd had the stronger – and more troubled – relationship as a girl and then, as a teenager. When he'd died, she and her mother had found themselves washed up high and dry with only each other for support. It hadn't taken long for this enforced closeness to have its consequences: Susan had moved to Oxford, leaving her mother to fend for herself. When she had thought about it – and that hadn't been often – Susan had felt ashamed of herself. And it was because of that shame that she had eventually, on one of her rare visits home, suggested that her mother might like to move into one of the rather smart retirement flats in Grandpont, a stone's throw from where she herself lived. To her surprise, her mother had agreed, and six months later they had become almost neighours. And then they had begun the awkward process of rebuilding their relationship.

'Ah, there you are.' Her mother opened the door, a smile on her face. 'Look at you!'

'It's been a bit of a day.' They exchanged kisses and Susan kicked off her pumps.

'Supper's almost ready. Why don't you unwind in front of the telly?'

Susan dutifully moved through to the drawing room, turned the television on, and slumped down on the sofa. Her mother had been an absolute brick since Karen's death. Her own suspension from work had followed, and then an extended break on medical grounds, and through all that desperate time her mother had been there for her. Feeding her, ringing her, calling round. The old Susan would have rebelled at the unwanted intrusion, but the fact was she couldn't get enough of being mothered. She had not had it for so long. She had fought against it all through her teenage years, and now extraordinarily she needed it more than she could ever have imagined. She felt tears welling up. She wiped them away with the back of her hand, and unconvincingly told herself to take a grip.

They ate in virtual silence, punctuated by only the occasional comment: 'Pass the pepper, would you?' 'This is very good, Mother.' 'It's nice to have someone to cook for.' Afterwards, Susan cleared the table, putting the dirty things in the dishwasher, and then she retreated again to the sofa, until her mother brought the coffee through.

'So,' her mother said, when they were both settled, 'how was your day?'

'Where to begin?' Susan balanced her mug on her lap. Now that she had eaten and unwound, she was more than ready to answer questions. It was good to have someone to use as a sounding board, and sometimes – as she knew from experience – her mother could be really quite perceptive.

The day had begun, of course, with Wilson and Lawson overhearing that lively encounter between Bella Sinclair and Peter Greenleaf. She recounted this to her mother, and then her own interviews of the two, with Greenleaf claiming that they had had a brief affair which he had terminated, and then adding the damning allegation that Bella was a pathological liar.

'Do you believe him?'

'I don't want to believe him, and yet ...' She tailed off, not finishing her sentence, took another sip of coffee, and then described her own conversation with Bella about the book *Unless*.

Mrs Holden frowned. 'I take it that you don't think that Bella was in the middle of reading that book?'

'No, I don't.'

'So maybe Greenleaf is right, and she is a pathological liar. Or,' she continued, raising her finger like a schoolteacher making a point, 'she was lying about the book because she was trying to distract you from something else she had removed from the locker.' Mrs Holden gave the smile of someone suddenly rather pleased with herself. 'You didn't search her did you, by any chance?'

'I had no grounds.'

'What about the ring she showed you?'

'It was a nice enough ring, but not exactly a knuckle duster.'

'That was probably to distract you too. I bet there was something else she removed from the locker. Some incriminating bit of evidence. The packaging of the morphine that she gave to the old woman, for example.'

'Mother! That's pure speculation.'

'Maybe, but hasn't the thought occurred to you?'

Of course the thought had occurred to Susan Holden, and the fact that it had occurred to her mother too gave her no satisfaction. She and her team had, in fact, searched all the lockers that afternoon, but if ever there had been a case of shutting the stable door after the horse had bolted, that had been it.

'The problem with this case is that the more you look, the more the possibilities open up. You see, we also bumped into Jim Wright at Sunnymede today.'

Her mother frowned, her recall of the detail of the case suddenly falling short. She was finding that more and more these days. Sometimes she knew a name, and yet when she twirled it round the computer of her brain, its significance failed to register.

'Jim Wright is Nanette's son,' her daughter said softly. 'Her only son, in fact, and he's rather short of money.'

'Of course he is.' Mrs Holden was cross with herself. 'So what was he doing there?'

'It turns out he's been doing odd jobs at Sunnymede. Greenleaf hired him to help out with the maintenance. What with the review of the place, there's been quite a bit to bring up to scratch, and so Jim has been helping out their regular man of all trades on the staff, Roy Hillerby.'

'Oh dear,' her mother said. 'I don't think I remember a Roy either.'

Her daughter leant across and gave her a comforting pat on the arm. 'Actually, Mother, I don't think I've mentioned him before. Mind you, he may be important. The gossip is, according to Lawson, that he's been pursuing Bella Sinclair ever since she started at Sunnymede.'

'So this Bella must be attractive.'

Her daughter swallowed the last of her coffee. 'Yes, she is.' She got up then, thanked her mother for supper, gave her a prolonged hug, and left. She could have talked more about the case, but suddenly tiredness had hit her, and she felt sure that if she could just get home and collapse into bed, she would sleep, despite the coffee. Thoughts and theories were spiralling around inside her like crazy bees, so as she walked slowly along Chilswell Road, she began to silently utter her own private mantra, in the hope that this would empty her head of at least some of them.

CHAPTER 6

She was there again at George and Delila's, and she had already chosen me a mango and passion fruit ice cream when I arrived. She said she was having one too. It was nice, though I would have preferred a chocolate nugget one. But I didn't tell her that. Instead I said, 'This is nice, Bella.'

'Do you remember what we agreed yesterday, David?'

I wasn't sure what she meant. 'No,' I said.

'You were going to call me either Mum or Mother.'

I looked at her. I wondered if I should call her Mum, but when I thought of Mum, it wasn't her I thought of. It was difficult. 'I'll call you Mother,' I said.

'Thank you, son,' she said. 'That sounds really nice.'

I ate my ice cream until it was all gone. Mother kept looking at me. I felt embarrassed. I don't like being watched.

'I think I'd better go,' I said.

'I'm so pleased we found each other,' Mother said.

I didn't know what to say. But I did want to ask a question. It had been battering my brain ever since our last conversation, but I was frightened. So I shut my eyes, took a deep breath, and then opened them again. Then I asked my question: 'Why did you abandon me, Mother?'

'Oh David,' she said, in a voice like velvet. 'I didn't abandon you. Don't think of it like that. I had you adopted because at the time that was the best thing for you.' There were tears in her eyes, and she wiped at them with one of the paper napkins on the table. 'Your father died in a car crash, and I got ill, David.

I couldn't look after you. So I had you adopted to keep you safe. But now I'm back. And I'll never go away again.'

'I think we should tell my mum.' I looked at her. There were tears in her eyes again. 'I mean my adopted mum. Maureen.'

'Not yet, David. It's too soon. One day, when we've got to know each other better, then we will tell her everything. It will come as a shock to her, David, and we don't want to upset her, do we?'

'No,' I said. Mother was right, I didn't want to upset Mum.

She looked at me and smiled. She has a nice smile. 'Just remember, I never stopped loving you David,' she said. 'Just remember that.'

I looked at my watch. 'I have to go now,' I said.

'This is fun.' DC Lawson's voice was pure sarcasm, but DC Wilson appeared not to have heard. For the last hour and a half, the two of them had been poring over the controlled drugs register of Sunnymede Care Home. Or, to be precise, Wilson had done most of the poring. He thrived on detail and order, and the painstaking task of tracking each batch of every morphine product as listed in the book, and comparing the balance against the actual drugs in the wall cabinet, was one that absorbed his every fibre. Lawson, however, was already bored. She knew the potential importance of the task: if they could identify a missing dose or two of morphine, that would be a huge step forward in the tracking of Nanette Wright's killer, and yet she had already abdicated responsibility to Wilson. She merely checked out each batch of drugs when Wilson called out a number, confirming the number of pills or capsules left. But her mind was elsewhere, turning and twisting the detail of the case as she currently knew it, and formulating theories about possible motivations for killing an old lady. Had it been an accidental overdose or a deliberate act of murder? What sort of woman had Nanette Wright been – a dear old lady, or a vicious old cow? Why would someone have wanted to kill her? Her gut feeling was that it was family, most likely her son and daughter-in-law trying to hurry her to an early death in order to get her money, but her imagination conjured up an alternative scenario, a warped mercy-killer stalking the care homes of Oxford, seeking victims to release from their mortal coil. Was this going to be the first of many? Were there other deaths in the offing, or indeed were there others already committed and yet undetected? The idea of being involved in a case of that magnitude excited her, conjuring up absurd romantic images, with herself as one of the key figures at the centre of the media scrum that would inevitably occur, and which would lead – equally inevitably – to her own promotion.

Wilson was working his way through the final page of the register, checking the doses of morphine given to a Mrs White. These had been regular daily doses, and the reduction in stock levels all added up. A last batch had come in a week before she died, and the dosage had been increased on a couple of days as – he presumed – the pain got worse, but there was no obvious discrepancy and nothing to set alarm bells ringing. When she died there had been eighty millilitres of morphine left, and these had, according to the list, been handed over to Oxford Waste Ltd, the licensed waste disposal company that Sunnymede used.

'Well, that's that then,' he said.

'That's what?' Lawson replied.

'I can't find any discrepancies.'

'Did you expect to?'

'It's our job to check it out.'

'It's also part of our job to use our brains. If I was a killer nurse trying to filch drugs, I'd take them from someone who had died. I'd pretend to have passed them over for destruction, and I'd doctor the paperwork to make it look as though that had happened.'

'That's why we need to check the paperwork at the other end.' Wilson felt irritated with Lawson. He wasn't so dumb this hadn't occurred to him. It was just that he believed in being methodical. 'And that is what I intend to do,' he continued quickly, before Lawson could butt in. 'Go to Oxford Waste and check that the paperwork at their end ties up with the paperwork here.'

'So you don't need me for that?' Lawson felt there were more interesting ways to pursue the case.

'I'll be fine.' Normally Wilson enjoyed working alongside Lawson. But not today. 'But we'll need to check it out with the guv.'

Lawson made a noise that might well have been a snort. 'Don't you worry your little head, Constable. I'll go and find her now, bring her up to date, and tell her where you've gone.'

Somewhere deep inside, Wilson's slow-to-flare temper ignited. 'Where did you learn to patronize, Constable? At your father's knee?'

Lawson felt a sudden nip of shame, a sense of having done wrong. That was certainly something she'd learnt from her father. 'Sorry,' she said abruptly. She considered saying more, but she could hear footsteps approaching along the corridor, and that was all the excuse she needed. 'See you later,' she said, as she opened the door wide.

Two corridors away, in the staff room, Paul Greenleaf had just sat down opposite DI Holden. She had wanted to interview him again first thing that morning, but there had been a crisis with one of the patients, and Greenleaf had insisted he needed to attend to that first. Holden wasn't sure why, when Fran Sinclair was there and Dr Featherstone had been summoned, but she knew it would have been churlish of her to insist he put police inquiries before the welfare of his patients, and so she had agreed to wait.

'How is Mr Osbourne?' Holden tried to sound concerned. At least she had remembered his name.

'We think he'll be OK, thank you.'

'Good.'

'What was it you wanted to ask me about?' Greenleaf leant back in his chair, as if suddenly he had all the time in the world.

'How long has Jim Wright been working here?'

'Jim?' He paused, running his two hands expansively through his long hair. 'He just does odd jobs for me from time to time.'

'That wasn't what I asked.'

'Hmm!' Again there was a delay. Greenleaf sucked in a breath of air and then expelled it. 'He did one or two small jobs for me in the summer, and then I got him in to help with some redecorating and general maintenance a few weeks ago.'

'Why him?'

'Why not?'

'There's a hundred and one odd-job men out there, Mr Greenleaf. How come you hired the son of one of your patients?'

Greenleaf lifted his hands theatrically. 'For that very reason. I met him when he came to look at Sunnymede for his mother. He told me he was a builder. I suppose I must have filed him away in the back of my head. We have our own odd-job man on staff – Roy Hillerby – but he has so many different things to do that when we had a couple of rooms that needed some serious work, I realized he'd need help. So I approached Jim.'

Holden nodded. It all added up, just about, but she wasn't completely convinced. 'Who did you use before Jim Wright came along?'

'A man called Alan Moore. But he's got asbestosis.'

'Why did you trust Jim Wright? If you'd done any checking around, you'd have discovered his business hit the rocks not so long ago.'

'Christ, what sort of woman are you, Inspector?' There was a sudden surge of anger. 'Do you write people off just because they get into financial trouble? Anyway, there was never going to be a risk to Sunnymede. We pay him, not the other way round, and we only pay him when the work is complete. In addition, given his situation, his rates are very competitive. And when you're on a tight budget, as we are, that's important.'

Holden was pleased at the response she had provoked. She didn't care what Greenleaf thought of her. What mattered was to try and get information out of him, and to probe his account for inconsistencies. And if getting him riled helped, then so be it. 'So he's been in a lot recently, has he? And visiting his mother too, no doubt, like the dutiful son.'

'No visiting of his mother during his working time. I made that clear from the word go. If he wanted to see her, then it had to be in his own time, after he had gone home and cleaned himself up.'

'Do you have a list of the days he has worked?' Holden couldn't help the feeling that Greenleaf's blustering manner was deliberate ploy, designed to distract.

'Of course I have. If you want, I'll get the timesheets he's submitted from my office. But basically he's been working here most days for the last month.'

'I'd like that,' Holden said. 'Sergeant Fox will come and get it all now.'

Greenleaf rose to his feet, as did the silent Fox. Holden waited for them to reach the door. 'One more thing,' she said, forcing Greenleaf to turn. 'Tell me about Roy Hillerby.'

'What do you want to know? He's our odd-job man, as I have already mentioned.' There was an edge of irritation in his voice. 'He's been working for us for about two and a half years. He's a very useful chap to have around.'

'I gather he and Bella Sinclair have a relationship?'

'You gather they have a relationship!' Greenleaf laughed dismissively. 'Where do you get your gossip, Inspector?'

'Oh, my constable is very good at extracting information from gossip, and usually it turns out to be remarkably accurate.' Holden knew that wasn't entirely true, but right now her only focus was to get Greenleaf rattled. 'Given that you've slept with

Bella, I thought you might be a good man to double check the gossip with.'

'Yeah!' he sneered. 'Well what I can tell you is that Hillerby has been buzzing round her honeypot ever since she started here. But I doubt very much if he's had even the slightest taste.'

Holden recognized the detective superintendent's voice instantly, and just as instantly she felt anxiety grip her stomach. 'How are things going, Inspector?'

It was the same question as before, and yet here she was three days later and there was nothing significant to report.

'I'm fine and the case in progressing, Sir,' she said, knowing that it wouldn't satisfy him.

'Is it murder or not?' Collins was in no mood to exchange politenesses.

'I'm not sure yet, Sir.'

'In that case, I need Wilson and Lawson back.'

'What?'

'Are they there?'

'Lawson is.' In fact, she was standing opposite Holden. She had just finished reporting what she and Wilson had been up to, and now she was pretending – and failing miserably – not to be interested in the telephone conversation going on in front of her. 'Wilson has just gone to check the records at Oxford Waste Ltd. We think morphine that should have been destroyed by them may never have got there.'

'Well, you and Fox will have to follow that up yourselves. We've got a big operation coming up tomorrow, so I need both Lawson and Wilson back at the Cowley station within the hour.'

'Is that absolutely necessary?'

'It's an order, Inspector, not a request. You can have them back on Monday. Maybe.'

*

'Hi!' A man had appeared in the doorway of the staff room. 'I understand you want to see me.'

Roy Hillerby was relatively short – about five foot eight, Holden reckoned – with dark curly hair, a lean face and an impressive scar on his right-hand cheek. He looked like a man who kept himself fit, and when he smiled it was with a slightly lop-sided grin. In fact, the first thing he did when he came into the staff room was to smile. Fox put it down to nerves – or maybe guilt. Guilt about what, it didn't really matter. Everyone feels guilty when they've been summoned by the police.

'Yes, we do.' Holden didn't bother introducing herself or Fox. The chances were that everyone in Sunnymede who wasn't suffering from dementia knew exactly who they were now. She waved him to the chair opposite her.

'How do you get on with Jim Wright?'

The question seemed to take Hillerby by surprise. He opened his mouth slightly, but two or three seconds passed before he actually spoke. 'We get ... get on all r ... right.'

It was Holden who paused now, taken off guard by Hillerby's stuttering. It wasn't something you came across so often these days, though she remembered being fascinated by one of her grandfather's friends, and her mother later telling her off for staring at him right the way through tea. 'How long have you known him?' she asked.

'He's been w ... working here f ... f ... for a month or so, h ... helping me.'

'Had you met him before that?'

There was another pause. 'N ... no!'

'Did he go and visit his mother when he was working? I mean, in his lunch break, for example.'

'No. You get d ... dirty when you're decorating, and Mr Greenleaf had asked him n ... not to.'

'It would be quite normal for a son to say hello to his mother, though. Didn't he ever just pop in to see her?'

'Not that I can rem ... rem ... remember.'

Holden nodded as she considered this answer, and what to say next. The stuttering was putting her off. She would have liked a wide-ranging chat, but it felt somehow unfair to keep asking questions of a man who had difficulties giving answers. 'Was it because he didn't like his mother?'

Hillerby shook his head. 'I don't know.'

Holden turned for support towards Fox. It was something he was used to. Holden would turn to him when she wanted him to apply pressure from another angle, but usually – almost always in fact – they discussed these tactics in advance. But not this time. Even so, Fox knew she wanted him to intervene. He cleared his throat. 'Was it because his mother didn't like him?'

Hillerby's eyes opened wide, and he sat up straighter. The question had clearly struck a nerve. 'His m … m … mother was a horrible woman. She was v … very unkind. To everyone. E … e … everyone!'

It was a moment of minor revelation for Holden. She had, of course, never met Nanette Wright, but she had assumed that she was essentially a nice old lady. That wasn't to say that Holden hadn't come across difficult and cantankerous old women, but her own mother was essentially nice – if a little overinterested in her daughter's life – and she wanted every-one else's ageing mother to be nice too. But it was an interesting thought – that Nanette Wright had actually been a right old cow who went around upsetting people and making enemies.

But that was for later. Right now, having got Fox to bail her out, she took back control and changed tack. 'I understand you and Bella are very good friends?'

'W … we are friends.'

'Are you lovers too?' There was no point in beating about the bush even with someone who stammered.

Hillerby's Adam's apple pulsated, bulging and contracting. 'Wh … what's that got to do with y … you?'

'I'm investigating a suspicious death. Bella Sinclair looked after Mrs Wright.'

'Lots of p … p … people looked after her.'

It was a fair comment. Lots of people had had access to her, and had cared for her in different ways. But Bella was the one who had been suspended, Bella was the one who had been accused of abusing another patient, and also of theft. If you were going to start with someone, then Bella was the obvious person. And if Bella had done something, then maybe Roy Hillerby was the man who might know. But if he was soppy about her, he was hardly going to split on her.

'If there's something you know, you must tell us, Roy.' Holden had leant forward, emphasizing her point. 'Because if you know something and you refuse to tell us, then that's aiding and abetting, and that's very serious. You could get yourself locked up if you don't tell me everything you know. You do understand that, don't you?'

Roy Hillerby's eyes narrowed, and the sinews in his neck tightened visibly. 'Don't treat me like I'm an idiot,' he hissed. There wasn't even a hint of a stammer. 'Bella and I are friends, and she has done nothing wrong. N … n … nothing!'

'So, what do you think?'

Holden and Fox had retreated outside Sunnymede, so that Holden could succumb to her third cigarette of the day. Until a few days ago, she had convinced herself that she had got her habit well and truly under control, but she knew now that her willpower was in serious danger of collapsing. She had smoked two cigarettes on the trot when she had got back home the night before, and she had even had one that morning before her cup of tea. She knew it was a bad sign. When the case was over, she told herself without conviction, things would improve.

'He never answered the question,' Fox said. There was a blank look on Holden's face, and Fox realized that she hadn't followed his thought pattern. 'About whether they were lovers.'

The blank look faded. 'Do you think they are? Or have been?'

'I don't know. But he was very protective of her.'

'Yes, I noticed. He's clearly fond of her.'

'But why would she kill Nanette Wright? There's no motive, is there?'

Holden took a final pull on her cigarette, dropped it onto the gravel, and ground it underfoot. 'If Nanette Wright was the vicious old woman that Hillerby said, then who's to say she didn't provoke Bella?'

'But murder?'

'Manslaughter, probably. Consider this. She puts morphine in Nanette's hip flask as some form of petty revenge, or perhaps just to quieten her down. The only problem is, she overdoes it, and the old woman reacts badly to it and dies. Anyway that's my best guess.'

Fox scratched his head as he wondered whether to say what he felt he should say. Now that Lawson and Wilson were both gone, there was only him to say it. He cleared his throat. 'Look Guv, where's the evidence? Because the way I see it, what you've said is an interesting theory, but that's all it is. In fact, not even a theory. As you said, it's a guess, even if it is a best guess.'

Holden wished she had another cigarette in her packet. Damn Fox! Damn him for his common sense. Damn him for being so damned steady! From behind her, she felt a sudden breeze. She shivered, and looked round, and then felt several spots of rain on her face, cold and unrefreshing. What a bloody rotten day it had turned out to be!

'Thank you, Fox,' she said sarcastically. 'In that case, we need to find some evidence, don't we.' And with that she started walking towards the front entrance.

At much the same time as Detective Inspector Susan Holden was irritably berating her sergeant, Mrs Jane Holden was stepping on a dog turd on the corner of Marlborough Road and Whitehouse Road.

Grandpont is an area that has seen something of a canine explosion since the late nineties. Perhaps because of its proximity to green spaces, or perhaps in response to the threat posed by burglars, or perhaps for other more complicated and ill-defined reasons, the narrow network of streets that make up the area immediately to the west of the Abingdon Road are home to a surprising number of dogs. From the ubiquitous collies and labradors to dachshunds (short-haired and long), from unkempt rescued mongrels to aristocratically trimmed schnauzers, they are to be seen dragging their owners out in all kinds of weather and at all times of day and, indeed, night. Dylan, Monty, and even – believe it or not – Freud, it is the dogs that control the exercise regimes of many a Grandpont household. Mostly they behave at least as well as their owners – and mostly they wait until they have the grass of the nature park under their paws before answering the call of nature, but occasionally accidents do happen in the streets, and even more occasionally (though still too often) their owners fail to clean up after them.

And this is what had happened on that miserable Thursday, when Mrs Jane Holden got to the crossroads of Marlborough and Whitehouse. She didn't see the turd. Of course she didn't, or she wouldn't have put her shoe in it. She had just been to see an ill friend from church. To find her sitting slumped and grey in her armchair, wheezing noisily as she fought for breath, had upset Mrs Holden. And now as she headed back towards her flat, it had started to rain too. As she huddled inside her coat and thrust her hands deeper into her pockets, her left foot made contact with a very fresh and slimy turd. At that very same moment she was twisting her not so flexible body in order to turn the corner into Whitehouse Road. She was not a particularly heavy woman, but her hands, being in her pockets, were in no position to break her fall. She plummeted sickeningly hard onto the pavement, and her head cracked against it with such force that she lost consciousness instantly.

*

If people really could turn in their graves, Nanette Wright would have been turning in hers. The only thing was, she hadn't yet made it that far. Instead she was locked up in the mortuary, cold and stiff, while the pathologist waited for the coroner, and the coroner waited for the police, and the police got on with more important things. As far as Detective Constables Wilson and Lawson were concerned (not that it had been their call, but actually they agreed with their detective superintendent on this), the death of a single old woman in a care home was less important than a major drugs bust. As for Detective Inspector Holden, Nanette Wright's death paled in significance compared to the damage that her own mother had sustained in Marlborough Road. So only Detective Sergeant Fox woke up on that Friday morning with Nanette Wright's death on his mind. He had received a phone call from his boss about nine o'clock on the previous evening; she had given him the full details of her mother's misfortune – her fall, her possibly cracked pelvis, how she was being kept in the John Radcliffe Hospital overnight, how she might need an operation, and, in that case, how was she going to cope? He had listened calmly, and assured her that he would manage on his own throughout Friday. Was he sure, she had asked? Yes, he was sure, he had replied. She would ring, maybe. No, really, there was no need. He would manage. And so they had left it. Fox would manage. And why not? For underlying their conversation – implied, but never stated – was the reality that Holden's mother was alive and was therefore more important than Nanette Wright, who was dead, and would have died sooner rather than later even if her whisky hadn't been spiked with morphine. And besides, was the accidental overdosing of an ill old woman really such a crime?

Fox spent Friday treading water. After reading through all of Wilson's notes, he drove to Oxford Waste Ltd and spoke to

Dennis Adkins, a rather podgy, moustachioed, petty function-naire, who took relentless delight in explaining his system, and in showing, item by item, how he had a matching receipt for each of Sunnymede's disposal records. Fox retreated as soon he was able, and spent the rest of the day back at the station, where administration and reviewing the detail of the case came as a blessed relief. And after that, of course, came the weekend.

CHAPTER 7

She was there at the game today. Hayes and Yeading in the FA Trophy. It was a rubbish game, but we won 1–0. I saw her with my binoculars. I always take them to a game. That way if there's an incident I can get a good close look. Like if someone is injured, or if I think the ref is going to send someone off. And especially if we get a penalty. If they get a penalty, I always shut my eyes, but when we get one I use my binoculars to watch. So I used my binoculars to look at Dad and Vickie in the executive box. I wish it had been Dad and David up there, but he said there were only two tickets. And, of course, Vickie is his real daughter, whereas I am just his pretend son. He didn't say that, but that's what he thinks. I know.

But guess who else was there? It's unbelievable. Mother! Not Mum, but Mother. My real mother. Why was she there? I don't understand. Dad said it was a special treat organized by someone at Sunnymede where Nan Nan was. They had hired a whole executive box for the game. He was given two tickets because he has been working there. So how come Mother was there? Has Mother told them? She said we shouldn't, not yet. So how come she was there? Are they plotting something? Maybe Mother isn't my real mother at all. Maybe she's been lying to me all along. I need to be careful, really careful. None of them love me. They only pretend.

'G ... G ... God!' Roy Hillerby was excited. He stammered when he was under stress and he stammered when he was excited.

And right now he sure as heck wasn't under stress. 'D ... d ...
did you see his face? Of c ... course you did. It was an absolute
cl ... cl ... cl ... classic!'

'Calm down, Roy.' Bella Sinclair spoke firmly, as if trying to
control a hyperactive kid. 'Just take a moment and calm down.'

Hillerby took not a moment, but a swig from his can of lager.
It was only a small one, out of Bella's fridge, but he'd had a
couple of pints before the game, and then one at half time, and
it was all starting to have an effect. He couldn't hold his alcohol
as well as he liked to pretend.

He could see it all, as clear as day. It had been priceless –
the look on Greenleaf's face when he walked into the executive box with Bella as his guest. He was glad she had been up
for it. Why the hell shouldn't she come with him? The fact that
she'd been suspended meant nothing. Innocent until proven
guilty, wasn't it? He smiled to himself, his eyes still shut. Not
that Bella Sinclair was a little Miss Innocent. God no! Maybe
she'd let him stay tonight. She'd better. God she'd better, after
everything he'd done for her.

Greenleaf had followed him to the loo at half time, and
they'd stood there side by side, pissing the beer away. 'What
the hell are you playing at, bringing Bella?' he'd hissed. 'She's
suspended from work.'

And he'd grinned back. 'This ain't work! And she's my guest
anyway. I'm entitled, as much as anyone.'

'You'll regret this!' he'd hissed again.

'I think you've got a bit of splashback there, my friend.' And
he'd laughed because Greenleaf's pale chinos were speckled
with urine.

Jim had been there too. He was a good laugh. Brought his
daughter along too. Twelve going on eighteen. Legs up to her
arse. She wouldn't be a little Miss Innocent either for long.
Played the shy one, kept looking down, but that only made look
her look like a tease.

'What are you grinning about, Roy?' The words were real,

not the product of his memory and imagination. Hillerby opened his eyes and saw Bella watching him.

'Just reliving every little detail. Reliving and savouring it.'

'Greenleaf won't forget, you know. You want to watch your back.'

Hillerby nodded, and took another swig. 'I know.' His voice was suddenly serious. 'You need to watch yours too, Bella.'

'Thank you, Einstein, for your words of wisdom.' Her tone was sarcastic, belittling, designed to keep him at a distance.

They both fell silent. Hillerby downed the last of his pint. She sipped at her ginless tonic, her eyes on him, but her thoughts elsewhere.

'Can I stay over?' he said, grasping at the straws of opportunity.

She frowned as she considered this. And then her mobile rang, saving her the need to answer.

'David!' She was genuinely surprised. She had given him her number, but she hadn't expected him to call. She had hoped he would, of course, hoped that he would choose to make contact, but she hadn't really thought he would. Not yet.

Hillerby saw the delight in her face, and felt a surge of jealousy. He wished he could listen in. There was a torrent of words from the caller. That much Hillerby could hear. But not what those words were.

'I can explain, David,' Bella was saying firmly. 'Just calm down....'

But there seemed to be no prospect of David calming down. Hillerby belched loudly, angered by the intrusion. It had been going so well. Why did the creep have to ring now?

'Why don't you come round to my flat?' Bella was saying. 'We can talk about it over some food?'

The torrent stopped.

'You live in Barns Road, don't you David? Well you're only a few minutes' walk from my flat.' She spoke calmly, soothingly, in a manner that was familiar to Hillerby. She used that tone with him sometimes, when she wanted him to do something for her.

'Well that's settled, then,' she said, winding down the conversation. 'I'll see you in a few minutes.'

She looked across at Hillerby. 'Sorry, Roy. My son is coming round. I think you'd better go.'

'I thought....' But his sentence died before it could take form. She had spoken to him in the tones she had used with David. Softly, firmly, and – as he knew from experience – implacably.

'I just need a pee first,' he said, conceding defeat. 'Then I'll shove off.'

'Thanks, Roy,' she purred. 'You're a star.'

Once inside her flat, Ania Gorski dropped her bag on the floor and went to the bathroom. She locked the door and sat on the toilet.

There was no real need to lock the door. It was her flat, and only she had keys to it. Sometimes, she deliberately left the bathroom door not only unlocked, but wide open while she urinated. It felt good, liberating even. But not today. Today she slammed the door shut and locked it, and sat on the toilet. She didn't urinate. She had not, she thought, had even a glass of water since she got out of bed. She should drink, she knew that, but her nausea was too overwhelming, and it was only as she sat there, that it finally began to recede. Locked inside her bathroom, locked inside her flat, she felt something approximating to safety. In the car with him, as he had driven her back to Oxford, she had been unable to think. She had shut her eyes in the hope that he would not try and talk to her, and had prayed for everything to be better – whatever that might be. She was not a praying person. She called herself a Catholic when required to fill in a form with the religion question on it, but that was as far as it went. For her parents and for her, that was all it had ever been.

She needed help. Not divine help, but practical, human help.

That is to say, advice. Guidance. Someone to tell her: *Do this* or *do that; dump him* or – God forbid – *don't dump him; go to the police* or *don't go to the police*. There was only one person she could think of. She was older and surely wiser than her. She had always been kind to her. She was, she supposed, a friend. She would ring her.

She stood up. The nausea, she realized, had receded. She knew what the next step was, and that in itself was a huge relief. She unlocked the door, and went through into the living room. Her bag was where she had dropped it. She kicked off her shoes, and knelt down on the floor next to it, scrabbling around inside until she had found her mobile. She found the number she wanted, and rang it, oblivious to the irony that as she did so she was on her knees.

'I've been praying.' It was the first thing Mrs Holden said when her daughter reappeared at 5.35 p.m. that Sunday evening. She was sitting in the chair by the side of her hospital bed, and her face was beaming.

The detective inspector smiled weakly in reply. Such comments by her mother still had the capacity to catch her off guard. 'What about?'

'That the doctors will let me home tomorrow.'

'What do the nurses think?'

'Sister says they very likely will. They need the bed space, anyway. But there's nothing like a bit of prayer to move things along.'

Her daughter nodded, but said nothing. Her mother's tendency to speak in such terms was both disturbing and a little embarrassing. She looked around the ward, in case anyone should be listening. The woman opposite was asleep, the woman next to her was watching TV, and the fourth bed in the area was empty.

'Well,' her daughter said finally, 'the question then is: how are we going to get you better? I think I'll have to ask for some compassionate leave and—'

'No, you most certainly will not!'

Susan Holden was taken aback by the sharpness of her mother's intervention. 'Why ever not?'

'Because you're in the middle of a case. And what do you think your Superintendent Collins will say? You've only just had six months off....'

'My sergeant can handle the case. It's only an old—' Holden ground quickly to a halt, suddenly conscious of what she had started to say.

'It's only an old lady,' her mother said quickly. 'An old lady who would have died sooner or later anyway. Isn't that what you mean? So it doesn't matter if she was murdered or not.'

'Of course it matters.'

But her mother had not finished. 'Suppose it was me. Suppose I had been that old lady. Would I be worth only a sergeant?'

Holden shook her head. 'That's not what I meant. What I meant was, it's important that you are properly looked after when you get home.'

'Don't worry. That's all arranged. Doris came in earlier, and she is going to take charge of me and organize a rota.'

Holden bowed her head in submission. Of course, the redoubtable Doris Williams would have been in to see her. And of course within minutes they would between them have organized a complete recovery programme. And no doubt after that they would have prayed for every other poor soul in the ward.

'So all you need to do is get me home tomorrow, and make sure there's some fresh milk in the fridge. Do you think you can manage that?'

Holden felt her hackles rise. What was it about her mother that even in these circumstances, she had the capacity to drive her nuts. 'Of course I can, Mother.'

Her mother smiled and settled back into her chair. 'Well, that's settled then.'

'And I am going to find out who killed Nanette Wright. You can be damn sure of that.'

'Good!' There was another beatific smile. 'That's my girl.'

CHAPTER 8

I told them at the end of Sunday lunch. I had just eaten my pudding – apple crumble with custard – and I was licking my spoon clean like I always do. But it wasn't just food in my stomach. Have you seen the film Alien, *where a thing bursts out of the chest of one of the spacemen? Well I felt like that would happen to me too if I didn't tell them, if I didn't bring it out into the open.*

So I said, 'I've got something to tell you, Mum.'

'Yes, David,' she said. But she wasn't looking at me. It was like she was humouring me.

'I bet you'll be cross,' I said. I wanted to get her attention.

'I bet I won't,' she said.

'It depends what you tell us,' Dad said.

I didn't look at him. I try not to look at him. I looked across the table at Vickie. She was making a face at me. Not a silly face, a serious one. I think she knew what I was going to say, and she didn't want me to. But I'm grown up now, and I can say what I want.

'I've met my mother,' I said.

'What do you mean?' This time, Mum did look at me.

'I mean what I said.' It felt good. I was telling them. 'The other day I met my real mother, the one who gave birth to me.'

'Don't be so bloody daft,' Dad said. 'What the fuck are you talking about?'

'You shouldn't swear,' I said. It was one of the rules in Mum's house. No swearing.

'It's my fucking house, so I'll do what I want in it.' He glared at me. His face was red, and so were his stupid sticky-out ears.

'Shut up, Jim,' Mum shouted. She hardly ever shouted, so I knew she was upset. Then she turned towards me and smiled her comforting smile.

'David, how do you know she's your real mother?' she said.

'She told me.'

'Did she?' Mum smiled again. 'David, darling, are you sure? You know how it is – people sometimes make fun of you and fib and—'

'She's my mother. She gave birth to me.' I was shouting now. Why do people never believe me? 'She wouldn't lie. She's lovely.'

'Lovely?' Dad bellowed. He suddenly stood up at the end of the table and slammed his fist down on it. 'Lovely? The woman who gave birth to you wasn't lovely. She was a crack head. Why do you think you were adopted? Not because she was a lovely mother!'

'I don't believe you,' I shouted.

'Well, it's true. I can tell you a lot more.' And he did. More lies came pouring out of his mouth, while Mum burst into tears and shouted at him to stop.

But he didn't stop and I wasn't stopping. I wasn't going to listen to his lies any more. I jumped up and ran out of the room. I ran to the front door, and then I ran all the way to my flat. And I locked myself in, and I turned off my phone.

When DS Fox arrived at Cowley police station on Monday morning, and found a yellow sticker on his monitor with the words 'Ring Holden' on it, his immediate assumption was that there had been complications with her mother. That was his first thought, and it proved to be an accurate one.

'They kept her in all weekend,' Holden confirmed, 'and now I've got to wait and see the consultant whenever it is that he does his rounds. But hopefully they'll be letting her out later today.'

'So you'll be in tomorrow?'

'I hope so.'

After the tedium of Friday, when he had uncovered nothing of interest at Oxford Waste Ltd, Fox felt an unaccustomed sense of disappointment. The investigation was slowing down, and he realized, with sudden insight, that it might not be going anywhere. An old woman who would have died soon enough has died from a morphine overdose, and the chances of them finding out who was responsible are reducing with every passing day. And in the greater scheme of things, did it really matter? In any case, one day very soon the chief super would ring up, mutter about budgetary constraints, and move them on to other things.

Fox went to the loo, got himself a coffee, and returned to his desk. His mobile, which he had left on his desk, was apparently able to detect his approach, for it beeped politely as he walked in. It was a text message, from Holden: 'Check out Featherstone!!!' A smile crept across Fox's face. Three exclamation marks! He liked that. He liked the fact that Holden was getting bored with sitting in the hospital and so was resorting to sending him texts and telling him what to do. Others might have resented it, but he grinned as he replied with three of his own exclamation marks: 'Will do, Guv!!!'

Three was also the number of hours that passed before he actually followed up her orders. The first was taken up with emails, the second with a fire alarm which went off and then proved to have been a false alarm with no obvious cause, and the third drifted by as he read right through several sheets of paperwork relating to an adjustment in his pension arrangements. He then he went to get another coffee via the loo (again). He is, he knows, putting things off. He checks his mobile. There are no new messages. Fox is not a man to encourage messages, but he rereads Holden's again. What does she mean by 'Check out Featherstone'? He isn't psychic. Check out his history? His personal life? His movements on the day of Nanette's death? Could Feathertsone have wanted Nanette dead? Or is he an incompetent doctor covering his tracks?

Well the place to start is Sunnymede. He gets up and instantly feels better. He will spend the rest of the day snooping round Sunnymede, asking question and checking records. And he will start in reception.

Twenty minutes later, he is chatting to Mary. Mary likes to chat. It was one of the qualities that got her the job as receptionist. After he has signed himself in, he answers her questions, about where he lives, what he does when he's not being a policeman, and whether he prefers the football or the dogs. He answers happily, until she asks him what his star sign is. Only then does he bring himself back to the job in hand.

'Mary,' he says, 'does everyone who comes in here have to sign in?'

'Of course,' she smiles. 'In case there's a fire.'

'Does that include the postman, for example?'

'No. There's no need. He comes in, leaves the mail, and goes.'

'Suppose he needs to use the loo?'

'Then I write him on a yellow Post-it note, and when he comes out I throw it away. I am very organized.' She smiles as she says this last thing. But it is not the cheery welcoming smile she had employed when he arrived, but one that challenges him to prove her wrong.

'Can I see the list for Tuesday 1 December?'

She has a large folder open in front of her. She turns back through several pages and then turns it round.

'There you are.'

There are names, times in and out, car registration numbers, and the name of the person being visited. He runs his finger methodically down the list, and stops near the bottom. Dr Featherstone had come in that day at 4.05 p.m. and had left at 5.35 p.m. But there was no car registration number recorded, and no person visited.

'We know which his car is,' Mary says quickly when he remarks on this. 'There's no need for him to write it down every time.'

'It's not his usual visiting day.'

'No, it was probably a minor crisis with one of the patients.'

'So why is the patient's name not written down?'

'Because it's not necessary!' The remorseless cheerfulness for which Mary is known is temporarily suspended. 'When someone comes to visit a patient, we record it because we don't necessarily know who they are. So we like to keep tabs. But everyone knows Dr Featherstone.'

Fox nods. 'Thank you.' He is aware he has upset her. 'It's all perfectly logical. But I do need a photocopy of this page.'

'Of course.' She stands up. 'If you can stand guard for me, I'll pop into the office and do it.' She is cheerful again.

In the middle of the afternoon, Fox's mobile rings again. It is Holden.

'How's it going?' she asks.

'How's your mother?' he replies.

'She's home. I'm here with her. I'm going to stay in the spare room for a few nights, and her friend Doris is organizing a rota for the days, just until Mother's a bit more mobile. But what I want to know is what you've been up to.'

'There have been some interesting developments.' He pauses.

'Well?' she snaps. Patience is not one of her virtues.

'Dr Featherstone visited Sunnymede on the day of Nanette's death. He was in the building between roughly four and half past five. A Mrs Jones had been taken ill – a chest infection, it turned out.'

'And he was there for an hour and a half? That's quite a time for one patient.'

'That was my thought too, Guv. And there's another interesting thing. Mrs Jones's room is in the same corridor as Nanette Wright's. In fact it's only two doors away.'

The jogger moved steadily round the Cowley Marsh Recreation Ground. He was a familiar sight to the footballers, dog walkers and sundry others who used the rec on a regular basis. Not that many would have known who he was, but the flapping hair, silver trainers, and red tracksuit were enough to make him notable. That and his strict adherence to his training pattern. He jogged, almost without fail, on Mondays, Wednesdays and (less reliably) Fridays. He arrived, almost without fail, a few minutes after five o'clock, winter or summer. In December, this meant it had been dark for some time, but this never appeared to worry him. He was rarely on his own, for even at this time of year there were always one or two people trailing their dogs whatever the weather after a day at their office or work place. Absolutely without fail, he would run three anti-clockwise circuits around the rec, or to be strictly accurate two and three quarter circuits, because before completing the third he would veer right onto the path that runs along the northern edge of the rec and beat his way remorsely along it until it became Barracks Lane. From there he would force his way up the hill, as far as the junction with Hollow Way, before turning round and accelerating with relief back down the hill, and then straight through the rec, this time keeping to the path. That was the pattern a keen-eyed stalker might have observed. And that was the pattern he followed this dank Monday, as if there was no other alternative. On this occasion, however, the imaginary stalker would have noticed that when he reached the Hollow Way Road, he stopped, looked at his watch, and for some thirty seconds waited, looking round, and jogging intermittently on the spot. Then with a sigh, he began to retrace his steps down Barracks Lane and into the rec.

And it was here, at this eastern entrance to the Cowley Marsh Recreation Ground, where bushes and trees press on either side, that he ran into a wire stretched tight across the path. It caught him full in the neck, and catapulted him off his feet. If this had been a cartoon it would have been comic: a man spinning in mid air, his feet going forwards and upwards, while his head rushed the opposite way, until it cracked against the unyielding pavement. Kerpow! The man would have got up, staggered, groaned loudly, and then within seconds have miraculously regained all of his faculties, except for the common sense that he never had. But this was brutal reality. For a moment the jogger lay still. The back of his skull was exploding with pain, but that was nothing compared to the multitude of nerves screaming in his throat. He wanted only relief from the agony of the moment, to be engulfed by oblivion, but the survival instinct is an overriding one, and with unconscious effort he pushed himself up onto his knees. He tried to suck in a breath, but the inferno of pain in his throat only intensified. Then – somehow – he became aware of someone else, someone who had pushed through the shrubbery and now stood looming above him. He looked up, trying to focus, trying to understand, but too late. He barely saw or even sensed the claw hammer which smashed into his right temple, and sent him sprawling onto to the ground again. Five, six, seven times, the tool bludgeoned his skull, shattering bone and gouging flesh. But there were no screams of agony and no yelps of pain, and long before the assault ceased, Paul Greenleaf lay still and twisted on the path, undeniably and irreversibly dead.

It was not until halfway through the following morning that Paul Greenleaf was identified, although he had been found almost immediately. Less than five minutes after he had breathed his last, a cyclist had to take sudden evasive action to avoid running over his inert body. The police were on hand less than six minutes later, but identifying him was not an easy task. This wasn't because his face was a serious mess – though it was. And it wasn't because nobody missed him – because one person most certainly did. It was essentially because he was carrying absolutely no ID. He carried no wallet with tell-tale plastic cards, because what need was there for them on a run? He carried a key, but the ring to which it was attached gave away no information about him save that he was a supporter of Help the Aged. He also, like many joggers, carried an iPod, but that offered no clues either, not even of his musical tastes, for it too had been smashed irretrievably in the frenzied attack.

Greenleaf lived in a flat at the back of Sunnymede, and given that he was not on duty that night, there was no reason for other members of staff to wonder where he had got to. His mobile phone rang twice later in the evening. On the second occasion, the caller merely left a short and brusque message, and gave up on him. She had been messed around by Paul Greenleaf before.

Only at round about 9.30 a.m. on the Tuesday morning – when he was half an hour late for a meeting, and when three attempts to raise him on his mobile had failed – did Fran Sinclair get sufficiently irritated to go looking for him. She started in the kitchen, in case he was cadging a late breakfast there (it wouldn't have been the first time!). Then she made a sweep through Primrose Wing, but he wasn't there either, and no one had seen him. So she made her way to his flat, and knocked loudly on his door. There was no reply. She tried the handle on the door. It was locked.

Fran Sinclair rang Greenleaf's mobile again, scratching her nose as she did so. She was inclined to leave an even stronger message than her previous one, but she realized that she could hear his mobile ringing inside his room. She killed the call, and unhooked her keys from her belt. There were nearly a dozen of these, including two master keys. These gave her access to every lockable door and cupboard in Sunnymede, in case of emergency, and that included Greenleaf's flat. It wasn't something she had ever discussed with him, but that was how it had always been in the eight years she'd been assistant manager. She fitted one of the keys in the lock and opened the door. She had, to be fair, never misused her powers of entry to the flat. The only other time she had entered it in his absence was when a plumber had needed access to replace the shower, and Greenleaf had been away on holiday. As she stood in the small hallway, she took a slight intake of breath, as if she had suddenly realized the possibilities that her unsolicited entry might present. She called his name once, and then again more loudly, but there was no reply. There were three doors off the small hallway in which she was standing. She pushed open the left-hand one, which she knew was the toilet and shower room. There was no sprawled body there, nothing out of the ordinary. She then opened the middle door into his living room. Again there was nothing to catch her attention and no sign of a mobile phone. She turned round, retreated to the hall, and tried the third door, his bedroom. On his double bed lay a disordered pile of clothes – faded jeans, navy-blue polo shirt, vest, navy-blue socks. The bed itself was tidy enough, the duvet straight and uncrumpled, the pillows plumped and in place. There was no sign of the mobile. She pulled her own out of her pocket, and rang his again. A ring tone sounded from the pile of clothes. She let it ring, lifting the shirt and then the trousers, pushing her hand into first his left pocket then the right, extracting the mobile, a wallet, a coin purse, and an electronic card key. But no flat or other keys. Not that that was a surprise. He had gone out somewhere, so he would need his key to get back. But without his wallet? She scratched her nose again. He had a house in Charlton-on-Otmoor, and he might have gone there for some reason, but if so, how come his car key was here? Maybe he had gone jogging? That was the simple answer. He was well known for his jogging. But that was invariably at the end of the day's work – Mondays, Wednesdays and sometimes Fridays. He had explained it to her once. It was his way of de-stressing. But if he had gone out jogging that morning, what had made him do that? And why wasn't he back for work? It wasn't like him. Whatever the bastard was, he was very committed to the job. She opened the wardrobe. It was one of those full-length ones, floor to ceiling, with lots of space to hang and fold and stuff everything out of sight. But she was only interested in shoes, and they were arranged on the floor – brogues, slip-ons, black lace-ups, but no trainers. She looked around the bedroom again, then went and scanned the rest of the flat once more – the hallway, the bathroom floor, the living room, the galley kitchen. Still no trainers. That settled it. He must have gone jogging. So why the hell wasn't he back yet?

Fran Sinclair let herself out of the flat, shutting the door firmly behind her. She would just check his office again, and then she would … well what? Wait and see for a bit longer? She was still considering this as she rounded the last corner on her trip and almost collided with DI Holden and her sergeant.

'Mr Greenleaf has gone missing!' she said all in a rush. 'It's most peculiar.'

It didn't take Fox and Holden long to look round Greenleaf's flat and agree that it was peculiar. They had been wanting to ask Fran Sinclair questions about Dr Featherstone, but that now got put on the back burner.

It also didn't take Fox and Holden long to put two and two together and come up with four. They had heard about the murder of a jogger in Cowley Marsh when they had called in at the station first thing, and by the time Fran Sinclair had finished her account, they both had their suspicions. They checked with her what Greenleaf's jogging clothes looked like, asked about the key and key ring – not that Fran knew what his key ring was like – and then they made their way to the mortuary. And there, to their own satisfaction, they identified the dead man as Paul Greenleaf. Not that it was entirely straightforward – his face had been smashed violently into a bloody pulp – but there really wasn't any doubt in their minds by the time they stepped into the spitting rain. Holden, oblivious to Fox's desire to get in the car, lit up her first cigarette of the morning – she had managed not to have one when she woke up – and sucked that first gulp of smoke into her lungs.

'Christ!' she said. 'This certainly changes things!'

'Do you think the deaths are connected?' Fox said after a pause.

Holden said nothing, and instead took another drag on her cigarette and then another. 'Why don't you ring up and find out where the hell Wilson and Lawson have got to. And tell them to get to Sunnymede a.s.a.p.'

'I hope you two aren't going to go walkabout on me again this week?' Wilson and Lawson were sitting down in the staff room drinking coffee when their DI stamped in, exuding foul temper. 'Fox and I have spent our weekend arranging another death for you, so I hope you'll do us the courtesy of staying around to help in its investigation!'

'We heard, Guv. We didn't want to start barging in until you were back and had briefed us.' Wilson had risen apologetically to his feet up as he spoke, spilling some of his coffee into his saucer. 'Do you think the two deaths are connected?'

'Do I look like Mystic bleeding Meg?' she snapped. It was an unfair response. Fox had raised the same question and she hadn't bitten his head off. But it was the obvious question. Could it be only a coincidence that an old woman had been overdosed and the manager of her care home had been beaten to death while out jogging? 'What I mean, Wilson, is that I can predict that Fox is going to pour me a coffee within the next thirty seconds, but that's where my psychic powers end.' She pulled with her left hand at her blouse collar, a mannerism of which she was totally unconscious. Wilson noticed it, however, and he noticed too a slight twitch of the head as she sat down. He hadn't appreciated her doing that before.

Wilson sat down opposite her, trying not to stare at her. He took a sip of coffee and then spoke casually. 'Lawson and I have been talking to Fran Sinclair.'

'I thought you said you hadn't wanted to start barging around?'

'We didn't, Guv.' Lawson had leant forward too, in automatic support of Wilson. 'It wasn't like that. Miss Sinclair brought the coffee in herself, and then she wanted to talk about it.'

'Did she now?' Holden took the coffee that Fox was offering her, and took a sip, her eyes watching Lawson and then Wilson as she did. 'So, what did you learn, Wilson?'

'The key thing is that he used to jog after work on a Monday as regular as clockwork.'

'So I gathered,' Holden replied quickly. 'And Wednesday too, and often Friday,' she added, to underline that none of this was new to her. 'I imagine it was pretty common knowledge.'

'Quite,' Wilson continued, earnestly. 'Common knowledge to everyone in Sunnymede, and, no doubt, to his friends too. Which suggests to us a premeditated murder by someone he knew.'

'As opposed to him having the bad luck to run into a mugger who needed some money for drugs?'

'But the killer used wire, Guv!' Wilson blurted out, more loudly than he had intended. 'He – or she – rigged up a wire at throat height across the path, and then used a heavy object, to finish the job. We spoke to Charlie back at the station. It doesn't look like a chance mugging, not to us, Guv.'

Holden looked at Wilson. He was, she reckoned, coming on. He had been so diffident when he first worked for her, and yet now he was learning to fight his corner. She was pleased. That was what she needed, a team who would challenge her and say what they felt. And who didn't just sit on their arses.

Holden took another sip of her coffee, and smiled. 'You have been a busy pair, haven't you! I don't suppose you've worked out who the killer is? And the motive?'

Lawson cleared her throat. She had been happy for Wilson to lead so far, but playing second fiddle didn't come naturally to her. 'I've been thinking about that. Who links the old woman and Greenleaf? Well, the obvious person in my book is Bella Sinclair. Greenleaf had got her suspended – that's a clear motive. And she looked after Nanette Wright.'

Holden cut in. 'As did many staff, in one form or another.'

'Agreed.' Lawson paused. It was the weak point in her theory, that Nanette Wright and Paul Greenleaf knew many people in common. Almost anyone who worked there might potentially have hated both of them. 'But I suppose my argument would be that you've got to start somewhere, and Bella seems as good a person to start with as anyone.'

Holden pursed her lips. Her coffee was only half drunk, but she put it down on the table in front of her. She could feel a headache beginning. She didn't need any more stimulation.

'What about Mrs Wright's son and daughter-in-law?' It was Wilson who jumped back in the fray, at the same time dissociating himself from Lawson. 'One fact we do know is that it is they who had most to gain from the old woman dying now. According to her accountant, her death is a financial life-saver for them.'

'But why would they have killed Greenleaf?' Lawson wasn't ready to concede ground, and certainly not to Wilson.

'There could be lots of reasons,' Wilson riposted, his voice now strident. 'Just because we don't know doesn't mean ...'

'Enough!' Holden shouted. 'Wilson is right in one respect. We don't know enough!' Holden spoke sharply now, the tone of her voice reminding both of her detective constables that when push came anywhere near shove, she was the boss. 'It's all very well to have theories, but what we need first and foremost is facts. So we need to dig deeper, not get fixed on one theory above all others.'

She stood up, and marched over to the window. She looked out into the bleak grey morning and began to shift rhythmically from one leg to the other. She was feeling stressed and irritated, and her irritation, she realized, was not with Lawson and Wilson. At least they were having a say. 'So, Sergeant,' she said loudly, without looking around. 'Do you have anything useful to add?'

Fox scratched his thinning hair. If he was hurt or annoyed by her tone, he didn't show it. His reply was measured, and some-what ponderous. 'I'm sure you're right, Guv. We do need to keep an open mind. But if you're asking me—'

'That,' Holden said, spinning round to face Fox, 'is exactly what I'm doing. Asking you! I'm hoping for the benefit of your experience, Sergeant. I am hoping you will demonstrate why you are a blooming sergeant and these two are not.' She stood, her hands on her hips, aware that she was pushing her luck with all of them, and especially with a man who had given her such solid support over the last three years or so.

Fox straightened himself in his chair, and returned his inspector's glare, but when he spoke he was still calm and infuriatingly unemotional. 'Guv, with respect,' he said – and that was an expression he never used when speaking to her – 'I think there's too much theorizing going on. We don't know much at all about this Greenleaf. So why don't we concentrate on him, find out all we can about him, and then we can compare that with what we've learnt about Nanette Wright, and see where it all leads.'

Holden looked around, at Lawson and Wilson, and then back to Fox. 'All right,' she said. 'If you say so, Sergeant.'

'I do, Guv. I do.'

It didn't take long for the four of them to search Greenleaf's flat. They found his clothes and personal effects on the bed, as Fran Sinclair had said they would. Wilson was deputed to check out the mobile, Holden herself began to scrutinize every card and piece of paper in his wallet, while Fox and Lawson took the living room and bedroom respectively.

'He must have some paperwork, somewhere,' Lawson said irritably. There was nothing of interest to her in his little bedside chest of drawers, and nothing that she could find stuffed in, under, or behind the immaculately organized clothes in the built-in wardrobe.

'There's something here,' Fox called out in response. 'In fact, it looks like our Mr Greenleaf has another house, out in Charlton-on-Otmoor.'

Holden, who had given up on the wallet, was leaning over Fox almost before he had finished speaking.

'It looks like he's been having some building work done on it,' Fox was explaining. 'Here's the address of the property.'

'And look at who's been doing it.' Holden's finger stabbed down onto the invoice, at the letter heading. 'JW Builders, Oxford. Look at the address! Lytton Road.'

'You mean, JW as in Jim Wright.'

'I'd put my mortgage on it.'

'There's something interesting here, too, Guv.' Wilson was brandishing Greenleaf's mobile phone like he was looking for bids at an auction. 'Ania. Isn't that the name of the nurse you interviewed?'

'What about her?'

'She rang Greenleaf last night. Or tried to. Three times.'

'Did she now?'

'In fact, looking back through the log, she quite often rang him, and he rang her too.' The grin on Wilson's face was Cheshire cat sized. 'Perhaps she and he were in a relationship?'

Fox laughed. 'You mean, they were fucking.'

Wilson blushed. He was strikingly coy about sex for a man of the twenty-first century.

Wilson's grin had, it seemed, migrated to Holden, for there was a look of delight written large across her features. The grin was not, however, aimed at anyone in particular. It was just that, all of a sudden, the whole investigation had become really rather interesting.

'They say Mr Greenleaf was killed by a mugger. Is that true?'

Ania Gorski sat opposite the detective inspector, her hands folded neatly in her lap. She had arrived at the interview with a red face and damp eyes, a clear indication that she had already heard about Paul Greenleaf's death. Her question confirmed it. Holden wished she could have put a lid on the news until she had confronted Ania with the question. To have seen her first reaction would surely have been instructive. But there's no stopping people talking.

'He was killed while out jogging. We don't know any more than that.'

'But why would anyone have done this?' Holden looked at her hard. She saw the round-eyed innocence of her face, and heard the shock in her voice. But she wasn't convinced, and she certainly wasn't distracted from her plan of action.

'Ania,' she said, with the most disarming of smiles. She too could play the innocent. 'Would you please tell us why you tried to ring Paul Greenleaf last night?'

Ania didn't answer immediately. It was only the briefest pause, the sort of pause that might indicate anything – shock, surprise, distress, or maybe several split seconds of thinking time. But undeniably she paused before she answered. 'Because I wanted to speak to him.'

'About what?'

'About ... about my job.'

'About your job?' Holden made no attempt to hide her disbelief. 'You rang him to discuss your job? But you were working yesterday? Did you not speak to him during the day?'

'I finished work at four o'clock. He wasn't in his office. So later I rang him.'

'Three times?'

'Maybe three times.'

'Definitely three times. Why did you ring him three times? Why did you not leave a message saying you wanted a meeting to discuss your job?'

She shrugged. 'I didn't want to leave a message. I wanted to speak to him.'

Fox made a snorting noise that indicated all too clearly his scepticism. Both women turned to look at him. But he was interested only in Holden. She gave an infinitesimal nod, and he switched he gaze back to Ania. 'Miss Gorski,' he said gruffly. 'Mr Greenleaf had your name and number stored on his mobile. And his call log suggests you often spoke to him by phone. Why was that?'

She paused, and chewed at her bottom lip. 'We were good friends.'

'You mean you were lovers?'

This time Ania made no reply at all, merely ducking her head as if embarrassed by the question.

'Were you lovers, Ania?' It was Holden asking the questions again. Gentle, encouraging, almost intimate. 'It's not a crime. But we do need an answer. Otherwise we'll have to take you down to the police station and it will all take a lot longer.'

'Yes.' It was a whisper, which Holden sensed rather than heard.

'How long have you been lovers? A week, a month, a year?'

'About two months.'

'What did you do yesterday, after you left work?'

'I went home to my flat.'

'Is there anyone who can confirm that? Was anyone there with you?'

Her once flushed face had now turned paler than pale. 'No,' she insisted, this time in less of a whisper.

'So when did you last see Mr Greenleaf?'

She shook her head, and then kept shaking it, harder and harder until her whole body was twisting from side to side in time with some monstrous unheard music. 'On Sunday,' she wailed. 'We spent the weekend at his house in Charlton-on-Otmoor. But we had a row, just as we were leaving for Oxford. It was a terrible row, and then we didn't speak all the way back to Oxford. But yesterday, when I had calmed down, I thought maybe I should try to talk to him at work, but I didn't see him, so in the evening I rang him on his mobile, but he never answered.'

'What did you row about?'

'Silly things.'

'What sort of silly things?'

'Private silly things.'

Holden leant forward, and raised her voice. She was confident that she only needed to apply pressure, and the woman would crack. 'What did you row about?'

Ania Gorski lifted her head, and stared back at Holden. Their eyes met head on. She would not be bullied. Greenleaf had not been able to bully her, and neither would the detective woman bully her. No one would, ever. 'It was private,' she said loudly. 'I will not tell you.'

Holden held the woman's glare. Ania was, she realized, more formidable than she had first appeared. Had that nervousness been an act? Holden pressed harder. 'I think you killed him, Ania. He always jogged on a Monday night, didn't he? You knew that. You knew the path he always took. So you waited for him in the bushes in the dark, and when he reached you, you tripped him up with a wire stretched across his path, and then you beat his head to pulp. A very messy, bloody pulp!'

But Ania Gorski was having none of it. She stood up, her face a mask of outrage.

'No,' she screamed. 'No I didn't. No! No! No!'

Elm Cottage lies at the western end of Charlton-on-Otmoor. It is set back from the grandly named High Street, a two-storey Cotswold stone building with leaded windows and a thatched roof. There wasn't, as far as Lawson could see, an elm tree in sight, but she couldn't help her mouth gawping as Wilson eased the car to a halt on the gravelled driveway.

'Wow!' Wilson said, echoing her thoughts. 'Not bad for a weekend hideaway!'

'Not bad at all!'

Once inside, their task was, of course, to look for evidence, whatever form that might take – evidence of a hatred so intense that someone chose to half garrotte Greenleaf with a

wire and then batter him to death with the bluntest of blunt
instruments. The two of them were used to working together,
and with barely a word Lawson headed up the narrow stair-
way while Wilson gazed around the main living room,
wondering where to begin. It wasn't, as far as he was concerned, a difficult decision: the escritoire. He knew it was called
that because his grandmother had had one and had told him
off for calling it a desk. 'It doesn't give it the respect it deserves,
calling it a desk,' she had said. And for some reason, that brief
exchange had stuck with him over the years, when thousands
of other more important ones had faded. Wilson pulled out the
two horizontal supports, and then lowered the hinged lid down
onto them. Inside a series of little vertical panels created six
cubby holes of varying width, plus a central one with a door,
and underneath each miniature cupboard was a miniature
drawer. He began to make his way methodically through each
segment, leaving the central cupboard and its drawer till last.
Leave the best till last. That was another thing he'd learnt
from Gran.

Upstairs Lawson was looking through a wedding album,
which she'd found stuffed in the long wide drawer at the base
of a rather pretty walnut wardrobe in what she assumed must
be his bedroom. The bed, she had noted, was a double. The
wardrobe contained a single, dark-blue suit, two white shirts,
and two ties, but beyond that the clothes were distinctly
casual. There were not, however, many of them, which tied up
with her understanding that he generally lived in the
Sunnymede flat during the week, and used this at the weekends. It was, she thought, a bit odd. It wasn't so far away, even
at rush hour time, so why didn't he use it more? Did he really
have to sleep on the premises during the week? She had been
pondering this when she found the wedding album underneath a spare blanket in the wardrobe drawer. He clearly
wasn't married now, so what had happened to Mrs Greenleaf
– had she died or were they divorced? Still if he had been

entertaining Ania here, it was no surprise that he had buried the album well out of view.

Half an hour or so later, the two detective constables were sitting in the kitchen drinking tea. It was Lawson who had found the half pint of milk in the fridge, and there had seemed to her little point in not making use of it. So there they sat, exchanging first banter and then information. Not that either of them had learnt anything obviously important. The place was neat and tidy, equipped reasonably but not excessively. There were a few CDs, two shelves of books, and a limited amount of food in the kitchen cupboard. More like a holiday let than a home.

So they sat and whiled away twenty minutes, before reluctantly agreeing they ought to get going. And it was as they were in the very throes of getting into the car to leave that a man appeared in the gateway.

'Who are you?' he demanded. He was a big man, with a huge bushy beard which hid much but not all of a ruddy face.

'We are detectives,' Lawson replied, turning towards the newcomer.

'So what are you doing in Paul's house?'

'We have a search warrant,' Wilson said defensively.

'That doesn't answer my question.'

'We not required to answer it,' Lawson said sharply. She pulled out her ID, holding it high for him to see. 'Who are you, anyway?'

'I'm his neighbour,' he said, his belligerence waning. 'I keep an eye out for him.'

'I see.' Lawson's tone eased too. 'I am sorry to have to tell you, but Mr Greenleaf was killed yesterday. We're here conducting inquiries.'

'God!' Behind the beard, there seemed genuine shock. 'How did he die?'

Lawson glanced across at Wilson, who shrugged. 'All I can say is that his death is suspicious.'

'You mean it was, like, murder?'

'I can't say any more than that at the moment.'

'But I saw him only on Sunday. Not to talk to, mind you. Him and his girlfriend.'

'They were here for the weekend?'

'Yeah, like most weekends.'

'Did you notice any other visitors this weekend?'

'Can't say I did. Not that I watch out all the time. I'm not a spy. It's just that he mostly only stays at the weekend, so it's only during the week that I tend to keep an eye open for intruders.'

'And have you seen any recently.'

'Not since the builder finished. It's been as quiet as the grave these last few weeks.' Then he laughed, realizing what he said. 'Sorry. That didn't come out right! I just meant—'

'That's fine,' said Lawson. She reckoned they'd got all they needed from this particular witness. And she was conscious too that she could have been kinder. 'And thank you for your help.'

'Oh, it's you.' The words were anything but welcoming. Maureen Wright shouldn't have been surprised to see Holden and Fox on her doorstep again, as they'd phoned her two hours earlier, but she stood in the doorway, one hand on the door, and her body fully in the way, as if they'd caught her on the hop. Her whole body language was telling them to bugger off.

'Is your husband in?'

'He's just about to have his tea.' She made no attempt to move aside.

'I'm sorry, but we need to talk to him. I'm sure his tea can wait.'

'Christ,' she snapped. 'You coppers! Don't you have a home to go back to?'

Inside, Jim Wright was watching the TV. There was no sign of his tea. He got up stiffly, killing the TV with the remote control as he did so. 'You've got some news about my mother?'

Holden shrugged. 'Actually we wanted to ask you about Paul Greenleaf.'

'Yeah, I heard about him. A mugging was it?'

Holden ignored the question. 'How long have you known him?'

'Maybe a year or so.'

'And how did you meet him?'

Jim scratched his hairless head. 'When I was looking round Sunnymede for my mother.'

'And then what happened?'

'Nothing really. Not then. A few months later he asked me to do some work on this house out at Charlton-on-Otmoor.'

'Yes, we found some invoices. And you did some work at Sunnymede too?'

'Yeah, just recently.'

'So you did well out of him?'

Jim's eyes narrowed with suspicion. 'I guess so.'

'It's just that we've been making inquiries, and the word is that you lost a lot of money in Spain.'

'Where the fuck is this all going to?' The feigned indifference had disappeared. 'I've had a few financial problems, and Greenleaf gave me some work. So what?' The four of them were all still on their feet. Jim Wright moved a step closer to Holden, thrusting his red face aggressively forward. 'Well?' he demanded when Holden said nothing. 'Well?'

She looked down at the floor, as if acknowledging his superiority, and only after several seconds did she look up.

'Who used to top up your mother's hip flask with whisky? Was it you?'

Holden's sudden change of direction took Jim Wright completely by surprise, and he gaped like a landed fish desperate for water. Then his red face darkened to puce. 'What's your fucking game, Detective? What are you trying to say?'

'Your mother had a hip flask. Someone topped it up with whisky for her. She came home most Sundays for lunch, didn't she? So was that when you filled it up with whisky again?'

'Not me,' he snarled. 'Not me, Detective!'

It was then that Holden noticed Maureen. She had made it as far as the archway through to the kitchen, but no further. She was watching her husband, and her two hands were attached to her hips like they had been stuck there with super-glue. 'Was it you, Maureen?' Holden asked quietly.

Her mouth opened as if to say something, but no words came out. Her face had turned a sickly, yellowish grey.

It was Jim who answered. 'It wasn't her who did it.'

Holden nodded, but her gaze was still fixed on Maureen. 'Who was it then, Maureen? We need to know.'

Maureen's eyes blinked. There was moisture in them, and distress too. 'Our son, David.' Her voice was barely more than a whisper. 'He used to do it. It was one of his Sunday jobs.'

'Actually,' her husband butted in, 'to be strictly accurate, David is our adopted son.'

'What bloody difference does that make, you bastard?' Maureen Wright moved a pace towards her husband, her hands detaching themselves from her hips. For a moment Holden saw them balling into fists, as if she was about to lash out at him, but Maureen stopped advancing, and unleashed instead a volley of words. 'Adopted or not, we chose him, so he's ours, full stop. Until we're dead, and maybe beyond that too. Not that you're much use to him as a father.'

'Is David here?' Holden didn't need to see more of this. Watching a couple hacking bits out of each other – that was something she took no pleasure in.

'He doesn't live with us,' Maureen said quickly. 'Not any more. He's twenty now, and lives in a flat on Barns Road. He needs his privacy at his age.' The words poured out, a protective torrent.

'Well, we will need to talk to him.'

'He's got Asperger's syndrome,' Maureen blurted out. 'He's not an extreme case, but you must treat him properly. And I'd like to be present.'

Holden nodded, as she assimilated this information. 'We do have to ask him some questions.' She tried to sound kind as well as firm. 'But you're welcome as long as you don't interfere.'

'OK,' she said.

'Good. Perhaps we should do that here, tomorrow morning.'

Fran Sinclair's mobile rang. She was halfway through *EastEnders* – not to mention her second gin and tonic – and she was tempted to ignore it. But she was tempted too to see who it was she was ignoring. She picked the mobile up. Bella!

On screen, Phil Mitchell was doing his one-man bore routine. Phil Mitchell was the character she would most readily push off the top floor of the Empire State Building if she ever got the chance, so she muted the TV with the remote control, and answered her sister.

'The police want to interview me again.'

'Do they?' Fran wasn't surprised. They were doing a lot of interviewing again after Greenleaf's death. She'd had that bear of a sergeant asking her for a minute by minute account of her Monday afternoon and evening. To see if she'd got an alibi. Which of course, she hadn't. She told them she'd been sitting at home on her own, but that didn't constitute an alibi as far as they were concerned. She took a swig of her gin and tonic, and swilled it round her mouth like mouthwash, savouring the sharpness.

'At Sunnymede,' her sister was saying. 'Tomorrow morning.'

'Well maybe I'll see you.'

'I'm worried.'

Fran giggled. The gin was doing its worst – or maybe best. 'You're worried? Why? Did you kill Greenleaf? Because if you did, you should be worried. And if you didn't, then what's there to be worried about?' She giggled again. She was pleased with that response. It sounded smart. Clever. Much cleverer than she could usually manage.

'He got me suspended!' Bella persisted. 'I'm an obvious suspect.'

'In that case, you'd better get your alibi sorted!' Fran belched, the tonic now taking its turn.

'Are you drinking?' Bella's irritation was apparent even down the rubbish phone connection they had got. 'Look!' she said, her voice growing more strident with every syllable. 'This is serious. What's going to happen to me? Do you think I'll get my job back now Greenleaf is dead?'

Fran wanted to laugh again, but she was seized instead by a bout of wheezing and coughing that betrayed all too vividly her years of devotion to cigarettes. Only when it had subsided was she able to voice a response. 'The police are investigating two suspicious deaths at Sunnymede, and you're concerned about your job. How very single-minded of you, dear sister! But to answer it, yes I'd say that your chances have very much improved with Greenleaf's death. But, of course, it is out of my hands. It's Margaret Laistor who will be making the decision.'

'But you will back me up, won't you, Sis? Tell the saintly Margaret what a bastard he was?'

'Sure I will. I'll cover your back, just like I always do.'

'Bless you, Sis.'

'Bye!' Fran killed the call. The credits were coming up at the end of *EastEnders*. Not that she cared that she'd missed some of it. There were more important things in life. Not to mention iPlayer and the Sunday omnibus.

She tipped her glass, until she had drained it, and then burst into giggles again. Bella saying 'Bless you'. Now that really did take the biscuit!

CHAPTER 9

Of course I put the whisky in Nan Nan's flask that Sunday. I always did. She'd get cross if I didn't, and when she was cross, she was really nasty. She could say terrible things. Not that I told the police that last bit. I don't want them to think badly of her. Anyway it was my job to do it. I always come home on Sunday. Dad would go and get Nan Nan from the old folks' home, and Mum would cook the roast dinner. When she arrived, I'd get her a drink, and she'd also give me her hip flask, and I'd top it up with whisky for her to take back to the home. Mind you, when I say top up, that's not really true. Usually it was empty, so it'd be a case of fill it up, not top it up.

'Did you ever add anything to the whisky?' the lady detective asked.

'Once,' I said. 'You see, once Dad told me to add some water. He told me she was drinking too much whisky. 'She's drinking me out of house and home,' he said. So I mixed some water with the whisky, but she knew, and the next Sunday she didn't half tell me off. I didn't like that. So I never tried it again.'

'David,' the lady detective asked, really slow, as if I was some sort of idiot, 'someone put some medicine into your gran's flask before she died. Something to make her sleep better. Only it went wrong and she went to sleep and never woke up. Was that you, David?'

Went to sleep and never woke up! Does the lady think I don't know what death is? Does she think I am completely brainless? She was accusing me of killing Nan Nan. I went mad then. I started shouting and all sorts. 'I didn't!' I shouted. 'I didn't! I didn't! I didn't!'

Then Mum started shouting too, shouting at the lady detective, and it was terribly noisy, so I stopped shouting and put my hands over my ears until it had all gone quiet.

'Sorry!' the lady said. But she wasn't sorry, I could see that. She looked at me like I was a dumb child. People often do. And she smiled a false smile. 'I just need to ask you where you were this last Monday,' she said.

So I told her. 'I went to work,' I said. 'I got there at 9 o'clock, and I had my lunch at 12 o'clock, and I went home at 4.30 p.m. like I usually do.'

'And what did you do in the evening? Did you go out at all?'

'No' I said. 'I stayed in all evening because I wanted to play on my new computer game. I also watched EastEnders. I like EastEnders.'

'Thank you,' she said. 'You've been very helpful.'

'I'm going to be late for work because of you,' I said.

'Don't worry,' said Mum. 'I've already spoken to Jaz.'

Doesn't Mum understand? That's not the point. I hate being late. I'm never late. Being late is bad.

So I went and caught the bus to work.

I'm not stupid. I know that the lady asked about Monday because that was when Mr Greenleaf was killed. Do I look stupid?

Mother doesn't think I'm stupid. She's told me. I'll send her a text. Perhaps she'll buy me an ice cream at lunchtime. I'd like a blackcurrant one.

'So, what do you think?'

They were at the end of Littlehay Road, waiting to pull out into the Oxford Road. It wasn't exactly a perfectly timed question from Holden, especially as it was Fox who was driving, and he was a man who liked to concentrate when he was behind the wheel.

Holden shut her eyes. She wasn't in a hurry for an answer, but she did want to hear what he had to say. The car lurched forward, and then very quickly stopped. It was well past rush hour, but the traffic heading into the city centre suggested otherwise.

'He's a bit odd,' Fox replied.

'Well, he has got Asperger's,' Holden said. 'But that wasn't really what I was asking. Do you think he could have put morphine in the flask with the whisky?'

'Maybe.'

'Maybe? Is that all you've got to say about it? Maybe?' Irritability had kicked in. Holden knew it, but felt unable to control it. Irritability was never far from the surface these days.

The traffic in front of them suddenly awoke from its torpor. Fox released the handbrake and moved forward, and as if the traffic and his own thought processes were linked, the words began to flow. 'It would be hard to prove, even if he did do it. And if he did do it, was it to kill her or maybe to help her? Maybe she'd been complaining about being in pain, and he got the idea into his head that he could give her some morphine to ease the pain.'

'So where did he get the morphine? Isn't it more likely the morphine came from Sunnymede, and was put into her flask there?'

'I thought we were concentrating on David,' Fox said quietly. He was not a butterfly when it came to analyzing a case, or indeed anything else. 'I thought we were constructing a scenario in which he killed his grandmother accidentally or otherwise. Personally, I don't see him as a killer, but maybe we shouldn't underestimate him. I watched a programme on telly about it once. People with Asperger's can be very bright and capable.'

Holden shut her eyes again, and allowed Fox to concentrate on turning right, off the main road. She agreed with him. David as killer was possible, but not probable. And where would David have got morphine from? Or, indeed, Jim or Maureen?

The smell of fresh coffee hit Holden as she walked into the staff room. Both Lawson and Wilson looked round, matching grins on their faces. Either there was something going on between them or they were after something.

'Coffee, Guv? Coffee, Sergeant?'

'You're not trying to soften me up, are you, Constables? Because if so I'd rather drink the dregs from the washing up.'

'Fran Sinclair bought it.' Wilson said. 'Specially!'

'I think,' Lawson added, raising her eyes as she spoke, 'that she's taken a bit of a shine to you, Guv.'

There was a silence then, very short, in truth, but a silence nonetheless. Holden's sexual orientation was understood, but never openly discussed by her team, and Lawson's sudden teasing was a step further than ever before. The young constable had a brief moment of panic, that it was maybe a step too far. She felt her cheeks flush and waited for a reprimand.

Holden, however, merely shrugged, and the silence softened as she did so. 'Whatever, Constable. I'll take my coffee black, unless Fran has splashed out and purchased cream for us.'

It took another minute for them to settle. Fox, Lawson and Wilson perched with their coffees on the rather worn armchairs round the low table, and waited for Holden to start.

'I've been thinking,' Holden said eventually. 'Has anyone checked Greenleaf's emails?'

'I took a look at the office PC yesterday,' Wilson said. 'But it didn't look as though he had any personal files there.'

'Does he not have a laptop?'

'I haven't seen one.'

Holden frowned at Wilson, and then turned towards the others.

'We searched his flat very thoroughly,' Lawson said defensively. She and Wilson had spent some time doing so the previous afternoon, and she was pretty damn sure that if there had been a laptop there, they would have found it.

'What about his cottage?'

'I didn't notice one there,' Lawson admitted, which she was beginning to realize was odd.

'Not everyone has a laptop,' Fox said firmly, thinking of himself. 'Not everyone feels the need.'

'But he must have had one!' Wilson blurted this out, more forcibly than he intended, and Fox coloured in anger. Sometimes, quite often in fact, he felt Wilson and Lawson didn't give him the respect he deserved, but at that moment Wilson was oblivious to everything except his own brainwave. 'He's got a wireless router in the cottage! On a little table in the corner of the living room. Why would he have that if he didn't have a computer?'

'Right,' Holden cut in. She wasn't oblivious to the tensions that were surfacing, but she didn't actually care about them either, at least not in comparison with finding Greenleaf's killer. 'So let's get on and find it! If it's hidden, maybe there's something on it he wouldn't want us to see.' She paused, and sipped at her coffee. There was something else she wanted to raise, something that she had noticed the night before as she had pored over the paperwork in her kitchen. 'Lawson. Wilson. Last night I was reading through your report of your visit to Greenleaf's cottage. There's something odd about it, you know.'

She sipped again at her coffee, savouring it. It really was rather good. She must remember to ask Fran what it was.

'What do you mean, Guv?' Wilson was conscious that it was he who had drafted the report.

'There was the neighbour you spoke to at the end. The one with a beard whose name you failed to record. He talked about the building work, and according to your report he said that it had been as quiet as the grave the last few weeks.' Holden had been studying her coffee as she spoke, but now she looked up at her two constables. 'Are you sure that is what he said? I mean, you must be sure, mustn't you, given that that is what you wrote down.'

'That is what he said,' Wilson said. He tried to sound definite, but there was a note of uncertainty in his voice.

'And you took that to mean there hadn't been any building work over the last few weeks?'

'Yes!' Lawson was not someone to duck out when the going got tricky, and Holden's implicit criticism was criticism of them both. 'That was exactly what he meant.'

'So how do you explain this?' Holden waved some sheets of A4 paper in the air. 'These are the invoices that we found in the flat. For building work done on the cottage. This is for work done in September, and this for October, and this,' she said with added emphasis, 'for work done in the month of November, when, according to your informant, it was as quiet as the grave. You see, that's what I mean by there being something odd.'

She slid the invoices across to them, and waited for a response. The three of them huddled round to get a proper look. Fox was as keen as the two constables to take another look at the invoices, and it was he who spoke first. 'Do you see that? In September, it was for the installation of a kitchen; in October it was for decoration of the kitchen, downstairs, living rooms, and downstairs toilet, but the one for November doesn't specify anything. Look! "General building and maintenance work". It could be anything.'

'Or maybe nothing,' Lawson added.

'Quite!' That was what Holden had decided for herself the previous evening. 'So now we've got two good reasons to make another search of Greenleaf's cottage. To find his laptop, and to check out Jim Wright's building work. And, of course, if we can, to have a chat to his neighbour, whatever his name might be.' And she flashed a sarcastic smile at her constables. She didn't want them to repeat the error – ever.

*

It took Lawson very little time at all to find the laptop. As before, Wilson took the downstairs and she took the upstairs. She started with the main bedroom, and stood in the doorway, scanning methodically from left to right. She had already been through the wardrobe, and found it hard to believe she would have missed a laptop if it had been stowed away there. Ditto the chest of drawers. The only other piece of furniture apart from the double bed was the bedside table. She had looked in the single drawer in that too on her last visit. Which left the bed. She advanced and pulled the cover and then the duvet back. She removed the four pillows, but there was no laptop under them. She shrugged and looked around. Where else could it be? And then it occurred to her. Not in a piece of furniture, but under it. She knelt down on the floor, to the side of the bed, and saw it almost immediately, not under the bed, but on the far side of the room, almost hidden in the shadow under the free-standing wardrobe. She wasn't sure it was a laptop until she'd crossed the room, and felt underneath. But her hand told her even before she saw it that she had hit the jackpot.

She handed it over to Wilson. Though it grieved her to admit it, he was better than her when it came to IT, and he had already informed her in the car that he'd brought along some password-cracking software just in case. Frankly, she was happy to let him have a go. It was enough to have found it. She wandered through to the kitchen. Fox was there, sitting at the table with the three invoices in front of him.

'So you found the laptop?'

'Yeah!'

'Good stuff.' Fox wasn't exactly a compulsive giver of praise, but he was in a good mood. And the reason for that quickly became apparent. 'I'm not sure what the deal was with Jim Wright and Greenleaf, but none of these invoices really add up. Look at this one. Nearly five thousand quid for a new kitchen! Well whatever he did in here, it didn't involve renewing the kitchen. There's some new tiling over near the sink, and that cupboard there by the door is new, but if you look, it doesn't quite match, not in colour or design. The flooring shows a lot of signs of wear and the work surfaces are scratched in several places. As for the decorating that he is supposed to have done in October, the only bit of new painting seems to be around the new tile work, and the toilet. Nothing like the four thousand quid he charged. And then, of course, there's all the general maintenance work he invoiced for at the end of November.'

'If he came here in November, he was damned discreet about it.' Holden had materialized at the doorway as if Scottie in *Star Trek* had just beamed her there. 'His neighbour, in case you are interested, is called Benjamin Croft. I have just been speaking to him, and he's adamant that it is more than a month since the builder was here.'

'So whatever Greenleaf was paying him for, it wasn't his building and decorating skills.'

'Indeed.' Holden was pleased. They were making progress, real progress. If Detective Superintendent Collins rang to ask if she was getting anywhere, she at last had some ammunition. They needed to pull Jim Wright in, and give him a proper grilling at the station away from his wife. But not quite yet. 'Did you find a laptop, Lawson?'

'Yes, Guv. Under the wardrobe. Wilson is taking a look right now.'

At that very moment, as if waiting in the wings for his cue, there came a shout from the living room. 'I've found something!' Wilson's voice was high and excited. 'Look at this!'

'This', as the others soon saw, was a photo, or rather a series of photos. The subjects of the photos were two girls, or at any rate two females dressed as girls.

'Isn't that Ania Gorski?' Fox said. He had sat through two interviews with her, and although she was dressed very differently from when she was at work, he was pretty damn sure that it was her.

'I think so,' Holden said, though she was having to peer to make sure. The figure was smiling rather unconvincingly at the camera. Her hair hung either side of her head onto her shoulders in plaits, and she was wearing the sort of uniform that all girls used to wear at school.

'So who's the other one?' Lawson said. The other one was dressed similarly, though her plaits were longer and blonder, and her grin more natural, and her face was flushed. She was, it seemed, enjoying it much more than Ania.

'I don't know.' Holden scratched her head. 'But she looks younger if you ask me. A real schoolgirl as opposed to Ania's pretend one.'

'So was Greenleaf into girls?' Fox asked the question that had popped into each of their heads. He laughed. 'Maybe Ania could only pull his bell when she was dressed in a pinafore dress and long socks?'

'In Ania's case, it's not a crime.' Holden said this firmly, though she felt slightly sick. 'But if this girl is as young as I think, then it most certainly is.'

'Should we go and pick Ania up, Guv?' Wilson had gone rather pale. The pictures themselves were little more than titillating, and yet they hinted at something altogether darker.

'Later. I think we've got a bit more to do here first. You, Wilson, see what else you can find on the laptop. I'll stay with you. Fox and Lawson, I want you to go and ask around the neighbours. See if they can confirm or add anything to Mr Croft's evidence. I'm especially interested in any visitors who may have come, especially at weekends, which is when Greenleaf seems to have spent most of his time here. Men, women and, of course, any girls.'

It was just gone 1.15 p.m. when the four detectives arrived back at Sunnymede. The interviews of the locals had done little except underline the reliability of the beady-eyed Mr Croft. Greenleaf was rarely in the village during the week. He turned up almost without fail on a Friday evening, and stayed through until Sunday night, or occasionally Monday morning. He had a girlfriend, a Polish woman who, the publican of the local confirmed, was indeed called Ania. 'Not sure how you spell it, mind you,' he'd said. 'She was quiet, but she had a nice smile. Sometimes, he'd bring friends in for a drink, or maybe even food on a Saturday night. And his mother sometimes for Sunday lunch. That was always without the girlfriend, mind you. I don't suppose she would have approved, him screwing a woman half his age.' And he had laughed. Fox had reported this conversation in detail, and with some relish, though Holden began to feel queasy as she listened. If Greenleaf's predilections were for women half his age, and then he liked them to dress as if they were still at school, it didn't seem at all funny to her.

Once at Sunnymede, Holden ruthlessly suppressed the urge to smoke a cigarette. She had realized as they drove back that she hadn't had one all day, and by the time they had pulled up on the gravel, the desire had turned into a craving. But there was too much to do. She needed to see Fran Sinclair for a start. If Fran did indeed fancy her, then Holden had no scruples about making the most of it. She found her not in her own office, but in what had been Greenleaf's.

'That was delicious coffee, this morning, Fran,' she gushed. 'Absolutely delicious. I hope it was fair trade, but if it wasn't I'd rather not know. I'll pretend it was.'

'Actually, it was,' Fran lied. It was a harmless lie, she reckoned. 'From Nicaragua.' That was true, at any rate. For a moment the two of them looked at each other. Fran wondered if possibly the detective fancied her, but decided even as she did so that Holden was way out of her league. Whatever else she had doubts about, she knew – had known from her teenage years – that she was attractive to neither male nor female.

Holden's thoughts were more focused: 'Has Jim Wright been working here today?'

'No,' she replied. 'There really isn't anything else we need him for. Roy is perfectly capable of coping on his own.'

Holden nodded, taking in the implication that under Greenleaf's charge Jim Wright's presence had not been entirely necessary. Was this bitchiness or fact?

'And is Ania Gorski working today?'

Fran looked at her watch with a frown. 'Yes, she finishes at four o'clock.'

'Ah, well I really need to see her now. More questions, I'm afraid.'

'That's fine.' Not that Fran had much option if it hadn't been fine. Ania might have had three patients with filthy nappies to be changed, but she doubted that would have made a difference to the inspector. 'Would you like me to go and find her?'

'Please! If you could send her along to the staff room.'

'And would you like more coffee?'

'Please! If it's no trouble.'

'No trouble at all, Inspector.'

Back in the staff room, Wilson was perched over Greenleaf's laptop. He had found little else of interest, and certainly not the evidence to suggest Greenleaf had been heavily into child pornography, but he wasn't prepared to give up yet. Lawson was scanning her mobile, while Fox was looking at a copy of the *Oxford Mail*.

'I need Jim Wright's mobile number,' Holden announced to them all.

'I expect it's on his invoices,' Fox said immediately. 'I'll dig it out for you.'

But when Fox dug out the number, and Holden called it, Jim Wright didn't answer. Instead, the answering service kicked straight in. Either he was on a call already, or the phone was turned off or out of range. Holden left the briefest message, asking him to ring back, and hung up.

'Right!' she said. 'You, Fox, and you, Lawson, take one of the cars and get round to the Wrights' house. See if Jim is skulking there. If not, maybe Maureen will be able to enlighten us.'

'So what do you think? About the guv?'

Fox had barely started the car before Lawson asked the question. He said nothing as he reversed the car, and then moved forward down the drive.

'In what sense?' he asked cautiously as he reached the gateway onto Fitzroy Close.

'Do you think she's still got what it takes? After, you know, Karen.'

'What are you suggesting?'

'She looks stressed to me.'

Fox said nothing. There was a private hire car half blocking the road, which he had to edge around with millimetres to spare. Only when he had done that, got to the end of Cumberland Road, and then turned left onto the Cowley Road did he explode. 'Of course, she's fucking stressed. Wouldn't you be if you were in charge of an investigation with two deaths and Collins breathing down your neck? Maybe, Constable, sometimes you should think before you open your mouth.' Fox was surprised at his own outburst. Often he would merely shake his head or make a face or just compose a tirade in his head, but somehow this time it had slipped out. He felt very defensive about his boss – he had, after all, seen her at her worst – and the fact that she was back leading her team was little short of a miracle in his book. But that wasn't the sum of it. The fact was that Lawson could be a right pain in the backside. She was so full of herself, and so keen to make a good impression on Holden. It was intolerable that she should question her behind her back.

They were silent for the rest of their journey. Only when Fox had brought the car to a halt in Lytton Road did Lawson speak, and then in a tone so respectful that Fox wondered for a moment if she wasn't taking the piss. 'How would you like us to play it, Sergeant?'

'Nice and steady,' he said, as he clambered out of the car. 'Nice and steady, Constable.'

Fox led the way to the house, and rang the doorbell. He didn't expect Jim Wright to be in. If he was at home, he'd surely have his mobile turned on. But if he wasn't, with a bit of luck Maureen would be. There was a noise from the hall, and then the tell-tale sound of the door being unlocked. Fox straightened himself. He had his opening gambit prepared, and a disarming smile on his face.

'Hello,' he said before the door was fully open.

'Hello,' said the girl.

'Oh!' He looked at her in disbelief. 'Who are you?' he said. Though in a sense he already knew who she was: it was her, the girl in the photos. The girl in the photos with Ania.

'I'm Vickie,' she replied brightly. 'Is it Mum or Dad you're looking for?

At almost exactly the same moment that Vickie Wright opened the door to Fox and Lawson, Ania Gorski appeared at the door of the Sunnymede staff room. By then, Fran Sinclair had herself brought in the promised coffee and had dallied unnecessarily as she assured Holden that Ania was just coming. Indeed it was only when Ania arrived that Fran finally departed. 'Give me a shout if you need anything,' she said, again unnecessarily. Holden was more interested in Ania, who seemed even more nervous than on the two previous occasions. She ought to have been getting used to answering the police's questions, but her eyes and the twitchiness of her hands suggested otherwise.

'Please, sit down.' Holden started with platitudes designed to put Ania at her ease. 'Thank you for coming. Sorry for interrupting your day. Do you want something to drink?' Ania accepted a glass of water, but Holden's small talk soon ran dry.

'We've found some pictures,' she said.

'Pictures?' Ania spoke as if she had never come across the word before.

'Photographs.'

'Ah, I understand.'

'Photographs of you.' Holden pushed one across the table, one of Ania on her own, with pigtails and a grey smock dress.

And only then did Ania did truly understand. Holden could see that from her face, which changed in an instant from blank incomprehension to patent alarm.

'Did Paul Greenleaf take this photograph?'

Ania said nothing.

'It was on his laptop.' Holden's voice switched from gently persuasive to not so gently assertive. 'Did he take this photograph of you?'

Again, Ania didn't speak, though she did nod.

'You're much younger than he is.'

Again she nodded.

'He liked you to dress up like a schoolgirl, did he? Is that how he got excited?' She paused, but there was still silence. Holden raised her voice even louder. 'You must answer me, Ania. This is not a game we are playing. If you do not co-operate with me, it will be very bad for you. Tell me, did Paul Greenleaf make you dress up as a schoolgirl?'

Gorski gulped. 'Yes,' she whispered. 'Sometimes he asked me. It was just a bit of fun.'

'So he liked to have a bit of fun with the two of you did he?' Holden pushed another photograph across the table, of her and the girl, both dressed as schoolgirls. 'It's just that the other girl looks like a real girl, maybe eleven or twelve.'

Gorski shook her head, but Holden wasn't satisfied. She leant forward and stabbed her finger down onto the second photograph.

'Did Greenleaf have sexual relations with the girl?'

Gorski shrieked. 'No! He never touched her. I would never

have let him. It was just a photograph. Nothing happened to her.'

'How do I know that?' Holden's voice was raised too, but more controlled. 'How do I know that nothing happened to her? I've only your word. How do I know that Paul Greenleaf didn't abuse her? How do I know you didn't help him?'

'Ask her!' Gorski was hysterical now. Her hands were clawing at her hair, and she had begun to rock backwards and forwards on her chair. 'Ask her!'

Holden's mobile rang. She saw it was Fox, and answered it. It wouldn't hurt to let the woman stew for a minute.

By the time she had finished speaking to Fox, she knew who the girl in the photograph was, and she knew, too, that both Jim and Maureen Wright were off the radar. Maureen had gone, according to her daughter, to Reading on a shopping trip. But she didn't know anything about her father. Or nothing that she was admitting anyway. Holden turned back towards Gorski.

'The girl is Vickie Wright, isn't she, Ania?'

Gorski nodded.

'When were the photos taken?'

'On Saturday.' She paused, and for a moment Holden thought that that was all she was going to say. But it was as if a log jam had been released, and all in a rush the words began to tumble forth. 'Mr Greenleaf took me to the football game on Saturday. Someone had hired a box, someone grateful for the care that Sunnymede had given to his wife, so Mr Greenleaf asked me if I'd like to go with him. And he asked other people, including Jim Wright and his daughter Vickie. I had met her a few times when she visited her grandmother in Sunnymede. Afterwards, they came back to Charlton with us. And we had some food and some drink, and then Mr Greenleaf said it would be fun if we both dressed as if we were sisters, sisters at school. So we did. And he took some photographs. But that was all that happened. Vickie said she wasn't feeling very well, so her father took her home. And that was all, I swear.' The effort of getting all this said with barely a pause for breath had taken a toll on Ania. She began to pant like a sprinter after a race, and sweat dribbled down her forehead.

But Holden was offering neither tea nor sympathy. 'Did you kill Mr Greenleaf, Ania?'

The question seemed to take her by surprise.

'You asked me that last time.' She was indignant, or was pretending to be. 'And I tell you again. I did not kill him. Why would I kill him?'

'Maybe because he was making you do things that you didn't want to do.'

'What do you mean?'

'I mean dressing up like a schoolgirl.' She stabbed her finger at Gorski and raised her voice. 'Sex games! Or maybe he was getting tired of you? Perhaps, instead, you were helping him find schoolgirls to have sex with?' She repeated the stabbing movement of her finger. 'I mean—'

The rest of what Holden meant was drowned out by the scream that erupted from Ania Gorski's throat. Holden had been half expecting it. She had pushed and pushed, in the hope that something would give. But what she hadn't expected was what happened next.

Ania Gorski flicked her wrist. The water in her half-empty glass showered across the table, into Holden's face. 'Hey!' It was Holden who shouted now, caught completely by surprise. Ania flicked her wrist again, this time downwards, glancing the edge of the table so that the rim of the glass cracked off. Then, with a huge grunt of effort, she hurled herself forward and swung the makeshift weapon towards the detective inspector's head. There was a squeal, like a piglet being slaughtered. Blood sprayed red, and Holden screamed for help.

'What on earth has happened to you? You look frightful!'

Susan Holden had tried to let herself into the flat quietly. Since her fall, her mother had conceded that it would be a good idea for her daughter to have a set of keys, though tonight Susan would rather have gone to her own home, bolted and chained the front door, and taken refuge in a bottle of wine, a microwave dinner, and some suitably undemanding tosh on the TV.

'Thanks, Mother.' It might, in other circumstances, have been a sarcastic reply, but after the shock of the incident, over two hours in accident and emergency, and seven stitches in her left cheek, Susan Holden was beyond sarcasm.

'Have you caught him then? The killer? Did he do this to you?'

'No.' She walked across to the sideboard, and poured herself a slug of whisky. She swilled it round the bottom of the tumbler, took a sip, and turned to face her mother.

Her mother, to her surprise, grinned. 'We are a pair, aren't we!'

Her daughter grinned back. 'The question is, who needs looking after most?'

They both laughed.

'I expect you'd like some supper.'

Susan sat down at the table, opposite her mother, and took another sip. 'In a minute.' She needed to talk first. To unload her day.

'There's a plate made up for you in the fridge.'

'You remember Ania, the Polish woman?' She paused. Her mother nodded. 'She did this. I was interviewing her, and she attacked me with her glass. I should have seen it coming.'

'You were playing the bad cop, were you?' Mrs Holden laughed.

'Sort of.' She frowned. 'I was on my own, and I pressed a bit too hard.'

Her mother got slowly to her feet. 'You stay there. I need to keep moving. I'll get your supper.' But she made her way round the table, not directly towards the kitchen. Gently she put her hand on her daughter's chin, and moved her head to the side so that she could get a better look. 'What a shame!' she said, and then kissed her on the forehead. 'My poor little girl.'

As her daughter ate her supper, Mrs Holden tried hard not to look at the stitches just above the jawline of her left cheek. Hopefully, in time, it would heal and the scar fade, and what nature couldn't fix, then make-up would surely cover, but right now it was hard not to stare. So she asked her more about her day and listened as her daughter told her. She listened right to the end, for it was in the end of her working day, the interview with Ania Gorski, that she was, for obvious reasons, most interested.

'So,' she said, when Susan fell silent, 'the question is why did she do it? I mean, quite apart from the obvious reason that you are prettier than she is and she was jealous!'

Susan shrugged, and laid her knife and fork down on her plate. Telling the story, reliving the experience, had helped. What was it that had triggered Ania's reaction? She could be a bully, she knew that. She wasn't proud of it, but sometimes needs must. But the fact was, when she had asked Ania bluntly if she'd murdered Greenleaf, there had been no sign of her flipping. She had denied it, and asked why she would have. No, it was what she had said next. About dressing up as a schoolgirl to satisfy Greenleaf. That had pressed Ania's buttons. She flushed, embarrassed to even remember what she had said to the woman next. She had accused her of helping Greenleaf find schoolgirls for sex. That was what had pushed Ania over the edge. And she couldn't blame her for that.

'You can tell me,' her mother said.

'No I can't,' she replied. That was a lie, of course, and yet it was also the truth. She just couldn't tell her mother.

She stood up, and felt a wave of exhaustion roll over her. 'I'm off to bed,' she said quietly, and this time it was she who moved round the table. She leant down and kissed her mother on the forehead. 'I'm so glad you moved to Oxford. So glad.'

CHAPTER TEN

Everything was dark. No, not dark. Black. Sightless. And there was a terrible pain in the back of his head. Not headache pain, but pain like someone had exploded a miniature bomb just behind his brain. There was pain in his back too, though this was nothing by comparison. And it was nothing compared to the panic that was rising though his whole being. Why the hell couldn't he see? He tried to feel for his face, but his right arm was stuck under his body behind him. Hell, he was lying on his back, and he couldn't lift himself up. At least his left arm could move. He felt for his face, and his fingers fastened onto something soft and woollen. It was his ruddy hat, and for some reason it was pulled down over his eyes. No wonder he couldn't see. He ripped it off, and felt the sudden shock of cold air on his shaven head. That was better. He could see shapes now, different shades of dark and light. Clouds up above him, and to the side the darker shapes of trees.

He pushed himself up with this hand, so he was sitting upright, and he became aware of something else. Beyond the pain which lanced through his head, there was a noise. It was a noise he recognized, and yet couldn't place. Where the hell was he? He was outside, he knew that, and yet there was no light. Nothing close anyway, though he could see two lights in the distance. The pain came surging up the back of his head again, and he shut his eyes against it. When he opened them again, the lights were brighter. 'Tiger, tiger burning bright'. Back from his past the words came. He had been crap at school;

the teachers were so boring. Only Mr Gascoigne had been any good, and it was he who had taught him that poem. God, he had almost forgotten it, just as he had almost forgotten Mr Gascoigne's piercing eyes, and soothing voice, and the brutal grip of his hand. 'Tiger, tiger, burning bright, In the forests of the night.' And the tiger's eyes were coming closer now, and closer, and behind his eyes the tiger was roaring. A sudden spurt of fear shot through him, and he struggled to his feet. He had to run, to get out of the way, before it was too late, but he couldn't move. His left leg wouldn't move. He pulled at it again, screaming at it. But his screams were lost in the roar of the tiger. He looked up again, into its eyes, and he knew it was too late. He knew there was no escaping the beast.

'Are you all right?'

Andy Stonehouse focused his eyes on the woman who was sitting opposite him and wondered if he had heard her correctly. She was his counsellor. He knew that because she had told him so. She had also told him her name, but he couldn't for the life of him remember what that was.

'Andy,' she was saying, in her softest, most encouragingly confidential voice. 'Why don't you tell me about it? Tell me what happened. You'll feel better if you do.'

He'd feel better! Was that a promise, a guarantee, or just the sort of psycho-babble shit she always churned out? How the hell would she know? He felt terrible. And not just in his head. He felt nauseous. He coughed, and for several moments thought he was going to vomit. He felt the bitter taste of regurgitated food in his throat, but fought it back. It was a natural reaction, to resist being sick, though if he'd been near a loo he'd have let it all come out. Sometimes you had to be sick before you could feel better, but sitting here in this grotty little room with this ridiculously overconcerned woman, he just wanted to get out and go home.

'Look,' she was saying, trying another tack, 'I'm not going to pretend that I know how you are feeling right now. Because I don't know. Only you can know. But you're not the first person to have had an experience like this, and I do know that it's important that you talk about it.'

He looked at her, and he laughed. Not loudly or unkindly. But he had just realized something. She had been looking at him intently, her face all serious and frowning, and her eyes wide and pleading. And then she had raised her hand and stifled a yawn. And realization had dawned on him. Christ, she was just as desperate as he was to get this over with and go home! For all her overt concern, he was just another job to her, at a bloody inconvenient time, and the sooner she had got him done and dusted, the happier she would be. Well, lady, so would he.

Stonehouse forced himself to speak. 'I didn't see him until the last second.' He paused then, and his face puckered as something occurred to him. 'Or was it a her?' He looked at the woman, properly this time, to check if she was really listening. 'I think it was a him. In fact, I'm almost sure, but it happened so quickly. Anyway, when I realized what was happening, in that split second I thought to myself, what the hell is he doing there? What the hell is that man doing there? And then, bang! Well, not so much bang as thud. It all happened so quickly. Of course I hit the brakes as soon as I saw him, but it was far too late. But I couldn't just keep driving, could I. Besides, that is what the emergency procedures are there for. We train for it, you see. We train for people throwing themselves in front of trains.'

He stopped, suddenly aware of what he had said, and he started laughing, though this time it was prolonged and highly strung laughter that see-sawed as violently as his emotions. It wasn't the first time his counsellor had witnessed hysteria, and she knew it wouldn't be the last either. So she waited for it to run its course, because what else could she do? And besides, there was a question she needed to ask. Eventually, she judged that Stonehouse had calmed down enough for her to continue.

'It's interesting that you talk about people throwing themselves in front of trains. Is that how you saw it? Someone throwing himself in front of your train? An act of suicide? Or could it have been something else? Someone wandering onto the track under the influence of drink or drugs, for example?'

Stonehouse winced as he tried to think. He shook his head. 'I don't know. Christ, that's the last thing you expect. Suddenly he was there, in front of me. He looked up at me. And then he was gone.'

The woman nodded. She was satisfied. Whatever the police might say, the guy had been through enough. And he had told her enough. It was up to them to work out how it was that the victim had ended up there in front of Stonehouse's train. Her job was to help the driver survive. That would be hard enough. Some drivers never got over it. She knew that. So the least she could do was protect him from unnecessary questions.

They drove in silence – round the southern ring road, over the endless humps which litter the road through the elongated village of Kennington, and past the umbrella of bungalows which mark the start of Radley. Fox was driving, Holden was sitting next to him, and in the back was one detective constable. Wilson had been late. Just as they had been drawing out of the Cowley station car park, he had hurtled in on his bike, and had almost skidded into them. 'Drive on, Sergeant,' Holden had rasped, sensing that Fox was about to stop the car. And she had held up her wrist so Wilson could see it, and tapped ostentatiously on an invisible watch.

No one was speaking. Even Lawson was improbably quiet. It wasn't just because she had been shaken by Holden's brutal treatment of Wilson. It was more what was in front of her. Train incidents were outside her experience, and she had realized that she was feeling rather unnerved at what she might see. She looked out of the right-hand window to distract herself. The bungalows had given way to farmland, and above it, no more than fifty metres up, a red kite was wheeling idly around the grey skies. She watched it briefly, but red kites are a common sight now in Oxfordshire, and besides, her mind kept lurching back towards the task in hand. Fox was turning left now, past the church of St James the Great, and she tried to focus on that. Her father had taken her there once as a young teenager. He had been invited to preach during an interregnum. Not that she remembered anything of the sermon (who would have?), but she did remember him telling her about how the church had been a battleground in the civil war, when royalist soldiers had taken refuge there from the parliamentarians. Or was it the other way round?

'There they are.' Fox's words dragged her back from her interlude. They were through Radley now, driving down a rough narrow lane with open farmland on either side. The 'they' were a pair of figures in the distance, one with an arm raised in greeting. The raised arm belonged to Nick Birch of the British Transport Police. Holden knew him vaguely. They had met on a training course, and sat together in some small group sessions. He had, she recalled, a taste for cheap aftershave and a tendency to apply it liberally.

Holden was out of the car almost before it had stopped moving. She shook hands with Birch and introduced her team. Birch's colleague had already wandered off.

'There's not much for you to see.' Birch launched straight in. He wanted to keep this short. He couldn't think they could gain much from the scene that he couldn't have told them over the phone or in an office, but Holden had insisted on it. 'Frankly, that's lucky for you. The train would have been going between fifty and sixty miles per hour, and at that speed it's going to make one hell of a mess of anyone stupid or desperate enough to get in its way. Sometimes they end up like a sack of jelly, but other times, like last night, they end up sliced and diced. We've picked up all the bits we've been able to find. That includes various items of clothing, both boots, and as I mentioned on the phone a wallet complete with credit cards. Which is why we can be pretty sure the victim is Jim Wright.'

'Were the boots on his feet?'

'Yeah.'

'Can I see them?'

Birch studied Holden. He remembered her from the course too. Nice enough, but talking of boots, she was as tough as the oldest. Even so, he tried to dissuade her.

'I wouldn't recommend it,' he said firmly. 'We're used to this.' And you're not, he implied.

'I need to be sure they are Jim Wright's boots,' she said with equal firmness. 'At the very least, I need a photo I can show Mrs Wright, and I need to know the size.'

'We can email you the details – size, make, distinguishing features – and photos within the hour. Is there anything else?

'I'd like to see where exactly you think the impact took place.'

'If you think it will help.' He spoke slowly, reluctantly, as if to demonstrate his own belief that it couldn't possibly help.

'I don't know if it will help or not!' Holden flared. Bloody men! Why was it they always had to know best? They always want to be in control. And Birch was no different from the rest of them. 'The fact is that yesterday we were trying to get hold of Jim Wright to question him in relation to a murder. And today he's dead. Now it could be suicide, and I dare say you'll trot out the statistics for railway suicides to underline your belief that suicide is most likely, but as far as I'm concerned, suicide is just too damned convenient. So if that is all right with you, Inspector Birch, I'd like to take a closer look at what may be the scene of a murder.'

'OK!' Birch said, looking down at the ground. Sometimes, a tactical withdrawal was the only option. 'But just be alert to the fact that the track is open and trains are running.'

Birch led them some twenty metres down the road, before cutting right through a narrow gateway. As if to prove his last point, a passenger train hurtled past from right to left, on the way towards Didcot, Reading and – most likely – London Paddington. He, however, led them in the opposite direction, towards Oxford, keeping tight to the side. 'We should be OK for ten minutes.' He had gone about fifty metres when he stopped and turned round.

'It's hard to be sure exactly where the impact took place, but this is where we started finding debris. Human debris. The actual impact may have been a bit further up the track, but in my experience not a lot.'

Holden looked around, half expecting to spot a severed hand that Birch's team had somehow missed. What had she come here for? She looked up the track towards Oxford, and tried to imagine how it might have been for Jim Wright, assuming it was him. It had been dark, of course, but trains had lights, and trains made a substantial amount of noise. It was hard to imagine that he could have been oblivious to the approach of the train unless he was drunk or unconscious or off his head on drugs. Or dead of course. There was no reason to think it was an accident. That much was pretty clear. Why would he have come here, except deliberately? Which meant he came here to commit suicide, or he came here to meet someone, and that someone ensured that he ended up in front of the London express.

She turned towards Fox. 'Sergeant, do you see Jim Wright as the suicidal type?'

'No, Guv.' The answer was immediate.

'So how easy would you reckon it is to murder someone with the assistance of a train?'

Fox sniffed, and looked around. At night it would be a fairly lonely spot. The road down here was going nowhere. How many people ever drove this way, especially at night? 'There are easier ways, no question,' Fox said, feeling his way. 'But it is isolated. If I was the murderer, then I might have lured him out here with the intention of killing him. Then I might have dumped his body on the track just to make identification a lot harder.'

'In which case,' Holden replied, 'why leave the guy's wallet in his pocket, for us to find?'

Fox shrugged. 'Panic maybe. Or maybe it all happened very quickly as the train was approaching. The killer wouldn't want to hang around. So he pushed the body on the track, and scarpered.'

'It might have been a she,' Lawson commented, anxious to get a toe hold in the conversation.

'If I can throw in my penny's worth,' Birch said, 'my understanding is that the man was alive when the train hit him. The driver said he saw him on his feet.'

'What?' Holden spat the word at him. 'How the hell do you know that?'

Birch held his hands up apologetically, as if fearful that DI Holden might pull out a gun and start shooting. 'The driver spoke to a counsellor afterwards.'

'So there's a report somewhere, is there? Why haven't I had a copy?'

'Hey, don't shoot the messenger. The report is probably being punched into the computer even as we speak. But it just so happens that the counsellor is my wife, and I rang her a few minutes ago.'

Holden opened her mouth to say something more, but bit back on the impulse. She suddenly realized she was trembling. She looked at her right hand, and tried to make it still, but it refused to co-operate. So she stuffed both hands in her jacket pockets, and took a deep breath in, and a long one out. Standing here, where Jim Wright had been mangled to death, where a train might hurtle by at any moment, it was no bloody wonder she was shaking. Had Wright been shaking? If he had been conscious and on his feet, why the hell hadn't he thrown himself out of the way? Like Fox, she didn't see him as the suicidal type. So what had happened?

She turned towards Birch. 'Any chance of me talking to your wife, Inspector?'

He nodded, dug his hand into his back pocket, and located his mobile. Within moments, he was passing it across to Holden. 'It's ringing. And her name is Dr Eileen Birch.'

'What the hell do you want now?' Dr Eileen Birch did not, it seemed, like being rung at work by her husband, at least not twice within the same morning.

'This is Inspector Susan Holden, Thames Valley Police.'

'Bugger!' came the reply. And then, almost as an after-thought. 'Sorry! I thought you were my husband.'

'He's kindly lent me his mobile.'

'Kindly!' There was an explosion of laughter. 'My husband doesn't do kindly. Not during office hours, and not much outside them either.'

'I understand you spoke to the driver of the train that—'

'Mostly I listened,' she broke in. 'That's what I do. Listen as much as I can and say as little as I need. More people should try it.'

Holden felt the rebuke like a slap round the face. 'I under-stand the victim was standing up at the time of impact?'

'Not that that did him much good!'

Holden paused, recognizing something of herself in the sharpness at the other end of the phone call. She'd like to meet her. Or maybe not. She took a breath and tried again. 'I don't want to be doing this, but the fact is that we have reason to believe that it may not have been suicide and—'

'Look, I'm sorry.' Again Dr Birch cut in before Holden had finished. 'You caught me on the hop. It's not something you get used to, listening to people's trauma. Sometimes, I wonder if I shouldn't go and run a B & B on the Cornish coast.' There was a sigh down the phone. Holden waited for her to collect herself. 'The victim was on his feet when the train struck. That really is as much as I can tell you.'

'Was he trying to get out the way, do you think? Or was he maybe drunk, and just staggering along the line oblivious.'

'Hey, listen Inspector. When I tell you that the victim was on his feet, that really is all I can tell you. The driver had only the briefest glimpse of him. He saw him at the last moment. A single nightmarish moment where a man appears in front of his train and disappears almost in the same fraction of a second, with a thud that will live on in the driver's dreams for months to come. Or maybe even years.'

'I see.' Holden paused, as she tried to frame her response. 'Do you think I might be able to talk to the driver myself?'

'Absolutely not.' The reply was emphatic. 'My concern is to protect the driver so he recovers. Nothing he can say to you is going to solve your problem, and even if there was a possibility, I wouldn't let you anywhere near him. His well-being is too important.' For a moment, neither of them spoke. 'So that's all then, is it?' Dr Birch said, bringing the conversation to an end.

'Yes,' Holden said. And then grudgingly added, 'Thank you.'

'My pleasure.' Dr Birch's tone was, as far as Holden could detect over a poor mobile signal, suddenly softer. 'I've enjoyed our chat.'

'So have I.' Holden wondered what Dr Eileen Birch looked like. It was a shame they had had to do this over a phone, and with an audience. 'Would you like a word with your husband?'

There was a guttural laugh. 'Just pass on my worst wishes to him, and tell him if he forgets it's his turn to do supper, he'll be sleeping with the dog.'

Holden passed the mobile back to Birch, but said nothing about supper. If he didn't remember, then he'd deserve everything he got. Besides, it was Jim Wright's death that she was interested in, and nothing else.

'I assume the victim was on this nearside track when he was struck?'

'Yes.'

Holden moved across and stood on the sleepers between the rails. Then she started walking slowly towards Oxford, her eyes on the ground.

'What are you looking for, Guv?' Fox had moved to her side, frustrated at the lack of anything to do.

'Rope, maybe. Wire. Something that might have been used to attach Jim Wright's leg to the track so he couldn't get away.'

There's a train due in three minutes,' Birch warned.

But no one was listening to him. Holden and Fox had stopped by Lawson, who was crouched down on her haunches by the side of the track, 'Take a look at this!' she had said excitedly, just as Birch had been broadcasting his three-minute warning. 'Is this what you're looking for, Guv?'

Lawson was pointing at a piece of wire that was looped twice round a sleeper. It was some eighteen inches in length, with a green covering, and it looked new.

As her latest – and, without question, most irritating – customer exited the shop, Jaz Green pulled out her mobile, flipped it open, and frowned. It wasn't the first time she had frowned at it that morning, but frown as she might, no text message, no missed call, no voicemail message displayed itself. It was very nearly eleven o'clock, and still David had not turned up. Normally, they'd have been fortunate to have had one customer by now, but it was Murphy's Law that on the day David went AWOL four separate and very needy customers should turn up before coffee break time. She had been sorely tempted to strangle the last of these four with some of her very best picture wire after the woman had fussed endlessly and very vocally about the boards and frames for two of her own very ordinary paintings. She had asked for advice, and then dismissed it with such condescension that Jaz had had to count silently to ten. Now all she wanted was to nip outside for a cigarette, and then pop up the road for a nice cappuccino. Only she couldn't because David still hadn't turned up.

It wasn't like him. He normally warned her if he was running even five minutes late. He was very precise was David. She rang his number, but as had happened when she'd rung an hour earlier, it went straight to his answering service. She killed the call. There was no point in leaving another message.

Jaz retreated to the yard at the back of the shop. If she stood by the small window – she really must get David to clean it – she could still spot anyone coming in the front door. She lit up, and waited for the tension to ebb. But she couldn't help but worry. The thing about David was he was so reliable. It just wasn't like him not to turn up. She took a final pull at her cigarette, dropped it on the ground, and crushed it under her heel. She flipped the mobile open again as she moved back into the shop. She hated ringing Maureen to ask whether she knew anything. It felt like a betrayal of David. She believed in treating him like an adult, and ringing his mother to check up on him was not treating him like an adult. But to do nothing seemed worse – suppose he had had an accident, or was so sick he couldn't get help. Perhaps he'd lost his mobile and couldn't call for help.

Maureen answered almost immediately. 'What is it, Jaz?' She spoke brusquely, which was unusual. They were good friends, and their conversations were typically anything but brusque.

'Is David all right? It's just that he's not turned up for work, and he's not answering his mobile.'

'He's not the only one.'

But Jaz failed to register the sharpness in her friend's voice. 'David is usually so reliable. Has he rung you?'

'No he ruddy well hasn't.'

Jaz said nothing, taken aback by her friend's answer and tone. It wasn't like her at all, at least not where David was concerned.

'Jim didn't come home last night.'

'What?' She wondered if she'd misheard. 'What do you mean? He's left you?' Mind you, she immediately thought, it wouldn't be the worst thing in the world if he had. He treated Maureen like shit.

'I don't know. Maybe he's left me, maybe he hasn't. Maybe he got as drunk as a skunk last night, and doesn't plan on coming home until my shift has started.'

'Maybe he's with David?' The thought had suddenly occurred to Jaz. 'Have you tried ringing him?'

But Maureen never answered the question. 'There's someone at the door.' And then, in a loud whisper, 'God! It's that bloody detective woman again and her sidekick. I'll have to go.'

'Ring me when they've gone,' Jaz said, but the line was already dead.

Back at the police station, Wilson was feeling very sorry for himself. Sometimes life – not to mention DI Holden – could be such a bitch. He'd only been a few minutes late that morning, and it wasn't as if it was his fault anyway. He'd been up half the night with his mother. She'd woken up feeling sick just after one o'clock, and she hadn't made it to the loo. His dad was in Manchester on business, so he'd had to clean up after her. Thick carpet impregnated with vomit – it had been disgusting. Sitting there at his desk, Wilson sniffed at the back of his hand. He reckoned he could still smell it, rank and rancid.

Eventually, he had got to bed, but he hadn't been able to get back to sleep for ages, and then he'd gone and slept right through the alarm. So all in all, what with speed shaving, and speed showering, and grabbing a banana on the run, he reckoned he'd done well to get to the station only twenty minutes late. But as he had pulled into the car park on his bike, he had almost collided with Holden, Fox, and Lawson coming out. He had skidded to a halt, expecting Fox to stop, but he didn't. Through the glass, he had seen Holden exaggeratedly tapping her forefinger on her wrist, and then they were past him.

Inside the station, he had soon discovered what he was missing – a death on the railway line – and he had sworn loudly. Wilson was not normally a man who swore. But inside the office that he shared with Lawson and two others, there had been no one to hear anyway.

There was a bright yellow sheet of A4 paper on his desk. It was Holden's writing. 'Find yourself something useful to do. We're working.' Terse, brusque and totally without sympathy.

For maybe half an hour, Wilson had seethed. At the injustice of it all. At his mum for not making it to the loo. At the ferocity of Holden. What a cow she could be! It just wasn't fair.

And then his mobile had rung. It was his mother. She never rang him at work. Never. And for a couple of moments, he was scared to answer.

'Sorry to bother you,' she said quickly, 'but I just wanted to say thank you.'

'Are you all right?'

'Much better, thanks. Don't worry. I'll be fine. I'm just sorry you had to clear up the mess.'

'That's OK, Mum.'

'Bye, then,' and she was gone.

For maybe half a minute he sat there, staring into nothing. A single short phone call, and his self-pity had evaporated like the early morning mist. What a bastard he was to have thought like that. He had helped his mother, but who wouldn't have in the circumstances? And then he had blamed her, just because he had overslept. How was that her fault?

He looked down at the desk, at the yellow paper which stared up at him. 'Find yourself something useful to do.' He made a face. He'd show Holden. He'd bloody well show her.

Holden was sitting on the same sofa as when she had first visited Maureen Wright, and she was feeling even more uncomfortable than the last occasion. This wasn't the sofa's fault; it was just that the impact of the morning was only now starting to kick in. She hadn't anticipated the emotional shock of walking along those railway tracks, imagining what might have happened, and she certainly hadn't been prepared for finding what they had found. And now she had to break the news.

'So are you going to tell me something?' Maureen had sat down in the armchair immediately opposite, and her hands were clenched tight together. 'I presume you're here because you know something?'

'Last night someone was hit by a train. It was travelling to London, between Oxford and Didcot, and it hit and killed someone on the line.'

'Someone?'

'We believe it may be your husband.'

'My husband?'

'We believe so. It's hard....' Holden paused. How do you say this to someone? 'In that sort of accident, identification is never easy.'

She was expecting Maureen to break down, to burst into tears or hysterics. But the woman's face was blank. 'It can't be him. What would he be doing on a railway line?'

'We don't know. Not yet. And maybe you're right.' Holden didn't feel this was going to plan, whatever that plan might be. But she had to carry on. 'It was on the line near Radley Village. We were wondering if he had any clients down there. Or potential clients.'

'Maybe.' Maureen shook her head, as it trying to clear it. 'I don't know. He sure as hell needed some more work.' She paused. 'He did say he was going to see someone about a job, but to be honest I wasn't really listening.'

'You mean he was going to see someone yesterday?'

'I think so.' She grimaced, trying to assemble her scrambled thoughts. 'Look, I don't—' She stopped, took a deep breath, and then started again. 'I didn't always believe Jim. When he said he was going to do this or do that, that he'd met someone who was going to put work his way, well I took it with a large pinch of salt. He was a bit of a bullshitter.' She paused again, looked down at her fingers, and then up again until her eyes met Holden's. 'Are you sure it was him?'

'We found his wallet. With a bank debit card, two credit cards, and driving licence.'

'Someone could have stolen it from him!' Maureen's voice had intensified. 'Then done a runner and got knocked down by the train. You can't be certain it was him. He could still be alive.'

Holden was watching her closely. Only DNA comparison could prove it beyond all doubt, but as far as she was concerned the victim had to be Jim Wright. The poor woman was clutching at straws – or possibly she was a very cool woman playing a very calculating game. If Maureen Wright had had even an inkling of what her husband and Greenleaf had been getting up to, then she had one hell of a good motive for murder. Genuine shock or crocodile tears? Holden needed to know. 'What size are your husband's feet?'

'His feet?' The surprise in her voice seemed genuine. 'Size ten.'

Holden turned slightly towards DS Fox, who was sitting to her right, an A4 envelope in his hands. He pulled out a photo and slipped it onto the coffee table around which they were all perched. It was a photo of a single brown boot. Holden opened her mouth to ask the question, but there was no need. Maureen Wright stood up from the table, staggered towards the kitchen door, and vomited.

Less than five hundred metres away, Wilson had, for the first time that day, a look on his face that denoted pleasure. Not intense pleasure, admittedly, and certainly not the pleasure of someone who has, maybe, just won the lottery. Rather it was a look of quiet satisfaction, one which his mother would have recognized, a look which indicated that Detective Constable Colin Wilson was on to something.

When he had finally recovered his equilibrium that morning,

Wilson had started with a sheet of blank paper, pushing the yellow one with its terse message from Holden to the side. On the white sheet, he had written the names of Nanette Wright, Paul Greenleaf, and finally Jim Wright. He had then added a question mark next to Jim's name, conscious that the identity was not certain.

His own initial theory, fuelled by his interviews of Nanette's solicitor and accountant had been that it was all about money, and that Jim Wright had slipped the morphine into the flask to bring about her early demise. But if it was Jim Wright who had been hit by the train, where did that leave his theory? Had Jim Wright committed suicide? After he had killed Greenleaf? But that didn't make sense. After all, Greenleaf had been paying him way over the odds for minor building work on his Otmoor house, and it was Greenleaf who had hired him to do some jobs at Sunnymede. So why on earth would Jim have killed Greenleaf? Was it something to do with the photos of Ania and his daughter, taken after that Hayes and Yeading game? He frowned, wrote 'Photos?' on the right hand side of the white sheet of paper, and tried to think.

And it was while he was thinking that Holden's text had arrived, as blunt and to the point as ever: 'Hayes and Yeading – who was in the box? Complete list. Pronto.'

So her thoughts were going along the same lines as his. He felt a sudden glow of pleasure, and picked up the phone.

The guy at Oxford United was helpful, and yet not helpful. There had been ten people in the box. At least he assumed there had been because they were designed for ten people and no more. But no, he couldn't give a complete list of who the ten people were because that wasn't how it worked. He could, however, confirm that it was Paul Greenleaf who had hired the box.

'He paid for it himself?'

'He paid with a business card – Sunnymede Care Home.'

'Right. But you can't tell me who actually came?'

'No.'

'What about CCTV?'

'What about it?'

'Was there any in the room?'

'No.'

'Outside the room?'

'No. Look, let me explain.' There was more than a tinge of irritation in the man's voice. 'We've got CCTV, of course we have, but we use it to spot troublemakers in the crowd, not spy on our corporate clients. Right? The boxes are for watching the football. They aren't part of the Big Brother studio.'

'Thank you,' Wilson said quickly, conscious that he was in danger of losing the guy's co-operation. 'It's just that my boss wants a complete list of everyone in the box that day and—'

'So get your boss to ask Mr Greenleaf. He'll know, won't he?'

There was an obvious answer to that, but Wilson had had enough. He thanked the guy for his time and rang off.

It was Greenleaf who had hired the box, using money donated by some grateful son or daughter. And it was clear from Ania's evidence that she, Greenleaf, Jim Wright, and Vickie Wright had been there. So who were the other six? And who could he find out from? Vickie maybe. But he couldn't just ring her up. So how...?

And then a thought occurred to him: Greenleaf's laptop. Maybe there was something on it. Mind you he'd already given it a pretty good once over. But Holden would want only answers, not excuses. He extricated the laptop from its case, and powered it up again. Then he logged on and opened up the email. The only problem with the email was that Greenleaf had been very careful when using it. Wilson had already discovered that. When he had cracked the password at Greenleaf's house in Charlton-on-Otmoor, he had discovered nothing in the deleted items folder, nothing in the sent items, and only three in the inbox, and they had all been marketing ones. But maybe, just maybe, there might be some new ones that might give a clue about something.

As he waited for Microsoft Outlook to do its check for new emails, he did a search for any file on the computer with the word 'Hayes' in it. Maybe, just maybe, Greenleaf had kept a file for the game. But the search revealed nothing. He flicked back to Outlook. Six emails had come in: two from Expedia with details of cheap flights to Minneapolis; one about parking at Heathrow; special offers from two supermarkets; and one from a money advice website. And then, as he looked at the screen in frustration, another one came in, from Facebook.

'God!' It wasn't a prayer. Wilson didn't pray. But it should have been, at the very least, a word of thanks to a higher being. 'Roy Hillerby wants to be your friend' the email said. Wilson clicked, confirming that he – or rather the dead Paul Greenleaf – would be happy to be a friend. So did that mean that Roy Hillerby didn't know about Greenleaf's death? But Wilson didn't dwell on the thought, because he was staring at Roy Hillerby's Facebook page, and a photograph. He clicked on it. It was one of only two in Hillerby's album. They weren't going to win any photographic awards, but they were clear enough. Nine people sitting round a table, each with a drink in his or her hand, and the same nine people sitting down in two rows of seats. Excitement flooded through Wilson: It was the Hayes and Yeading game. It was a result.

'What happened to you, then?' Wilson looked up to see Lawson standing smugly in the doorway.

'I overslept.' He had no intention of going into detail, not to her anyway.

'It looks like Jim Wright was tied to the railway.'

'Tied to it?'

'With garden wire.'

'Shit!'

She walked over to Wilson. 'Checking your Facebook, I see,' she smirked. 'Naughty boy!'

'Not mine, actually. Greenleaf's.'

'Greenleaf's?'

'Yeah, Roy Hillerby from Sunnymede has asked Greenleaf to be his friend, and look at these photographs he posted. From the Hayes and Yeading game.'

'Hey, that's Jim Wright and his daughter, and Greenleaf and Bella Sinclair.'

'Yeah, I'm not sure about the others. Hillerby hasn't tagged anyone or written any names, so I was thinking we should go and show it to Fran Sinclair. She ought to know everyone on it.'

'OK, let's go.'

'I ought to speak to the guv first.'

'She won't want to be disturbed. She and Fox have gone off to tell Maureen her husband has been marmalized.'

'If you're sure.'

'She wants a list of names of everyone in that Oxford United box. If you want to avoid a bollocking, I suggest you ring her when you've got them, not before.'

Maureen Wright had changed her clothes. The pink blouse and black slacks had been thrust into the washing machine, and had been replaced by a blue T-shirt and jeans. She had brushed her teeth to get rid of the taste of the vomit, applied some perfume, and brushed her hair. She was ready for whatever came next, as long as it didn't involve photographs.

'When did you last see your husband?' Holden asked. She was sitting opposite on the sofa as before, leaning forward, eager to get on with it, a terrier worrying at a bone.

'Yesterday morning, just before I went to Reading.'

'What time was that?'

'About half past ten, maybe eleven.'

'And Jim was at home?'

'That's right. He was at home. Sitting on his arse, because with Greenleaf being dead, that cow at Sunnymede didn't want him doing any more work there.'

'So he had no work to go to?'

'He told me he was going to finish off Mr Jones's patio. He

lives three doors up. Jim laid it all a couple of weeks ago, but he needed to go and finish it off. I warned him I'd finish him off if he didn't get it sorted because we needed the money, but that was Jim Wright all over. Never quite finished what he started unless you planted a bomb under him.'

'And you said earlier he was planning to call on someone about a possible job?'

'Oh, you were listening then.' Maureen's answer was savage with sarcasm.

'But you don't know who it was?'

'No, I still don't know.'

Sometimes, when she questioned people, Holden got a strong sense that they were telling the truth, and sometimes she felt instinctively that they were spinning a line. But right now, she had neither. The only sense she had was that Maureen Wright was spurting out vitriol in the same way – and perhaps for the same reason – as an octopus ejects ink, to protect itself and confuse its enemy. Holden was encouraged. 'Look,' she insisted, 'I do need to ask these questions if I'm to—'

'Bugger your questions, Inspector.' Maureen Wright stood up abruptly, catching the edge of the table on her knees so that it lifted and jumped with her. 'And bugger my husband. There are more important things in the world than him. David has gone missing. My son has gone missing.' And then she started howling.

Wilson and Lawson found Fran Sinclair in Greenleaf's office – or rather it had been Greenleaf's office, but it was clear that Fran Sinclair had already staked a permanent claim to it. It wasn't as if she had heavily feminized it – far from it – but the walls proclaimed that this room was now under new owner-ship. In particular, an oversized graduation photo of her confronted the visitor as he or she entered the room, and to the right of it a framed certificate proclaimed Frances Alison Sinclair as having been awarded a degree of Bachelor of Arts (Second Class) in Applied Social Studies.

'I wonder if you can help us with identifying the people in these photos?' Wilson waved the photographs as he asked the question. Fran Sinclair leant back in the swivel chair she had inherited from her unlamented boss, and scowled.

'I do hope this isn't going to take long, young man. I have a business to run.'

'Of course not. It's just that you seemed the obvious person to ask,' he continued. 'We wanted to identify all the people who attended the Hayes and Yeading match in the Sunnymede box.'

'Talk about a waste of money! If someone wants to give us a present of several hundred pounds, there are better ways they could spend it than splashing out on a football game, ways that would help lots of people here, and not just a few favoured workers.'

Lawson had already heard enough. She took the photographs from Wilson's hand, and thrust them at Fran. 'There are ten people in these photos. We know six of them – Paul Greenleaf, Ania Gorski, Jim Wright and his daughter, Roy Hillerby, and your sister Bella. Just tell us who the others are, and then we'll get out of your hair.'

Fran took the two photographs and laid them carefully on the desk. Then she spent at least fifteen seconds studying them as it they were rare prints of some Oxford college rather than a pair of cheesy, slightly out of focus photo prints.

'These two here,' she said eventually, stabbing her finger into the centre of the left-hand picture, 'are Mr and Mrs Thorpe, who paid for it all. And these two over here are Justin, who works in the kitchen, and Dr Featherstone.'

It was Dr Featherstone's name which caught the attention of both Wilson and Lawson. They knew who he was, of course, but neither of them had been there when Holden interviewed him.

'So Justin and Dr Featherstone are keen on their football, are they?'

'Justin yes, he's mad keen. But I wouldn't have said so about Dr Featherstone.'

'Oh?' Lawson tried not to sound too interested, though obviously she was. She wasn't much of an expert on football herself, but she was pretty damned sure that Oxford United versus Hayes and Yeading wasn't exactly the match of the season unless possibly you were a football nut living in the flight path of Heathrow airport.

'The good doctor has short arms and long pockets.' The contempt in Fran's voice was unmissable.

'Sorry?'

'I've told him more than once he needs to work on those arm-stretching movements, but he never changes. He's game for anything if there's a chance of a free lunch and several free drinks.'

'And as a doctor?' Again Lawson left the question hanging. In this mood, who knew what Ms Sour Face might say.

'As a doctor, he's getting near his sell-by date, and I sure as hell won't be sorry when he reaches it.'

'I see.'

'This place needs a bit of fresh blood.'

'You have plans, do you?'

'I'm not in charge. Just holding the fort. But if I had it my way, yes there'd be quite a few changes.'

'Like Jim Wright?' It was Wilson who said this, keen to get a foothold in the argument. 'He was fresh blood, wasn't he? Brought in by Greenleaf to help Roy Hillerby. Yet I understand you didn't approve.'

'Jim Wright was a waste of money. Roy could have managed on his own. Would have done if we'd given him a bit of overtime. But Greenleaf and he fell out. Greenleaf even wrote him a disciplinary letter. He wanted to get rid of him, if you ask me, and then hire Jim Wright in his place. That was his long-term plan.'

'So what was the disciplinary matter?' This was Lawson

again, trying to wrench control of the interview back from Wilson.

'Nanette Wright complained about him. She claimed she caught him snooping through her cupboard when he was meant to be replacing a tap washer. Greenleaf believed her, and so Roy got a disciplinary.'

'So what does that mean?'

'It means one more incident and Roy would have been in serious trouble. Two strikes and you're out.'

'And Jim Wright would have been in? Thanks in no small part to his mother.'

'I guess so.'

'But now that Jim is dead ...' Wilson butted in, though he left the sentence unfinished. He wanted to see Fran Sinclair's reaction.

'Dead?' The surprise in her voice sounded genuine.

'Hit by a train.'

She stared at Wilson for several seconds and then exploded into laughter. 'Sorry!' She held her fist up to her mouth, and pushed hard, as it trying hold the laughter in, but it burst out in huge gulping guffaws. 'But it's impossible to feel anything for those two bastards except relief that they're dead.'

'And Roy must be relieved too.'

'Sure. Why not?'

'And Roy is fond of your sister, I understand.'

Fran looked at Wilson, and then laughed. 'Fond of her? He sniffs round her like she's a bitch on heat. But there's no law against that now, is there?'

CHAPTER 11

I like it here. It's the best. It always was. They won't find me here. I wasn't sure I would find it, but I have a good memory for places. When I've been somewhere once, I can usually find it again. And so here I am, back safe and sound.

I slept here once before. When I was on camp and they were mean to me. They were always being to mean to me, and Mr Miller called me stupid, so I just packed my bag when they were all singing songs round the fire, and I escaped.

I've got everything I need. My sleeping bag is a four-season one. It's got a hood with a drawstring so I can pull it up tight round my head. I can't possibly get cold, not when I've got good protection like I have here. Even if it rains, I'll be all right because I won't get wet. I've got food, and water, and a little camping stove. The stove is brilliant. It's really light, and it means I can have hot food when I want to. Water is the biggest problem when you're camping. If you run out, you're done for. But there are houses round here. You wouldn't believe it. There really are quite a lot of houses in these woods, so when I need water I just need to find one with an outside tap. But I have to be careful. I don't want them to find me. Because I need time to think. Time to work out what to do next. Time on my own.

Holden got back to the Cowley Road station with Maureen's wailing still echoing in her ears. She went straight to her office and slammed the door like she was shutting out the hounds of hell. Then she walked over to her grimy window and gazed out.

A broken-down lorry was causing traffic chaos on the Oxford Road. Two men in high visibility jackets were gesticulating wildly, and an unseen driver was taking out his or her frustration with the hooter, but Holden barely noticed. All she could think of was Jim Wright's boot. The photo had been unexceptional: it was just a boot, a size 10 working man's boot. It was exceptional only because she knew – as Maureen had known when she had vomited so spectacularly – what the boot signified, and where it had come from, and that inside it there remained a remarkably intact piece of foot (Nick Birch had rung her to tell her that!). For a moment, she wondered if she wasn't going to be sick too. She stuck her hand out to steady herself against the window sill. Christ, she really was losing it.

There was a bang on the door. She turned to see Wilson standing flush-faced in the doorway. 'Dr Featherstone was in the box too!'

'What?' Holden looked at him as if he was speaking a foreign language.

'And Roy Hillerby was on a disciplinary.'

This time Holden said nothing, as she tried to assimilate this new information.

'Because of Nanette!' Wilson continued.

'What?'

'And if you ask me, Fran Sinclair would have loved to murder them all.'

It took Holden five minutes to extract from Wilson (and Lawson, who had been parking the car) a more complete and coherent account of their visit to Sunnymede. But at the end of it, she felt only confusion. If knowledge was meant to bring clarity, it had, on this occasion, singularly failed. She tried to organize her thoughts but they refused to be marshalled. Featherstone had been in Sunnymede shortly before Nanette's death. He was in the box at the Hayes and Yeading game despite not liking football. And yet it was hard to see him murdering Greenleaf so violently, or indeed overcoming Jim Wright and dragging him onto the railway track. But Roy Hillerby – he was a man to wonder about. All the evidence was that he fancied Bella like crazy; he was one incident away from getting dismissed from his job, with Jim Wright waiting in the wings. He sure as hell had motives for murder. Nanette Wright had made the complaint that got him his disciplinary letter, and now she was dead. Hell, maybe that was it? Maybe it was Roy Hillerby who had spiked her whisky? Why not?

'So what do you think, Guv?' Wilson was bobbing with excitement, like a cork on the high seas. 'Should we pick them both up, Featherstone and Hillerby? Maybe we could sweat them a bit – see who breaks first?'

'Personally,' Lawson broke in, 'I think we need to look harder at Fran. She sure as hell had access to morphine, didn't she? And she's Bella's sister, so anyone who attacks Bella, attacks her. And then—'

Lawson never finished her theorizing because Holden suddenly skipped forward two, three steps and swung her right leg at a grey plastic waste-paper basket that stood next to her desk. It soared and spun and crash landed in the doorway, causing Wilson and Lawson to scatter.

'Where in God's name is the evidence?' Holden held her hands up, fingers splayed wide, as if she was in the presence of the supreme being, entreating him (or her) for the answer to the meaning of life. 'Because theories are ten a penny. And theories aren't what I want. What I want are hard, relevant facts, evidence that points us directly to our killer or killers. Are you with me?'

Neither of them said a thing. Wilson knelt down on the floor, and started to pick up the tea bags, plastic cups, and other detritus strewn across it. Lawson, after a brief hesitation, recovered the bin and placed it near her colleague.

'Fox!' Holden bellowed her sergeant's name as if she was auditioning for the position of Oxford City's town crier. 'Where in hell's name are you, Fox?'

*

Holden rang Detective Superintendent Collins from the car, as Fox drove her to Barns Road. She probably wouldn't have bothered if Fox hadn't suggested it.

For all his own lack of ambition, Fox knew the importance of keeping superior officers on side. And he knew too that it wasn't something that came naturally to Holden. What came naturally to her – so naturally that Fox imagined her having ingested it with the milk from her mother's breast – was a heady mix of assertiveness and aggression. She seemed to believe that she could get anywhere by insisting on it, and if that didn't work, demanding it. And if that didn't work, demanding it again and again increasingly noisily, until the other party conceded defeat.

'Did you see the super?' Fox had asked as he started the car. He knew she hadn't.

'No,' was the blunt reply.

'It might be a good idea to keep him in the loop,' Fox had said, as he turned into the peculiarly named Between Towns Road.

Holden had emitted a guttural noise that might have meant 'yes' or 'no' or indeed anything.

'You know what he's like,' Fox had pressed.

This time, Holden had made no audible response beyond a slight sniff.

But Fox, having started, had no intention of stopping. 'Why don't you ring him before he rings you?'

'Christ, Sergeant,' she had exploded. 'You're not my mother. I've got one of those, and one is quite enough.'

Fox had said nothing. How had Lawson once put it? That half the time it was as if Holden didn't want to be mistaken for a member of the human race. Lawson could be an irritating so and so, but she had got that right.

'All right then, I'll ring him,' Holden had snapped, suddenly conceding. 'I'll ring the detective superintendent, and then, Sergeant, perhaps you'll revert to the role of detective.'

Fox said nothing.

After all this preamble, it was inevitable that Murphy's Law kicked in. Holden's phone call was answered by Amanda Blenkinsop, the DS's guard dog of a secretary.

'I want to speak to Detective Superintendent Collins.'

'He's not available at the moment,' came the reply. Ms Blenkinsop was notorious for her ability to not give out information.

'When will he be available?' Holden asked testily.

'Would you like me to pass a message on to him?'

Holden was conscious of Fox's presence next to her. They had stopped at a pedestrian crossing, and she had glanced across to find him watching her, though whether to give her moral support, or whether to check she didn't misbehave, she wasn't quite sure. Whatever the reason, it had an effect.

'Thank you, Amanda,' she said with a huge effort. 'The message is this.' And she proceeded to tell her, in short sentences, about the death on the railway, the identification of the body – or rather its remains – and the disappearance of David Wright.

'And this David Wright, the adopted son,' Blenkinsop said, 'who has disappeared.' She liked to demonstrate her ability to summarize. 'Am I to tell the detective superintendent that you believe his disappearance to be connected with the death of Mr Jim Wright?'

'No, you may not,' Holden replied firmly. 'You may tell him the facts only. If he needs to know more, or if he wishes to know my current thinking, then he can ring me. Can't he?'

'I understand.' Blenkinsop spoke smoothly and calmly. Getting flustered, getting irritated, indeed getting any sort of emotional high while on duty, was quite out of the question. 'Rest assured, Inspector, I will pass your message on.'

Holden terminated the call with a snort. Rest assured! Who did the woman think she was?

'Happy now, Sergeant?' she snarled.

Fox again said nothing. All his energy and attention was being poured into parking the car tidily and turning off the engine. They were halfway down Barns Road, outside a featureless three-storey block of flats. Holden had despatched Wilson and Lawson to pick up Maureen Wright from her house, so now they had at least five minutes to check David's flat out before they arrived, just in case there was anything there that Maureen would be best not seeing. Like David's dead body.

Maureen had given them the entry code for the main entrance, and her spare key for the flat, so they gained access without a problem. The studio flat – essentially one large room with kitchen facilities at one end, a bed, desk with computer, one armchair, two upright chairs, and a built-in wardrobe, plus a door which opened onto a tiny en suite shower room – was tidy. Whatever and whenever he had had his last meal there, he had washed up and put everything away afterwards. The flat was also, thankfully, free of human corpses.

Holden opened the wardrobe. Clothes were hung and folded with a neatness and sense of order that matched the rest of the flat. Underneath the rack of shirts, T-shirts, and trousers lay a small suitcase with wheels and a handle, small enough to be treated as hand luggage if you're flying off on holiday or business. Next to it was an empty space.

'If that's a missing case,' Fox said, 'then it looks like he's done a runner.'

Holden nodded. It seemed a fair enough inference, but she didn't want to jump to conclusions. 'We'll see what Maureen can tell us.'

When Maureen arrived, she soon demonstrated that she wasn't going to jump to conclusions either. She looked at the gap by the case, and then she opened the other end of the wardrobe and looked there. She studied the footwear. 'Oh!' she said. Then she stood up and moved over to the cooking area, opening a cupboard above the sink. It contained various food items – a tin of tomatoes, two jars of pasta sauce, a bag of white rice, a box of cornflakes, a carton of apple juice, gravy granules and tomato sauce.

'There's no baked beans,' she said.

'No baked beans?' Holden felt she needed some guidance.

'No baked beans, and no camping gear.'

'You mean he's gone camping?'

'It looks like it. He loves camping.'

'Well that must be a relief for you. That he's only gone camping.'

Maureen looked at Holden, but there was no sign of relief in her face. 'You don't understand. He always tells me if he's going off anywhere. Always. And it's us he goes camping with. Twice he's been camping with my friend Jaz. But never on his own. And anyway, why would he go camping at this time of year? Don't you understand? Something is wrong. Something is very, very wrong.'

It took them several minutes to calm Maureen Wright down. The two female detectives sat on the bed either side of her, trying to reassure her. It was the younger woman, Lawson, who put her arm round her, consoling her, while Holden sat slightly further away, maintaining a distance physically and emotionally. Meanwhile Fox and Wilson tried to conduct a search as quickly and discreetly as the circumstances allowed.

Wilson found something almost immediately. Fox had started to make a more thorough search of the wardrobe, whereas he had gone straight to the chest of drawers by the bed, and there in the second drawer, under a collection of rolled-up pairs of socks, he located a diary. He sat down on the side of the bed, his back facing the backs of the three women, and opened it. David Wright had filled in his personal details on the page for them near the front: name, address and mobile number. There was no email address, Wilson noted, and the name of his employer was Frame It, which Wilson knew to be just off the Cowley Road – Princes Street, he thought.

He leafed forward, into January. It wasn't exactly, Wilson reckoned, stream of consciousness stuff. He wasn't sure quite what stream of consciousness was, but he remembered the expression from school – as far as he could recall, it was when someone writes long and rather tedious, badly punctuated, self-centred sentences that ramble all over the place without ever getting anywhere much. Anyway, whatever it was, David Wright didn't do it. What he did write was arguably duller, but from Wilson's point of view it was no less useful for that. For example, the week beginning 5 January 2009: on the Monday there was the single word, 'Work'; on Tuesday, 'Work'; on Wednesday, 'Work'; and underneath that 'Dinner at Mum's' (not 'Mum's and Dad's' Wilson noticed); on Thursday, 'Work' again, and on Friday, '10.00 a.m. Dentist – no work'; on the Saturday, 'No Oxford game'; and on the Sunday 'Roast lunch at Mum's'. It was a similar pattern the following weeks – work, meals on Wednesdays and Sundays at his mum's, and on Saturdays and other days Oxford United games to which he'd normally 'listen on radio' or 'go to'. Occasionally he would record another activity.

Wilson took a wedge of pages in his right hand, and began to flick quickly through them, allowing himself the opportunity to check for any obvious change of pattern. He knew that the most interesting and probably most useful material would be at the back of the diary, in the month of December, but he was methodical and thorough by nature. There was nothing, however, that caught his eye. 'Camping with Mum and Dad and Vickie in the New Forest' was the longest entry, repeated eight times, for a whole week at the end of May. He paused briefly over that – Vickie's half term, he told himself – and then moved steadily on through the summer and autumn until he got to the beginning of December.

The first week of that month (and including the Monday 30

November) had five days of 'Work', two Oxford games, a 'Dinner at Mum's' and a 'Roast lunch at Mum's'. Wilson had kept a diary once, though not for that long. Every night for several weeks he had sat in bed and laboriously recorded the events of that day, and sometimes his own reactions to those events, until the entries had got so short he gave up. Other people, like his mum, had kept a diary to organize her and her son's life. Those, he reckoned, were the two types of diary, one looking back, one forward. David's however, was a mixture of the two. He used his diary as a planner – work, visits to his mum's, the dentist, and Oxford United – and yet he also used it to record what had happened. Against each Oxford game, for example, he recorded the results and the Oxford players who had scored.

Wilson turned to the following week. The general pattern was the same – work, meals at his mum's, and two more Oxford United games – but there was more than that. 'Fish and chips – Vickie' on Tuesday; that was clear enough. But it was the entry for Saturday that caught and held his attention: underneath the expected reference to Oxford's games against Hayes and Yeading (a rather dull 1–0 win – Wilson hadn't gone, but he had read the reports), were two words: 'Mother's flat!' Wilson stopped reading. Now that was odd. David's mother didn't have a flat, did she? He looked again, and noticed the exclamation mark. That was odd too. He flicked back through the last few pages to check he hadn't missed something. No. The fact was that David Wright didn't really use punctuation at all except for dashes. No full stops, no commas, no semi-colons or colons, and certainly no exclamation marks. So why this? And then he spotted it. The most obvious thing. 'Mother's flat!' Not 'Mum's flat!' but 'Mother's flat!'

'How's it going, Constable?'

He stood and turned round. Holden was clearly talking to him, because Lawson was guiding Maureen Wright out of the flat. He paused, waiting for them to leave. It wasn't something to raise in front of Maureen, without first sharing it with his DI.

'It's David's diary, Guv,' he said quietly, as if afraid his words might pursue Maureen down the stairs. 'And there's something very odd about it.'

Lawson drove Maureen Wright back to Lytton Road in silence. It was a short trip and the woman was in a fragile enough state, and Lawson didn't want to risk any more emotional storms until they were both sitting down with a soothing cup of tea. The others would be following in due course, but she reckoned that would take a while.

Maureen insisted on making the tea herself, and even dug out some chocolate digestives. Then they sat at the kitchen table, sipping and chewing, until Maureen suddenly looked up and broke the silence.

'I really don't know what to think.'

Lawson couldn't come up with an immediate response. If she'd had a husband who had been hit by a train and a son who'd gone missing, she doubted she'd have known what to think either.

'Maybe you should just try and think about where David might have gone camping. Does he have a favourite place, for example?'

'He came wherever we went. The New Forest, Devon, Cornwall and the Forest of Dean. I don't know that any of them were his favourite. He liked them all.'

'And he never goes camping on his own? Not even for the weekend?'

'No.'

Lawson frowned. She needed to come at it from a different angle. 'Does David have a car?'

'A car? How could he afford a car? He's not even attempted his driving test either.'

'So how does he get around?'

'How does anyone get around? He walks when he comes to see us, and he catches the bus to work. Occasionally he'll get a taxi.'

'Has he ever been camping in Oxfordshire?'

Maureen opened her mouth, but didn't immediately say anything. But a thought had occurred, and Lawson could almost see it circling her brain. 'When he was a scout,' she said eventually, this time in a much less irritable tone. 'He was in the scouts for two or three years, but he found relating to all the other boys tricky. In the end the scout master told us that David just didn't fit in, and that it was bad for general discipline …' She never quite finished the sentence. Her eyes, Lawson couldn't help noticing, had gone all damp again. Oh shit, she said to herself, with sudden insight; that poet who said that parents fuck up their children, didn't he realize that children fuck up parents too?

'They used to camp up at Boars Hill. He loved it there. He used to say it was like being lost in a forest miles from anywhere, but he always knew he was only a few miles from home.'

They never got any further in the conversation. The doorbell rang. Lawson went to answer it, and found Holden, Fox, and Wilson outside.

'We're just having a cup of tea,' she said.

'I need to ask Mrs Wright some more questions,' Holden said softly.

In reality, nearly ten minutes elapsed before Holden started asking her questions. That was because she needed to go to the loo. She had wanted to at David's flat, but what with it being small and with Fox and Wilson hanging around, it had all felt a bit too public. Maureen offered her a choice – the one by the front door or the main bathroom up the stairs. Holden opted for upstairs.

When she came down, the four others were sitting in the

living room. More tea had been made, and a full cup sat in front of the one free chair. Holden sat down and took a sip.

Fox passed David's diary to her. She picked it up and looked at it, and then at Maureen. 'This is David's diary.' It was a statement, but she said it as if it was a question.

Maureen nodded. 'I know.'

'You've seen it before.'

'Seen it, yes. But I've not looked inside. Diaries are private,' she added reproachfully. 'David didn't let people read what was inside.'

Holden frowned, the implications of Maureen's tone apparently lost on her. She opened the diary at random near the beginning, and showed it to Maureen. It was a week from the beginning of March. 'There's nothing very private here. Look! Merely what he was planning to do. Go to work, watch the football, come to you to for a meal. Look here, for example, on the Sunday. "Roast lunch at Mum's".'

'So why are you showing me it?' There was more than a tinge of aggression now.

Holden pulled the diary back to herself, turned to somewhere near the back, and pushed it in front of Maureen again. 'Last week was a bit different though. Busier for a start.' She paused, letting Maureen take a look. 'But it's the entry for Saturday that intrigues me. Not the football game, but the rest of it. Here.' And she pressed her finger down on the page. '"Mother's flat"!' she read, as if Maureen was an illiterate 5-year-old. 'What do you make of that?'

Maureen studied the page for several seconds. 'I don't know,' she said firmly. 'I really don't know.'

'He didn't come and see you on Saturday night, did he?'

'No.' She spoke the word reluctantly, wishing it wasn't the truth.

'And you don't have a flat, do you?'

'No,' she repeated, even more reluctantly.

'So, Maureen, who is Mother?'

'I'm his mother!' She bristled, a hen protecting its chicks. 'You know I'm his mother.'

Holden stabbed the diary with her forefinger, and when she spoke, tact and diplomacy had been tossed out the window. 'So what is this all about?'

'I don't know. You'll have to ask him.'

'David's adopted, isn't he? I remember that's what your husband said. Vickie is your own child, but David was adopted.'

'Jesus!' Maureen stared at the woman who was tormenting her. 'What the hell difference does that make?' she hissed. 'They're both my children. Equally! And they always will be. You wouldn't understand that, though. You don't look the type to have children. You wouldn't know what it was like to care for them for all those years, through the good times and the bad, the sleepless nights, being hauled into school because someone's complained. Or to see your son heartbroken because some creep with a Hitler complex has thrown him out of his beloved Boy Scouts.' She dribbled to a halt.

'I think this refers to David's birth mother,' Holden said quietly, as if the torrent of abuse had been directed at someone else altogether. 'He calls you "Mum" in the diary, always. This here is "Mother", and she appears to live in a flat. Do you know who she is?'

Maureen said nothing for some time. She was having to think quickly – whether it was best to tell the truth, or to lie, or maybe a bit of both. 'Sorry,' she said eventually, and sat down again. 'That was over the top.' And now, for the first time, she looked Holden in the eye. 'I did know something had happened. I knew something had changed for David. I could tell by his behaviour. But on my life, I didn't know he had met up with his birth mother. But if he has, then that would explain an awful lot.'

Holden nodded, more thoroughly than she intended, for she too was having to think quickly. 'It wasn't just a diary we found at David's flat,' she said. 'My sergeant found something else too. A number of drawings. Portraits of people.'

'Those would be David's,' Maureen replied quickly. 'He's good at drawing.' The pride she took in her son, adopted though he was, was obvious.

Holden gestured to Fox, who passed over a sheet of A5 paper. 'Do you recognize this person?'

Maureen looked at it for several seconds before she spoke. 'It looks like the auxiliary from Sunnymede. Bella. She was very good to David's gran.'

'We thought it looked liked Bella too.'

'What's your point? He must have done it one day when he was visiting her at Sunnymede.'

'I don't think so. She's not in uniform. And it looks to me like she's sitting in a bus.'

'I can't say I'd noticed. Anyway what does it matter?'

'Look at the date,' Holden pressed. 'He's written it on the bottom: 4 December 2009. So you see, Maureen, what we were thinking, putting two and two together, was maybe Bella is David's mother? What do you think?'

'I don't know,' came the instant reply. Too instant, Holden thought. She is too nonchalant. She is not surprised. She is lying.

'Maybe you're right,' Maureen conceded. 'How should I know? We never met his so-called parents when we adopted him. There was no contact. Not then, not ever.'

'I see,' Holden said in a tone that implied she really didn't see.

'Anyway,' Maureen snapped, 'what does it matter? Right now, what matters is that David is missing, and you're doing nothing. I was telling your constable that David used to camp up in Boars Hill, when he was part of the Boy Scouts, so maybe he's gone there.'

Holden nodded, as if giving due consideration to the woman's theory. 'Or ...' She paused, determined to get Maureen Wright's attention. 'Or maybe he hasn't run off at all. Maybe he's gone to his birth mother.'

'Why the hell should he have?'

'Perhaps he likes her.' As replies went, this was about as low as Holden could possibly have gone, except perhaps by adding the words that she had left unspoken, but hanging in the air: 'more than you'.

Maureen Wright looked at Holden as if she couldn't believe what she'd heard. 'You bitch,' she said quietly. 'You fucking bitch.'

Holden should have apologized. Immediately. She knew that. But knowing was one thing and doing was another. And besides, how do you behave towards a woman who may have lost a beloved husband, or alternatively may have anchored him to a railway line and watched as the London train ran him down.

'She's not herself, today, Inspector.' The voice came from the doorway, where a girl had appeared.

'Vickie,' her mother said, plaintively, 'there's no need—'

'There's every need, Mum,' she cut in, and moved forward to give her a prolonged hug. Then she stared down at Holden. 'My mother has been through a lot this morning, Inspector. In case you haven't noticed, her husband's been murdered, and her son has run away, so maybe you should try being nice to her.'

Holden bowed her head. It might have been an apology, but she said nothing to support that theory. Fox, watching from the sidelines, reckoned it was at least half way to one. He had seen his boss in many situations, but rarely had he seen her apologize. And yet this time he sensed that she was at least embarrassed by Vickie's challenge. Fox tried to suppress a smile. DI Holden taken to task by a 12-year-old. Now that was something.

'I didn't recognize you, Vickie.'

'Why should you? We've never met.'

'You're not like the photos.'

'Photos?'

'The school photos. You and David. In the upstairs loo.'

'Best place for them.'

'It's funny though.'

'Funny?' Vickie, who had perched on the arm of her mother's chair, stared at Holden, suspicion in her eyes. Not that it was easy for Holden to see them, for her long black hair fell lank down either side of her pale face, like half-pulled curtains.

'Most girls – most women in fact – would give their eye teeth for your blonde hair....'

'What's that to you, Inspector?' Maureen Wright, sitting next to her daughter on the sofa, had no intention of putting up with any crap. 'It's a free world, and if she wants black hair, that's her choice. End of.'

It wasn't just black hair, though. It was the clothes too – black long-sleeved blouse, black skirt, dark patterned tights, and black Doc Martens boots – not to mention the black eyebrows and black lipstick. The whole Goth transformation.

'I dyed my hair black once,' Holden said, dropping her voice as if this was something secret that only they were sharing. 'I was older than you, maybe sixteen or seventeen. My father went spare.'

Vickie lifted her head a bit more and gave it a shake. She looked again at Holden, her face tilted at a slight angle. 'Really?'

'Look, what's this got to do with anything?' It was Maureen cutting in again, a mother trying to protect, and maybe control too.

'Just small talk,' Holden replied, though her eyes were still on Vickie.

Maureen gave a snort. 'You coppers don't do small talk!'

Vickie looked at her mother, defiance in her eyes. 'Actually,' she said with exaggerated pause, 'Mum did go spare.'

'Did she?' Holden, like Vickie, turned to look at Maureen.

'Yeah, she had a right go at me.'

'Did you, Maureen?'

'Yes I blooming well did,' she snapped back. 'Not because of her going Goth in itself. Hell, we all do stupid things when we're young. It was all to do with the timing. It was about respect, of rather her lack of it, for her grandmother. Nanette was very good to her, very good to us all, and I thought she could have had the decency to wait until after the funeral before she entered her Goth stage. She can be a Goth for all I care, but yesterday, while I was out in Reading buying myself a suitable outfit, she was spending money on black spiky hair and make-up. And she skipped school to do it! Jesus bloody wept!'

'Only the afternoon,' Vickie responded sharply. 'One lesson was sport and Mr Ford was sick. It would only have been a crappy supply teacher.'

Holden turned to Fox, trying to get her head round all this new information. 'Sergeant, when you called in here yesterday, Vickie was blonde, wasn't she?'

'That's right, Guv.'

'Yeah, that's right!' Vickie drawled, her confidence growing with every word she spoke. 'I was nearly late for my appointment, because of him and that female with him. She insisted on going to the loo, and was ages in there, and I ended up having to run to the hairdresser.'

'And this was when?'

'Half past two.'

'And you got home when?'

'Just before five.'

'Oi!' Maureen had had enough. 'Why all these questions? What has my daughter's skipping school and getting her hair messed up got to do with anything?'

Holden ignored the question. 'So Vickie, did you skip school in the morning too?'

'No.'

'But you came home at lunchtime.'

'Yeah.'

'And did you see your father?'

'No. He wasn't in.'

'And you were out of the house between half past two and five o'clock.'

'Yeah.'

'And when did your mum get back from Reading?'

'Maybe ten or fifteen minutes after I got back from the hairdresser.'

'And did you go out again?'

'No, she did not!' Maureen was standing up and her eyes were flaring. 'I grounded her. I got a text from the school. That's what they do now. They send you a text telling you if your child has skived off. So I was hopping mad by the time I got home. I grounded her, and I stayed in all evening to make sure she stayed grounded.'

'I see.' Holden tried to assess this new information – or was it disinformation? It would be easy enough to check out their story – the hair appointment, the text message from the school – and it certainly put Vickie in the clear, but Jim died at 7.27 p.m. and if Maureen was behind that, then Vickie was lying for her. But if Vickie was telling the truth, then the obvious suspect had to be David. 'Tell me, Vickie. Do you know where David is?' She spoke casually, as if the answer was barely consequential.

The girl began to study her fingernails, which were painted alternately deep crimson and black. She said nothing. Gave no indication.

'We're worried about him. If you know anything, you must tell us.'

Vickie's hand moved involuntarily to her neck, remembering the aftermath of the fish and chip supper. 'He can look after himself.'

'I'm sure he can. It's just that we're worried in case he does something silly.'

Vickie's earlier confidence had faded, and been supplanted by mere stubbornness. 'I can't help you.'

'You know where he is, don't you, Vickie.'

'No.'

Holden had been leaning forward confidentially, but now she leant back and took stock. Was it time for a change of tack? David wasn't going to go far. No doubt he was camping somewhere in the Boars Hill woods. Sooner or later a search team would find him. And then, if he was the killer, there was a good chance they'd be able to get him to confess. But what if he wasn't? Holden leant forward again. She had another weapon in reserve, and now was the time to deploy it.

She opened the folder in front of her, pulled out a piece of paper, and pushed it across the table towards Vickie. 'Talking of photos, Vickie, as we were a bit earlier, what can you tell me about these ones?'

'These ones' were three of the photos of Ania and Vickie, dressed as schoolgirls and smiling unconvincingly at the camera.

Vickie said nothing. It was her mother who stretched forward, picked them up, and studied them one at a time for several seconds. 'Where did you get these from?'

'They were on Paul Greenleaf's laptop.'

It was just a bit of fun,' Vickie jumped in. 'After the fooball game. We went to Mr Greenleaf's house, and had supper, and Ania and I dressed up for a bit of fun, like we were sisters, and they took photos.'

'They?'

'Mr Greenleaf really. But Dad was there, so I knew it was all right.'

'Did anything else happen, Vickie?'

'No. Course not. I got a headache, so Dad brought me home.'

'And I guess that was quite late, was it?'

'Half past ten.' Maureen cut in firmly. 'Or thereabouts. I was still up. Jim turned on the TV to catch *Match of the Day* but it had already started. I gave Vickie two paracetamol and saw her into bed.'

Holden picked up her mug and slowly drained the tea in it. Mother and daughter were united now: Maureen was sitting bolt upright in the armchair, while Vickie perched on its arm, her right arm across her mother's shoulder. The question was how to separate them.

'Weren't you worried, Maureen?'

'Why should I have been? It was a Saturday night. She was with her dad. What was there to worry about?'

'Sorry, that isn't what I meant.' Holden tried to look apologetic, as she set her trap. 'I meant, weren't you worried when you saw the photos?'

'What are you talking about? I've never seen them until now.'

'No, of course not,' Holden said quickly. The trap had snapped shut on thin air. 'You wouldn't have. But I assumed that Vickie would have told you about them. Or maybe your husband would have.'

'Why would they have told me? It looks like just a bit of fun. Harmless fun. What's the big deal?'

'The big deal, Maureen, as far as I can see, is that they are motive for murder. Paul Greenleaf and your husband took the photos, and now they're both dead.'

'That's ridiculous. They're just stupid photos. They were probably drunk when then took them.'

'Stupid photos?' Holden spat the words back. 'Is that what you really think, Maureen?'

Maureen flinched. Whatever thoughts she had about the photos, she wasn't going to share them with Holden. 'I don't give a shit about them!' She waved the photos wildly in front of Holden's face. 'Right now, all I care about is David. You should be out there looking for him, not showing us stupid photos.' And she started to rip them up into pieces.

It was Fox who intervened. He could read the signs, and they were flashing red for danger. 'Mrs Wright,' he said, because at that moment anything else seemed too casual, 'let me reassure you. We'll soon have a search party out on Boars Hill. I'm sure if David is there, they'll soon find him.'

She looked at him, glad of his assurance even if she wasn't convinced. 'I can't wait here,' she said simply. 'I'd like to join the search. David may be frightened. I should be there. I'm his mother.'

'I understand,' he said. It wasn't his call to say 'Yes' or 'No', but he felt he had to say that much.

They both turned towards Holden. 'DC Lawson will drive you up there,' she said quickly. There was no need to deny the woman's request. In fact, it was a damned good way of keeping tabs on her. 'You can both join the search.'

'What about me?' It was Vickie. She had retreated to the door, watching, listening, and silent. Behind the black curtains of her hair, there were dark smudges down her cheeks.

'I want you to stay here,' Maureen said firmly. 'In case David phones. Or comes home.'

'Is he here?' Holden had pushed past Bella Sinclair as soon as she had opened the door of her flat.

'Who are you talking about?'

'Your son, Bella. We know all about you and your precious son, so why don't you just tell us where he is?'

Bella didn't say anything, not for several seconds. She looked from Holden to Fox to Wilson as if sizing up her options.

'David is your son, isn't he?' It was the big male detective speaking now, more quietly than his boss, seeking confirmation.

She nodded.

'So do you know where he is?'

'Isn't he at work?'

The man leant forward. 'Has he been here today?'

She shook her head.

But Holden had had enough of Fox's softly-softly tactics. She wanted answers, and being nice wasn't going to get them, at least not as quickly as she wanted them. 'Ms Sinclair,' she snapped, stabbing her forefinger at the woman's face. 'Your son is wanted for murder. For three murders, in fact. His grandmother, your boss and his adoptive father. Now, when did you last see him?'

Bella's mouth opened, shut and then opened again, but no sound came out. Her face, however, had turned a sickly white.

When she did speak, she did so with anguish in her voice. 'Why would he have killed them? Why would he have killed Greenleaf? He didn't even know him.'

'What on earth makes you think that?' Holden had her line of argument prepared. 'He used to visit his grandmother in Sunnymede, didn't he? So he could easily have met Greenleaf there, couldn't he?'

'Believe me, Greenleaf wouldn't have wasted his precious time talking to someone like David.'

Holden smiled bleakly, and delivered her coup de grâce. 'But Greenleaf spent his precious time chasing you, didn't he Bella. And then he suspended you. So you had a motive to kill him. Maybe you told David, and out of misguided love for you, David killed him?'

'That's ridiculous!' She sounded angry, but her face had paled. 'Absolutely ridiculous.'

'What's ridiculous?' Holden hadn't finished yet. 'Are you saying it's ridiculous that David should love you, then? Or that he should do something to demonstrate his love?'

Fox flinched. Sometimes, he found Holden quite terrifying. First it had been Maureen, and now Bella. Find the weakest point – and in both their cases it was a mother's love – and then stick the knife in and twist.

But if Holden's intention was to get Bella to react, to say something that she instantly regretted, something incriminating, she was to be disappointed. The woman sank down onto her sofa and began to drag her fingers through her red hair, tugging viciously when they met resistance. When she looked up, her eyes were moist, Fox noticed, and her face a picture of misery. 'He hardly knows me,' she said plaintively. 'We've had such little time.'

Fox almost nodded in sympathy. To him, the woman's grief seemed genuine. But Holden's features were as unrelenting as granite. And she hadn't finished yet. 'Where is he, Bella?' she demanded. 'We need to find him. Before he does any harm to anyone else. Or even to himself.'

'Himself?! What are you suggesting?'

'Where is he, Bella?' Holden persisted. 'You'd better tell me before it's too late.'

But Bella was saying nothing. Instead she just sat there, looking over Holden's shoulder, and out through the window beyond. It was as if she had entered another reality.

'If you don't co-operate,' Holden said, raising her voice, 'then I'm going to have to ask you to accompany Detective Constable Wilson down to the station until we've more time to interview you.'

Bella focused her eyes back on Holden. 'Now that really would be stupid,' she said. Her eyes didn't blink, and she continued speaking as if explaining a rather dull concept to a rather dull set of children. 'You don't look stupid to me, Inspector. Behind that miserable face of yours, I bet you're really rather smart. But what good is taking me to the station going to do? It will occupy your constable here, and leave my flat empty. And when David comes to find me, I won't be here.'

'And what makes you think he'll come and find you?'

'Where else can he possibly go? The world is against him. I'm his mother. His real mother. He'll come home to me sooner or later.'

Holden looked at Bella, and wondered if the woman looking back at her was completely deluded. Would David really come to Bella rather than Maureen? Surely not. Maureen had been his mother for some twenty years. How could this woman replace her? And yet. The words of doubt were there in her brain. What would it be like to be David – to have your mother return from the dead after twenty years? What might it have done to him?

'Very well.' Holden had made her decision. 'You can stay here, in case David comes or tries to contact you. But Detective Constable Wilson will remain with you.'

She turned to him. 'You stay here whatever the circumstances, Wilson. Any news and you report to me immediately. And you don't let her out of your sight. Understood?'

Wilson tried not to show his dismay. 'Yes, Guv.'

Holden and Fox had barely stepped out of the lift when her mobile rang. The caller's name did not register.

'Who are you?' she demanded. She dared it to be someone selling something. Dared it and willed it. She was in the perfect mood to rip a call-centre operator limb from limb.

'Nurse Straker,' the answer came. 'I'm calling from the hospital.'

'The hospital?'

By the time the conversation with Nurse Straker had finished, Holden's face – and probably every other part of her body – had gone puce.

'Is your mother OK?' Fox asked.

Given that a string of expletives had started to erupt from his guv's mouth, it was, Fox knew, not the most sensible question. But he reckoned he had to say something before he had half the inhabitants of Blackbird Leys turning up for the sideshow.

'My mother has only gone and fallen over in the hospital! Why didn't she tell me she was going? Or Doris at least. But oh no, not my mother. She takes a taxi up to the JR for a check up, and then faints right in front of the consultant. So Nurse Straker rings up and insists someone picks her up. And by someone she means her daughter.'

'So let's go.'

'I'm in the middle of a murder case, Sergeant.'

'She's your mother, Guv.'

'I could strangle her.'

But Fox had already got his door open. 'I reckon I can do it in six minutes with the light on.' And with that, he slipped into the driver's seat, and started the engine.

'Would you like a cup of tea, Constable?'

'Please. Milk one sugar.' Wilson picked up the copy of the *Oxford Mail* lying on the sofa, sat down and turned to the back page. At least he could catch up on the local sport. 'United missing out' the headline screamed. It seemed appropriate.

In the kitchen, Bella switched the kettle on, prepared two mugs with teabags and sugar, and waited for the kettle to create some noise. Then she switched her mobile onto silent, and composed her text.

'You must ring me. The police are looking for you. I can help. Mother.' She looked at it, frowned, added 'xx' at the end, and sent it.

CHAPTER 12

For the third time in less than three hours, Fox felt acutely embarrassed by DI Holden. Previously it had been because of the terrible things she had been saying – first to David's adoptive mother and then to his real mother. But now it was because she wasn't saying anything at all. Here they were, taking her own mother back to her flat, and Holden had sent her to Coventry. The two of them had exchanged words at the hospital along the lines of the 'Why didn't you tell me?' and 'You're always too busy to help' variety, but now his DI was refusing to communicate with her mother at all. It was, he couldn't help thinking, ridiculously childish.

'This is why I never told you,' her mother was saying. It was a variation on a theme she had been playing ever since her daughter and the nice sergeant had turned up at the hospital. 'I didn't want to distract you from your big case.'

There was no reply. Holden was sitting in the back of the car. She was hiding. She knew if she said something, anything, it would be unforgivably rude.

'We're very glad to be able to give you a lift, Mrs Holden.' Fox realized it was up to him to intervene.'

'You're only saying that.'

'No I'm not,' he said calmly, easing to a stop at the traffic lights. 'I mean it. And despite what you might sometimes think, your daughter is very fond of you. It is just that the case is at a very difficult stage.'

'Is it now?' Mrs Holden paused. But almost immediately pressed on. 'What has happened today, then? Or is that something that you can't tell me? My daughter is always refusing to tell me things, but I can keep a secret.' Neither of these statements was entirely true, but right now she was more interested in provoking her daughter than being entirely straight with the sergeant.

'Jim Wright has been killed,' Fox said. He could see no reason not to say it. If it wasn't all over the local news now, it almost certainly would be at six o'clock.

'Really? Murdered, you mean?'

'And David has run away.'

'David? You mean he killed his father and has gone on the run?'

'We don't know. That's one possibility,' he admitted cautiously. 'But the key thing is to find him.'

'I feel sorry for the boy,' the old woman said.

'He's a grown man, nearly twenty,' DI Holden interjected suddenly from the back of the car.

'But inside, I bet he's a small insecure boy.'

'What do you mean?'

Mrs Holden, who had finally provoked her daughter into life, had no intention of not telling her. 'He's had a terrible shock. After all these years, his birth mother turns up, and tries to reclaim him. Suddenly he's got two mothers and doesn't know who to trust, who to love. He's got Asperger's, hasn't he, and maybe sibling rivalry with his so-called sister, Vickie. And remember his grandmother has just died, and she must have doted on him.'

'Why must she have?' Holden's tone was acerbic.

'I can't imagine any woman who's lucky enough to have grandchildren, not doting on them. It wouldn't be natural.'

There was no quarter being asked, and certainly none given. The production of a grandchild had been a taboo subject ever since her daughter's traumatic affair with Karen Pointer, but now, it seemed, the knives were well and truly out. And there was bright red blood dripping from both blades.

'Here we are!' Fox said loudly, like a boxing referee trying to part two boxers at the end of a particularly gruelling contest. 'Home sweet home!'

But his words were falling on deaf ears. 'You're living in cloud cuckoo land, Mother. For all we know, it was David who killed his grandmother. For all we know, he was so fed up with her nagging him that he laced her whisky with enough morphine to kill a mule.' Holden had no compunction about exaggerating when it suited her argument.

'But why would he have done that? After all Nanette had done for him. I mean, have you thought how on earth this Bella found out that David was her son? Would she really have recognized him after all these years? Of course not! I bet it was Nanette. Somehow she must have realized that David, her adopted little grandson, was none other than Bella's abandoned baby. And so she brought them together.'

Fox had got out of the car, and had opened Mrs Holden's door. 'Thank you, Sergeant,' she beamed. 'So kind of you.' She eased herself out with as much alacrity as her legs and hips allowed, expecting a riposte from her daughter. Getting in the last word was not, she knew from experience, very easy with her daughter. But the detective inspector said nothing. She too extricated herself from the seat belt and car. Then she tucked her left arm inside her mother's right, and motioned her forward.

'Come on then, Mother. Let's get you upstairs. I think Sergeant Fox has heard enough from the two of us.'

Vickie was studying her nails when the phone rang. She wished she hadn't painted the red ones red. It wasn't even a nice red. It was garish, disgusting. They should be black too. They should all be black.

The cordless phone was on the arm of the sofa. She watched it ring – two, three, four times – and only then did she lean over and pick it up.

'Hello?'

'It's me. David.' He was whispering.

'Where the hell are you, David?'

'I've run away.'

'That's stupid.'

'Don't call me stupid.'

'Sorry.' It was a trigger word with David. She knew that. 'Mum's out of her mind.' Involuntarily, she was whispering back. 'She's looking for you.'

'I'm not coming home. Ever.'

'You must, David. We'll look after you.'

'Never, ever, ever, ever.'

'David.'

'Dad is a bastard. He's a lying bastard. I'm never coming home.'

'David, Dad is dead.'

There was silence.

'Dad is dead,' she repeated. 'Somebody killed him.' She paused, willing him to say something, but he didn't. 'Was it you, David? Because Mum and I will protect you. We'll lie for you. They'll never know.'

There was silence, except for the sound of heavy breathing. She tried to think. She had to say something else. Keep him from hanging up. 'I'm glad he's dead, David. If you killed him, it's the best thing you ever did.'

She paused and waited for a response. But this time there was no breathing to be heard. David had terminated the call.

'You weren't very kind to your mother.' Fox spoke with care, a man treading gingerly through a minefield, conscious of the explosion that one wrong step might provoke.

They were standing in the parking area designated for the use of residents of the south-eastern corner of Grandpont Grange. They had seen Mrs Holden up to her flat, and left her in the rather fussy hands of her friend Doris. Fox was by the driver's door, but had made no attempt to get in. Holden glared at him. 'Wasn't I!' It wasn't a question. It was a red and white 'No Entry' sign, and spoken in a tone that told her sergeant to drop the subject.

But Fox wasn't quite ready to give up. 'You weren't.'

'Thank you, Sergeant. But if you don't mind, we've got a murder case to solve.'

'She's your mother, for God's sake.'

'Don't I know it!' Holden gave a sigh. She felt tired all of a sudden. She looked up towards her mother's flat. There was no sign of her at the window, but she was there, inside, an old lady longing for a grandchild, for something worth living for as death loomed larger and closer. And she, her only daughter, was failing her.

Fox shrugged and unlocked the car. 'So where do you want to go?'

'Let's go and see Vickie.'

'Why?' Fox was startled. 'We saw her earlier.'

'I want to ask her some questions while her mother isn't there. Why the hell do think, Sergeant?'

'But she's a minor, Guv! You can't just turn up and question her without an appropriate adult present.'

Holden was about to bite back, but beyond Fox's head she could see an elderly couple in matching tan mackintoshes making their way unsteadily across the quadrangle towards them. She opened the door, got in, and slammed it shut.

'Whose side are you on, Sergeant,' she demanded as soon as he had shut his door. 'Do you want to find out who the killer is, or not? Because let me assure you that it certainly matters to Detective Superintendent Collins, and for that reason it sure as hell matters to me. It is Vickie's father who has been murdered. It is Vickie's brother who is on the run. And in case your memory doesn't stretch back that far, let me remind you that it was Vickie that Paul Greenleaf was taking dodgy photos of shortly before he was murdered. So maybe, just maybe, Sergeant, Vickie hasn't told us everything she knows.'

Fox nodded, acknowledging her authority. 'Even so, Guv, she is a minor.'

'Which is why we are only going to have a chat. A nice, informal, off the record chat. And you're going to be there bearing witness to the fact. OK?'

Fox said nothing. The act of manipulating the car out of its parking place had suddenly become a thing that demanded all of his attention.

'Is that clear, Sergeant?' Detective Inspector Holden had raised her voice even more. She had no intention of being second best to a driving manoeuvre.

'Absolutely crystal, Guv.'

The call came when Wilson was in the loo, and before Bella had got round to taking Wilson his cup of tea. It was either luck or fate, but she didn't give a stuff which. She moved back into the kitchen, as she answered it. 'Hello, David. It's Mother. Where are you?'

'I'm scared.'

'Of course you are.' She spoke in lowered, reassuring tones.

'I don't know what to do.'

'I'll look after you. Tell me where you are. I'll get a car. Tell me where you are, and I'll rescue you.'

'They think I killed Dad. What will they do to me if they catch me?'

'I won't let them catch you, David. I promise. Just tell me where you are, and I'll come.'

She would have said more, but she could hear the sound of Wilson exiting the loo. 'Keep calm,' she whispered, 'and wait for me.'

'David, why won't you ring me?' It was the fourth time Maureen had rung him since leaving her house, and for the fourth time he didn't answer.

Again she left a message. Not a new message, just the same

message in slightly different words, but each, as Lawson was fully aware, increasing in intensity and desperation. She wasn't at all sure this was going to help, but for once the self-confidence that the young DC normally displayed had collapsed under the pressure of the situation, and she had said nothing to dissuade her.

'For God's sake, David, you must ring me. I will protect you, but you must tell us where you are.' Maureen paused. Lawson opened her mouth to say something reassuring, but Maureen hadn't finished. 'David, you must give yourself up. Otherwise, how can I help you?'

Roy Hillerby parked his car in Knights Road, locked it, and walked reluctantly towards the bus stop. The wind was blowing sharply from the east and he pulled his coat more closely around him, but it made no difference. He looked up high, at the flats, as if in expectation that she would be there leaning out of the window, waving him a thank you. But, of course, she wasn't. She wouldn't. She didn't need to. All she had to do was whistle, and like an obedient dog he'd come running, panting and grateful just to be noticed by her. What a bloody fool he was! And why on earth had he given her his spare set of keys, because now it was as if she had a divine right to the use of his car.

He stopped, sent her a text as he had promised he would, and then looked around. A number 5 bus was coming up Blackbird Leys Road. He waved his arm to get the driver's attention, and broke into a jog, because the last thing he wanted was to end up waiting at the bus stop in this godforsaken weather.

'Are you OK, Constable?'

Detective Constable Wilson, who had just emerged from a five-minute stint in the loo, flushed crimson. 'Sure! Absolutely.' He spoke quickly and awkwardly. 'Just a call of nature. A bit of an urgent one, I'm afraid.'

'Never mind.' She smiled. 'I'll take a turn now, if you don't mind, and after that I'll make you a nice cup of tea.'

'Thanks.' Wilson slumped down on the sofa. The copy of the *Oxford Mail* he had been reading was lying where he had left it, and his hand reached over to pick it up, but his eyes had other ideas. For they were fixed not on the newspaper, but on Bella Sinclair's legs and arse as she stepped her way across the living room. Only when she and her kitten heels had disappeared fully into the loo did he pick the *Mail* up, with an audible sigh, and turn to see what was on TV later that evening.

Bella didn't need the loo, at least not for the reason that people normally need a loo. Once inside, she bolted the door, and then unlocked the glass-fronted wall cabinet. It took her a minute or so to inspect the labels of several items until she had found what she was looking for: one reading 'temazepam'. She opened the box. There were four small capsules inside. They weren't hers, at least not originally. She'd 'borrowed' them, in case she needed a bit of night-time help, from Mrs Jeffrey's stash. It was, as she saw it, one of the perks of the job, to pick up drugs here and there. You never knew when they'd come in handy. It was lucky Mrs Jeffrey had had such trouble swallowing in her final days. Liquid capsules were so much easier to administer. Especially in a nice cup of hot tea.

'Hi, there!' Holden put on her most cheerful voice, but Vickie Wright was having none of it. After Fox had rung the bell, there had been a rattle of a chain, and the door had opened only a few centimetres. A pale-skinned, black-eyed face had peered out unenthusiastically.

'What do you want?' a voice demanded.

'Can we come in?'

'Have you found David?'

'Not yet.'

The door was pushed shut, there was another rattle of the

chain, and then it swung half open. But Vickie Wright kept her hand on the catch, and her body in the doorway, challenging them to enter without her say so.

'So why aren't you out looking for him?'

It wasn't an unreasonable question, and yet Holden was initially stumped to give a reasonable answer. Or any answer. Though given her limited experience of Vickie, and given that she was Maureen Wright's daughter, Holden shouldn't have been surprised by Vickie's demeanour.

'We have a team of people out there looking.'

'Yeah, right. You have a team.'

'We've ordered up a helicopter too.' Holden was conscious that she sounded like she was making excuses. Maybe she was! After all, why on earth was she here, knocking on Vickie's door when David – maybe the murderer, or at least the key to the murderer – was out there on the run? The 12-year-old with black hair, white face and pretty much black everything else was staring at her like she was a piece of particularly smelly dog shit. Holden felt embarrassed.

Fox intervened. 'Do you mind if we come in for a few minutes?'

'I suppose not.' Vickie shrugged and retreated inside, leaving them to follow. Keeping the police waiting while she decided whether to let them in had, apparently, stopped being fun.

Vickie sat down in one of the armchairs in the living room, but said nothing. Holden sat down opposite on the sofa, while Fox sat to her left in the other armchair. Holden wasn't quite sure what it was she was going to ask, except she couldn't help feeling that Vickie and Maureen hadn't, between the two of them, been telling her the truth, the whole truth and nothing but the truth.

It was Vickie who eventually broke the silence: 'My Mum'll kill me if I don't do my homework.'

'Good for her.'

Silence again. It was a game. Like staring at each other –

the first to blink loses. They could both feel it, and Fox wondered if Holden had forgotten that Vickie was a minor and also
(as far as he was aware) not a suspect. Vickie, however, was
interested only in winning. She was saying nothing more. Not
until the bitch opposite asked her a question.

'Has David been in touch?' the bitch said eventually.

'No,' Vickie lied.

'Why don't you ring him now?' the bitch pressed.

'Ring him? Why would he answer?'

'Why wouldn't he?' The bitch leant forward, unblinking.
'Humour me, Vickie. Ring him.'

Vickie reluctantly unfolded her hand from around her
mobile and made the call. She put it on loudspeaker. They all
heard it ring twice, and then the call was killed. David, it
seemed, did not want to speak to his adopted sister.

'Tell me what really happened at Charlton-on-Otmoor.'

'What do you mean?'

'I mean, after they took the photos of you and Ania dressed
as schoolgirls.'

'I told you, I got a headache, so my dad drove me home.'

'What caused the headache?'

Fox's mobile rang. Holden made a face that Medusa would
have been proud of. But she waited nevertheless.

'He's not at the scout camp,' Fox reported.

'I want you to go.' Vickie stood up as she said this, and her
voice was wobbly. She rubbed her right eye, smearing mascara
across her cheek as she did so. 'I want you to go and find him.'

Maureen had pinned her hopes on David being at the
Youlbury Scout Centre. If he had gone off camping somewhere
nearby, this had to be the obvious place, surely. The last time
Maureen had been there was eight years ago, but she remembered it like it was yesterday. How could she not? The only
problem was she kept expecting that bloody scoutmaster,
Peabody, to suddenly materialize from behind the next tree or

bush, with his moustache, beaky nose, and sweaty forehead. She looked around and tried to concentrate. There were ten of them out looking for David – two constables, six community support officers, Lawson and herself. But they had found no sign of him. Mind you, there were loads of signs of people having camped, but that meant nothing. People were always camping there, every weekend, and during the weeks often enough. So one lone person was hardly going to leave an unmistakeable trail. To know that David had been there, they would need to find something that belonged to him, or maybe one of his empty baked bean cans. She had told the police about his baked beans, and how they were bound to be Heinz, but they had found nothing, and were now gathered in a group while Lawson and the two uniformed constables discussed what to do next.

It was as she watched them, with a sense of growing despair, that she had her moment of enlightenment. She shouted across the clearing. 'You're wasting time here!' Nine pairs of eyes swivelled to look at her. Given that it was she who had insisted this was the best place to look for him, this wasn't going to win her any favours or friends.

But Maureen didn't care, because suddenly it had all become only too clear. Of course he wouldn't have slept here. It was the last place he would have slept. He had run away from here the last time, ran away from the bullying boys and that bloody little Hitler, to sleep on his own, well away from them all. That was what had brought it all to a head. That was why he had been expelled by that bastard Peabody. Because Peabody had had to spend half the night looking for David in the pouring rain, and at the end of it they had found him asleep and dry in an old brick-built shed near the Jarn Mound. The Jarn! Of course! Maureen felt an almost physical leap of hope. That was where he would have slept if he had come up here. She would find him there. And then he would be safe.

*

It was the sound of the helicopter that caused him to panic. He was sitting in his den, with his arms wrapped tightly round his knees and his rucksack ready and packed. He was sitting and waiting because that was what Mother had told him to do. 'Keep calm and wait for me.'

Unlike Mum, who had left four voice messages, and in the last one told him to give himself up. Give himself up! Like a criminal. That was it. She and the police thought he was a criminal, and they were hunting him down. Like Tommy Lee Jones hunting down Harrison Ford in *The Fugitive*. He loved that film, but now it had come to life and he was in it, and he was the one fleeing for his life. And the woman who claimed to be his mum was Tommy Lee Jones.

And now, up above, he could hear a helicopter. He waited and listened. He knew that was what he had to do. To wait until the helicopter had passed over, and then to start running.

He stood up, hefted the rucksack onto his back, and waited. And then, as the helicopter's engine faded into the distance, he began to run hell for leather. He wasn't quite sure where he was going, but he knew which direction the main road was, and he knew he had to get there if he was ever to meet up with Mother.

'Here's your tea, Constable.'

Lawson put the *Oxford Mail* down, and took the mug that Bella was offering. 'Thanks.'

'You've got the short straw, babysitting me, haven't you?' She smiled her brightest smile as she said this, daring him to agree.

Wilson took a sip from his mug. It wasn't as hot as he expected. There was more milk in it than he ideally liked. But he wouldn't have dreamt of complaining about it. 'Not at all.'

'Liar', she said, and walked back into the kitchen. For the second time Wilson admired her back view. She dropped something on the floor, and Wilson continued to watch, as she bent down to search for the recalcitrant object, and then slowly raised herself up again. She turned round, and momentarily they locked eyes. Then he ducked his head and busied himself with his tea.

He heard rather than saw her walking back across the room, and only when she slumped into the armchair next to him did he look up. She was leaning back, observing him. 'Sometimes, lying is good. Better than the truth,' she said. And she crossed her right leg over her left so that it dangled dangerously close to him. Wilson, suddenly flustered, sat himself up straighter, and took a sip from his tea. Lawson flirting with him was one thing, but this was altogether something more complicated. It wasn't as if Bella Sinclair wasn't attractive. Far from it. But to have someone of her age making a play at him was unnerving.

Bella sat up too, mimicking his posture. She demurely pulled her legs close together, and leant forward earnestly. 'Tell me,' she said, as seriously as if she was interviewing him for a job. 'What made you want to become a policeman?'

Wilson did a double take, momentarily flummoxed by the sudden change. 'I guess I always did.'

'Your father wasn't a copper, then?'

'No.'

'Nor your mother?'

'No.'

'Your grandmother, then? I bet she was!'

Wilson almost laughed. 'You're teasing me!' he exclaimed. As she was, of course.

'Me, Constable! Not me!'

They both laughed. Actually, Wilson admitted silently, for all her age, she was bloody attractive. For several seconds they looked at each other, in silence. Bella smiled again. 'Is the tea all right?'

'Yes, thank you.' Wilson looked down, took a long sip as if to demonstrate how much he appreciated her tea-making skill, and then glanced up at her.

'Waste not, want not, Constable.' The smile had become a grin. 'That's what my mother always told me.'

He wasn't sure he was interested in what her mother always said, but he was finding Bella herself hard to ignore. In fact, he was returning her grin now. He was a puppy, eager to please. If he'd had a tail, it would have been wagging like crazy. Maybe Bella did fancy him. You read about it often enough in the papers – older women and younger men. Why not? He felt flattered. He felt light-headed. He felt, he suddenly realized, very tired.

He yawned. Bella was still watching him, her head now cocked to one side, but the grin had been replaced by a quizzical frown, as if she was weighing her chances. He suddenly felt unsure of himself. Suppose she did make a make a move on him? He was meant to be watching her, not.... He tried not to finish the thought. Instead, like a toddler with its security blanket, he put the mug to his lips again, almost draining it. It tasted, he realized, slightly funny. And slightly sweet. But he didn't mind. Suddenly, he didn't mind at all.

Bella Sinclair was just past the Littlemore roundabout when she finally got hold of David.

'Where the hell are you?' she demanded, her mobile clamped to her ear. 'I'm on the way. I'm coming to get you. But where are you?'

There was no immediate reply, for David was bent over in the undergrowth, panting. He was young and naturally fit. He often walked around Oxford, but running helter skelter through the undergrowth with a pack on his back was altogether different. Yet that wasn't the only reason he was temporarily speechless. He had avoided Jarn Way, and had instead followed the path that ran roughly parallel to it through the trees. He had kept running until he reached the road – and had almost run slap bang into the police. Fortunately the van carrying them was noisy, and he had stopped in the undergrowth moments before it drove past from left to right, followed by a police car. He knew the road. It led to the scout camp. That was where they must have been, so where were they off to now? He edged forward, and watched them disappear down the road, and then turn right. They were going up towards the Jarn. He bent over, trying to think what to do, and that was when his phone rang. He saw it was Mother, and answered it. But Mother was shouting, and he was panting and shaking, and the police were headed for the Jarn which meant … which meant what?

'I'm headed for the main road,' he said firmly to his mother.

'What main road?' She was still shouting.

He tried to think. 'The main road over Boars Hill. That leads to the pub. The Fox.' That was it. The name of the road. He remembered it from looking on Google Maps before he had left home. 'Foxcombe Road.'

The name of the road meant nothing to Bella, but the pub did. Roy had taken her there once. She'd let him drive her up there, and she'd let him pay. And then she'd let him take her home and had let him stay. 'Right,' she bellowed. 'Wait there, on the main road. I'll be with you in five minutes or less.'

'OK.' He thrust the phone into his anorak pocket, clipped the pocket shut with its popper, and began to jog up the road. By the time the police had finished searching up near the Jarn, he would be safe in Mother's car. In five minutes he would be safe.

Rob, the spotter, had a bad feeling. He'd woken up feeling the day wasn't going to be a good one, and right now as he gazed down over Boars Hill, with its thick green woods, he wasn't feeling any more optimistic. The guy could be anywhere. A guy in a red anorak – probably with a rucksack. That was the description, which wasn't so bad. Red was an easy colour to spot, and a rucksack too if they flew low enough, but the bloke could be anywhere in the woods. And if he stayed there, undercover, only the guys on the ground would find him. Larry, the pilot, peeled suddenly to the left. Rob looked forward briefly, wondering what the cause was. He turned further, saw that Liz, his fellow spotter, was staring intently out of her side of the helicopter, and swivelled reluctantly back to the task. They had been scouring the far side of Boars Hill – the far side, that is, if you lived in Oxford, which he did. But now Larry was making a wide looping arc across the fields to the east of Wootton.

Rob, who was on the right hand side of the helicopter, watched as the Wootton to Abingdon road slid past. A single red figure briefly caught his attention, but the red coat was a long one, a woman's. The helicopter tilted further to the left, signalling a turn towards Oxford. The Harley Davidson dealership appeared down below them and Rob stared enviously down, envious because his wife wouldn't let him have one, while Liz turned up for work every day on hers. Bitch, he thought. Bitches, they were, both of them.

They were travelling straight now, though climbing gradually, as they followed the line of the road and the contours of the hill. In fact, they were as near as dammit right over The Fox pub now. Rob couldn't see it from his side, but he knew it well enough. Below him, the open fields had given way to woods, to the large houses and larger gardens of the rich. He fought hard to concentrate, scanning the open spaces for a red man with a rucksack, but no joy. Typical! He was muttering to himself, now, giving full rein to his innate pessimism. A wild bloody goose chase!

'There he is!' The shout came from behind him, from Miss Harley Bloody Davidson herself. 'And he's getting in that car!'

David had barely shut the passenger door before the car jumped forward. Bella wrenched hard down on the wheel and rammed her foot hard to the floor, so that the rear wheels spun as the back end slid round.

'Where are we going?'

'Somewhere safe.' Bella's face was set in a mask of concentration as she accelerated the Peugeot back up towards the top of Hinksey Hill.

'But where?'

'For Christ's sake, David, not now!'

Where? She wasn't sure. She wasn't sure what she was doing at all. Except that she was rescuing David. She – not Maureen – was rescuing him, because she was his real mother, and after this he would appreciate it. She just had to get him somewhere safe, and when it had all calmed down, when she had gained David's trust, she would take him to the police station, and everything would be all right.

At the top of Hinksey Hill, she braked late at the junction and swung right, all in a single movement. A car approaching fast up the hill hooted angrily, but she stuck up her middle finger and hit the accelerator pedal hard.

'I know what you did to me.'

'Shit!' It wasn't David's statement that had caused her to swear. In fact she hardly noticed it. It was the fact that out of the corner of her eye, up to the right, she had just spotted a helicopter. The pilot was descending fast, towards them. She knew with a start what it meant.

Coming up fast on the left was the turn for Kennington. She delayed to the last moment, then hit the brakes and spun the wheel, and then she was off down Bagley Wood Road, the car bouncing around like it was a crazed kangaroo.

David raised his voice, and said it again. 'I know what you did to me!'

She flicked a glance at him. 'What do you mean?' she asked, but her head was elsewhere. How the hell was she going to get him somewhere safe now? How could she lose a helicopter?

'I know you were a drug addict.'

They were right in Kennington now. She wrenched the wheel right, squealing round the mini roundabout, towards

Radley. But where the hell then? Abingdon? Maybe, amidst the traffic and the side streets, she could lose them there.

'I know!' David was shouting now, screaming. 'I know what you did! Dad told me. My dad Jim told me. He told me everything.'

'Don't be stupid, David. The man's a liar.'

Don't be stupid. The trigger words. David began to scream. 'Stop the car!' he wailed. 'Stop!'

But she wasn't going to stop. Not until they were safe. David, however, was scrabbling at the handle of the door, trying to push it open against the slipstream. There was a sudden blast of air and Bella knew she had no choice but to stop. She hit the brakes, and the passenger door swung wildly open, so that David half fell and half rolled out. She screamed in sudden terror, but David bounced back up onto his feet like a crazed jack-in-the-box. For a second he looked at her, and then he spun round. In front of him, and dropping away from the main road, was a lane, and it was down here that he now began to run, legs pumping and arms flailing, like a marionette that had snapped its strings and was making a desperate break for freedom. Bella gunned the car into life again, and followed.

'The car's stopped' a voice was telling Holden. 'He's out. He's running off down the lane there.'

'Which bloody lane?' Holden snapped. 'I don't live in Kennington. Give me instructions!'

'Sandford Lane. And the car is following him.'

'Sandford Lane,' Holden shouted, though this was for the benefit of DS Fox, not the moron in the helicopter.

'I know it, Guv.' Just when it was needed, Fox's local knowledge and unflappability rose triumphantly to the fore. He was driving fast down the same bump-strewn Kennington street that they had travelled much earlier that morning, but this time he was driving fast, lights flashing, siren wailing, testing the vehicle's suspension to the limit.

'It's a left turn. There are trees close up on either side of the road.' The moron in the helicopter had woken up and was actually giving helpful instructions. 'I'm hovering over it,' the moron continued. 'I'll wait here and guide you in.'

'Ouch!' Holden's head hit the ceiling as Fox hit a speed bump harder than ever.

'Sorry, Guv!'

'Shut up, Sergeant!'

Up in the helicopter, Liz was straining forward in an attempt to see where the car and runner had gone. They had been out of sight for over a minute, but that hadn't stopped her scanning left to right and back again for any sign of them.

'Here come the cavalry!' Larry could see the police car now, hurtling down the hill towards them.

'Thank God,' Liz muttered under her breath, almost meaning it. For she had just seen her quarry again. Her binoculars and her eyes were now trained forward, on one spot. 'Red-coated subject in view,' she called out. 'He's standing on the parapet of the bridge! By the railway.'

Halfway down Sandford Lane, Fox brought the car to an abrupt, juddering halt. He was forced to, because another car was slewed across the road. Holden was out of her seat before the engine had died, and set off at a sprint towards the red-headed figure of Bella Sinclair, who was standing in the middle of the road looking up at her son. She was holding her hands up, though whether in surrender or supplication only she knew.

'What the hell are you doing here? And where is Wilson?'

'David rang me. I had to come. On my own.'

'Where is my constable?'

'Asleep.'

'Asleep?' The incredulity in Holden's voice was obvious.

'Do you think he'll jump?'

Bella had dropped her hands to her sides, but was still

looking up at her son. She hadn't even glanced at her questioner.

Above, the helicopter drifted closer, its rotors beating their remorseless rhythm. Holden felt its sudden downdraft, and waved it angrily away. 'Jesus,' she shouted against the engine noise, and to no one in particular, 'do they want to scare him witless?'

Holden walked a few paces forward. Fox and Bella both advanced with her. The helicopter was already wheeling away into the distance, taking its noise with it.

'Hi David,' Holden shouted. 'Do you remember me?'

'You're the police.'

'My name is Susan.'

'You've come to lock me up.' David was shouting back at her, but in a matter of fact way. 'You think I killed them.' And he raised his arms, like a diver preparing to spring off the high board. He was, Holden reckoned, some twenty-five feet above the road. If he jumped he'd damage himself badly, maybe fatally.

'I know you didn't,' she said, speaking slowly and loudly in imitation of him. 'You're a good man, David. I just need to talk to you.'

'Why should I believe you? Everyone lies to me.'

'I just want a chat, David. Just you and me, and your mother if you want her there.'

David said nothing. His arms were still raised, though they had lowered from the position of a high diver to that of a man about to be crucified. Otherwise, there was an almost unnatural silence. The helicopter had disappeared, and somewhere in the bushes to the right a blackbird was defiantly singing its song of existence.

'I'm here.' Bella had taken half a step forward. 'Mother is here. She will look after you, David, I promise.'

'You promise.' David's arms dropped further, until they were hanging down either side of his body, as if in agreement or resignation. But his voice told a different, harsher story. 'Why should I believe your promises? You abandoned me.' He raised his right hand, pointing it directly at her. 'When I was a baby, you abandoned me. You left me. You betrayed me.' His voice had reached a crescendo now.

But as Holden opened her mouth to intervene, she became aware of other noises. A car was approaching from behind them. She turned and saw it skid to an untidy halt beyond the others. Two figures got out: Lawson from the driver's seat, and Maureen. Thank God! Holden turned back. 'Here's your mother now, David. I promise she'll be there at any meetings we have. I promise.'

There was the noise of a train too, but so distant that it didn't immediately register with any of them.

Certainly not with Maureen who was running towards them as fast as her squat body would allow. And not with Holden who had turned to see how David was reacting to Maureen's arrival. And not with Bella either, whose brain was screaming at the injustice of life and the ingratitude of her son.

Maureen was panting as she pushed past Holden and stopped just in front of them all.

'David,' she shouted, through the gulps of air. 'I want you to keep very calm.'

'Mum!'

'Do you understand, David? Keep very calm.'

'They are going to arrest me, Mum.'

'I won't let them.' The words were firm, decisive, allowing (she hoped) no argument.

'They are going to lock me up. They think I killed Dad, and that other man. And Nan Nan. They think I murdered her too. My Nan Nan!' His voice rose to a crescendo of pain, as he strove to be heard over the noise approaching from his right.

'You didn't kill them, David, did you?' She shouted back. 'So they can't lock you up!'

But the logic of this argument had no impact on David. 'I

won't let them lock me up. I won't.' And he turned round, and slowly raised his arms up high again.

Everything then happened in slow motion, or that was how it seemed to Lawson, rooted to the spot by her car.

Bella was shouting: 'Don't be so bloody stupid, David!'

The Oxford-bound express was greedily devouring the space that separated it from the bridge.

Holden, Fox, and Maureen were setting off at a run towards the bridge, but doomed never to get there in time.

David's arms were almost vertical. Against the pale blue sky, Lawson could see his whole body quiver uncertainly in the air.

And then, even above the roar of the oncoming train, Lawson heard Maureen wail in agony. She was shaking her arms. 'I killed them, David!' she screamed. 'I killed the bastards. So the police won't lock you up.'

David may have heard. He half turned, and for the briefest of moments his eyes locked with Maureen's. And then his wavering body lost all balance, and Lawson saw him fall forward into the path of the train.

EPILOGUE

They sat either side of a featureless rectangular table – Holden and Fox nearest the door, Maureen Wright and her solicitor (disconcertingly surnamed Constable) opposite. The room itself was featureless too – a door that might briefly, in the 1980s, have seemed modern, a single double-glazed window some six feet from the floor (and so offering only delinquent basketball players a view), and a flooring so inoffensive that Holden, who had been in there often enough, wouldn't, if asked, have been able to describe its colour, let alone its pattern. They sat on moulded plastic chairs with metal legs, and both Fox and Constable had a sheaf of paperwork on the table in front of them.

Holden had already completed the formalities – pressed the record button, announced the date and time, and listed the persons present – but there was a hiatus of several seconds before she asked her first question.

'Maureen, yesterday, at a time of intense pressure, you claimed that you killed Paul Greenleaf and your husband Jim Wright.'

'Yes.'

'I am now asking you to confirm and clarify that statement.' She paused. Maureen was looking directly at her, head up. 'Did you kill Paul Greenleaf?'

'Yes, I did.'

'And did you kill your husband, Jim Wright?'

'Oh, yes. I most certainly did.'

'Tell me how you killed Mr Greenleaf.'

This question surprised her. 'How? You know how.'

'I need you to tell me.'

'Why?'

'In case you're lying.'

'Why should I be lying?'

Holden leant forward. 'You wouldn't be the first parent who lied to protect a son or daughter.'

Maureen glanced across at her solicitor. He nodded. She turned back and leant forward too, so that her face was barely eighteen inches from Holden's. 'I used a piece of garden wire, stretched between two trees. It caught him round the throat. At least I think it did, only it was hard to see clearly, and I wasn't actually that bothered. What I was bothered about was beating the bastard with a hammer until I was sure he was dead.' She leant back, and folded her arms. 'Is that enough detail?'

'And your husband?'

'I only needed to hit him once. He went down like a sack of potatoes.'

'And then what?'

'I thought he was dead. I dragged him onto the rails. I wanted to be sure. I wanted to watch him be obliterated.'

She fell quiet, and a smile crept across her face as she remembered. She shook her head as if she could barely believe what she was remembering, and she laughed. 'Then he gave a groan. Christ, he didn't half make me jump. If I'd had the hammer with me still, I'd have given him another thump, but I'd had to put it down while I dragged him onto the tracks, the fat bastard. What I did have in my pocket was some garden wire. In case I'd needed to tie his hands with it. It's very handy stuff, garden wire. So I pulled his stupid bloody woollen hat over his face in case he opened his eyes, and I looped the wire under a sleeper and then round his leg several times. His left leg I think it was. And then I sat on top of him. I could hear a train, so I waited, and when I saw its lights and I knew for sure it was coming straight for us,

I got off him and walked over to the bushes. It was dark, but I could see enough. I saw him clutching at his hat, trying to pull it off his face. I saw him stagger to his feet, and I saw and heard him die.' She had a faraway look on her face, the look of someone remembering, and enjoying the memory.

She rocked forward. 'Is that enough detail, Inspector?'

Holden flinched. 'Yes, thank you.'

'Is that it, then?'

'Is there anything else you'd like to tell me?'

Maureen frowned. 'I don't think so.'

'Did you kill Nanette too?'

The question seemed to startle her. 'Nanette, no of course not. Why would I?'

'Money, maybe?'

Maureen eyes narrowed. They were hard eyes, Holden reckoned, behind which a formidable woman lay. A tough woman, capable of who knows what. Lying certainly. And more if necessary. 'If,' Maureen said, 'you want my opinion, I think Jim did it.'

'What makes you think that?'

'Like you say, money. Jim was short of it, whereas his mother had money in the bank. The only problem was the nursing home fees were racing their way through her savings like a bush fire.'

'So you knew this, but said nothing?'

'Hey, that isn't what I said. I don't know. It's just that it makes sense.'

'I need proof.'

Maureen considered this for at least ten seconds. She sat back and massaged the bridge of her nose with her thumb and forefinger. 'Not proof. Intuition. Woman's intuition.'

'Intuition doesn't tend to stand up in court.'

'Well it bloody well should do.'

Holden smiled. 'I agree. But unfortunately I don't make the law. I merely enforce it.'

Maureen grunted, unimpressed. An uncertain silence descended.

Holden looked down and inspected her fingers. Not that there was much to inspect on them. She wore no rings, the nails were cut short and were unpainted, and there were no discernible spots or lumps that might have been worth inspection. Eventually, she raised her head: 'You see, Maureen, I have another theory. Would you like to hear it?'

Maureen shrugged. 'If you want.'

'My theory is that you are lying through your teeth.'

Maureen returned Holden's stare. If there was any emotion in her face, it was well hidden. She said nothing. Cat and mouse watching each other, though who was cat and who was mouse was hard to say.

'My theory is this,' Holden continued. 'That you are lying to protect your son. That you know that it was he who put the morphine in the whisky flask. I also have a theory that it wasn't you who killed your husband or Greenleaf, but David. And you know that too. And yet you are prepared to lie for him, and to take his punishment, to prove that you love him.'

Maureen shook her head in an exaggerated gesture of disbelief. 'That's plain ridiculous. You haven't a shred of evidence to link David to any of the deaths. And why on earth would he have killed Greenleaf? What's his motive, Inspector?'

'Love for his mother, of course, Maureen. That is to say, love for his birth mother, Bella.' Holden let this sink in for several seconds, and wondered if perhaps Maureen really hadn't considered this as a possibility. Then she continued. 'Greenleaf got Bella suspended from work after she laughed off his sexual performance. She told David about it, and he killed Greenleaf for her. It seems a strong motive to me.'

'But you have no evidence.'

'What makes you think that? David ran away, after all. That implies guilt, if you ask me.'

'Jesus wept!' Maureen slammed the palm of her hand on the

table. 'It could imply anything. Fear. Confusion. But actually, David ran away because of Jim. Do you know what that bastard did? He told David the truth.'

She paused, checking that she had got Holden's attention. She had. 'The other Sunday David told us that he had met his birth mother, his real mother as he called her. You can't imagine how much that hurt me. But he was so excited. I tried to be calm. I asked him if he was sure. Sometimes David is easily led and I was genuinely worried that he had somehow got confused. It was the last thing that I wanted to hear, but I tried to not to show how upset I was. "She's wonderful!" David kept saying at the top of his voice, and there was such a grin all over his face. Only Jim soon wiped that off. "Wonderful?" he screamed. "Your mother wasn't wonderful, you stupid fool. Why do you think we got you, you bloody idiot. Why? Well I'll tell you why. Because your so-called real mother was a crack head, and so was your useless father. The reason we were lumbered with you, was because both of them were constantly doped up to the eyeballs."

'David went crazy, calling him a liar, but Jim hadn't finished. "I'm not a liar, David. Just the opposite. I'm going to tell you the truth. Listen. I'll tell you what happened. One day, when you were a little toddler, the social services came round to your parents' flat, and they found you lying on the floor eating cat food. Out of the cat's bowl! That's the sort of mother you had before you came to us! She let you eat cat food, and she let you shit all over the floor like a dirty little kitten." What he said … it was unforgiveable. I had spent a lifetime building my son David up, and in a few moments of utter spite he destroyed him. Because as far as I was concerned, whoever this other woman was, David was my son. I tell you, when David ran off down the road screaming, if I'd had a gun I'd have killed that husband of mine then and there.

'I finally saw what a complete bastard I had married. I saw how I could never trust him. And, of course, you were right about those photos. They had really freaked me. Ask Ania Gorski. She told me about them later that day. She rang me up before Sunday lunch in hysterics, so I'd agreed to meet her. We'd hit it off at Sunnymede. She was very good to Nanette. She told me how they'd taken these photographs of her and Vickie on Saturday night, and how she was really worried about Vickie because of the way Greenleaf had been looking at her. I knew I had to do something to protect Vickie. So I killed them both.'

'But not Nanette?'

'No. And neither did David kill her.'

'How can you know that?'

'A mother knows, Inspector. I know David. David doesn't lie to me. He never did. He topped up her flask with whisky that Sunday as he always did, but he told me he never put anything else in it. And I believe him. He had no reason to kill her. And in his own way, he was very upset when she died. He doesn't show it, the way you or I might, but I know he was upset. He couldn't have killed her. You've got to believe me.'

Holden leant over and clicked the recorder button off. She stood up, and brushed a crumb off the sleeve of her jacket. She gave the faintest of smiles to the woman who had just admitted two murders. 'Actually, Maureen, in my experience, any man or any woman is capable of murder. And that would include David. But as it happens, I agree with you. I don't think David killed Nanette.'

'How are you feeling, David?'

The room into which Holden and Fox had just walked was significantly more comfortable than the one from which they had come. There were two people there already. David Wright was sitting on a sofa; he was wearing brown whipcord trousers and a navy-blue cardigan zipped right to his neck. He was rocking ever so slightly backwards and forwards. Next to him, her hands folded across her stomach, was Jaz Green; she wore jeans, a pink T-Shirt and denim jacket, and she looked up at the sound of their entry, anxiety smeared across her face.

'He'd be feeling a lot better if he wasn't stuck here.'

Holden acknowledged the criticism with a nod of her head.

'You were very lucky, David.' He didn't look up, but she continued nevertheless. 'For a moment, when you fell onto the track I thought ... I thought....' But what she thought refused to materialize.

David looked up now. 'You thought I was dead.'

'Yes.'

'I wish I was.'

Holden nodded again, but again found she had nothing to say.

'What will happen to Mum?' he asked. 'Can I see her?'

'Later. But first I need you to answer some questions. Is that all right?'

'Yes.'

'Do you remember when your Nan died?'

'Yes. On a Tuesday night. I was listening to the football.'

'Two days before that, she came home for Sunday lunch, didn't she, like she always did. And you filled up her flask, David, didn't you. Like you always did.'

'With whisky.'

'Did you add anything to the whisky, David?'

'No.'

'Not even just to help her sleep, maybe?'

'I've told you before. No.'

'Are you absolutely sure, David?'

Jaz made a guttural noise that signified disgust. 'He's said no, he means no. He's a good lad. He wouldn't have hurt his Nan.'

'I know it's difficult,' Holden said, trying to be sympathetic.

But Jaz Green had had enough. 'No you fucking well don't. You've no idea what it's like for him. I certainly don't know, and I've known him since he was little.' The two women eyed each other.

It was David who interrupted. 'Are you going to lock me up?'

Holden turned towards him. 'No. In fact, Jaz can take you home.'

'Are you going to lock Mum up?'

'Would you like to come and visit her tomorrow?'

David stood up, ready to go. 'I visit her on Wednesdays and Sundays,' he said, and he walked towards the door. Jaz got up and followed him out.

'We found some interesting things in your flat, Bella.'

'What were you doing there? You can't just walk into my flat and—'

'We had a search warrant, Bella, so we have every right to turn your flat upside down if we so wish.'

'Well, fuck you.'

The woman sitting on Maureen's left flinched perceptibly. Holden hadn't come across Ms Althea Potter before. She was dressed the part – dark suit, white blouse, discreet necklace and earrings – but Holden sensed a fragility in her.

'We found this, for example, in your kitchen bin.'

Fox leant forward and placed a polythene evidence bag on the table. Inside was a small white cardboard box, with a printed label on it.

'Haven't you got better things to do than go through my rubbish?'

'On the label it says temazepam.'

'So?'

'We found traces of temazepam in Detective Constable Wilson's bloodstream.'

'Did you, now.'

'My guess is you added it to the cup of tea you made for him.'

'Really?'

'Because you wanted him to go to sleep so you could go and find David.'

'And my guess is that you haven't got any proof for any of

this. And besides, your detective constable is OK isn't he? He just had a nice long sleep.'

Holden gestured with her right hand, and Fox placed another polythene bag on the table with another white box inside it. 'We also found this box in one of your drawers. It once contained morphine capsules, though there's only one left now.'

This time Bella said nothing. She turned briefly to Ms Potter for support, but the solicitor was writing something on her notepad.

'Did you give the rest of it to Nanette Wright? Did you put it in her flask?'

'No.'

Althea Potter looked up, and adjusted her glasses. 'Unless I am mistaken, Inspector, this is all only circumstantial evidence.'

Holden turned to her right. 'We have another piece of evidence, don't we, Sergeant? Two in fact.'

Fox leant forward again. This time it was his turn to speak. 'We found this photograph in your book. You remember the book, don't you? *Unless*, by Carol Shields. With all those funny chapter titles. Well, the photograph was inside it, at the beginning of the chapter titled "Forthwith".'

Fox laid two more polythene bags on the table, one containing a paperback copy of the book, and the other a small photograph. Bella ignored the book, and picked up the photograph. Its faded colour betrayed its age. A small child, maybe six months old, sat on the floor. It was looking slightly to the side, directly perhaps at someone trying to catch and keep its attention while the photographer focused.

'Who is that?' Holden asked quietly.

'David.' There was no delay in the answer. 'I want to keep it,' she said firmly.

'It's evidence, I'm afraid, but I'll see if I can have a copy made.'

'It's mine. You can have a copy. I want the original.'

'It's only yours because you stole it.'

For the first time in the interview, a look of uncertainty crept into Bella's eyes. Holden saw it, and pressed on. 'You stole it from Nanette Wright. This was her photo. Maureen has confirmed it.'

'You can't believe that murdering bitch.'

'Vickie has confirmed it too.'

There was a silence. It was almost over. They had reached the end game. Holden sensed it. Even Fox could feel it.

Bella picked up the plastic cup of water that was sitting in front of her, and drank it all. 'That woman was a miserable cow. She was always complaining. I shouldn't have called Maureen a bitch. Maureen is OK. It was Nanette who was the bitch. Maureen, David, Vickie, even that miserable arse Jim visited her regularly, took her out every Sunday, and she wasn't the least bit grateful. She was particularly unpleasant about David. Used to call him a stupid spastic. Not to his face, of course. But that's how she described him to me. Anyway, one time after I'd had to clean her up after she'd messed her bed, she grabbed my arm, and said she wanted to show me something. So she showed me this photo of David as a baby. Of course, I recognized it. It was the only photo I ever remember us taking of him. It was my child.' Bella stopped talking, and sank her face into her hands. Holden waited. Outside, from down the corridor, there came the sound of laughter, that soared and dived like an out-of-control submachine gun. Holden thought she recognized DC Rachman, and vowed to strangle him later.

Inside the room, a huge sob erupted from somewhere deep within Bella, causing her trim figure to heave and shudder. Then she looked up and rubbed at her eyes. 'Imagine! David, the big gawky guy who came to visit her, was my son. Christ that was a shock. Not that I told her. Not that I had a chance to tell her, because she then started to spout off about how David wasn't really her grandson. "He's adopted," she said. "You can see he's not our flesh and blood. He's not like Vickie.

But what can you expect? His mother was a slut. A drug-addled slut. Tell me, Bella," she said, looking straight into my eyes, "what sort of chance does a boy have when his mother feeds him cat food off the floor?"'

Bella picked up the plastic cup in front of her, realized it was empty, and crumpled it in her fist, before tossing it onto the floor.

'So I decided to do two things. To teach the vicious old cow a lesson, and somehow to make it up to David. To get to know him. To show him that I wasn't bad. To get him to understand that I'd been through a rough time then, but that now I was OK. I wanted to be his mother. Do you understand?'

'So you put morphine in her whisky flask?'

'It seemed like a good way to do it.'

'And how did you get the morphine?'

'From my flat.' Holden made a face, indicating that this was hardly an answer. 'It wasn't difficult. I often used to nick the odd pill or capsule. In case it came in useful. Occasionally, I'd give them to friends.'

'But stuff like morphine is under lock and key and carefully monitored.'

Bella gave a snort of derision. 'Sleight of hand! I'd help hand the drugs out sometimes. Fran or someone else would hand them to me, and I'd administer them, but if she gave me two, it was easy enough to slip one into my pocket and give the patient only one. They were so dopey they didn't notice. Anyway, my next shift I brought some in, and when I was tidying her bed and stuff, I opened some of the capsules into her flask. To be honest, I didn't think it would kill her. But was a very nice surprise when it did.'

'Even though it put David in the frame?'

'That was unfortunate.' She pursed her lips. 'I hadn't realized that he was the one he who filled the flask for her at home.'

'So, just for the record, you admit that you wilfully murdered Nanette Wright?'

Ms Potter stretched her hand across her client, motioning her to silence. 'Please don't try and put words into the mouth of my client, Inspector. What she actually said was that she wanted to teach the vicious old cow a lesson. I am fairly sure those were her words. She has also stated that she did not believe that the dosage of morphine she put in the hip flask would kill Nanette. That is all she is going to say for now.'

'I merely wanted to establish—'

But the not so fragile Ms Althea Potter had had enough. 'My client has said all she is going to say until we have had a chance to discuss the matter further. I suggest you formally charge her, or release her.'

It is 7.45 p.m. on 21 December. Mrs Jane Holden and her daughter sit in the dining room of the Shillingford Bridge Hotel and watch in silence as the waitress removes their plates. The dining room is quiet, too, the other occupants are speaking in hushed, intimate tones. Several tables have been placed together for, presumably, an office party, but if the staff attending have arrived, they are still lubricating themselves in the bar. Apart from the Holdens, there are five other couples of various sorts taking advantage of the last Monday before Christmas, treating themselves to a restful meal out before the frantic assault of last-minute shopping, demented cooking and dreaded relatives overwhelms them. Not that this is the type of festive season that awaits Jane and Susan. There is no family beyond themselves, and a quiet, even lonely Christmas awaits them.

'I do miss Karen,' Susan says. Christmas has that effect, making you miss those who will not be there. She looks down, not able to look at her mother, but she yearns to be comforted by her, to be hugged and told that it will be all right.

Jane merely nods. 'I know.'

Susan's eyes grow moist. A tear runs down her right cheek, but she makes no attempt to rub it.

'You do know that Karen would want you to move on.' It is not a hug, but advice that Mrs Holden gives.

'Yes.'

'We are not designed to live alone.' Susan looks up, and finds her mother looking at her with a glare of such intensity that she flinches. 'Believe me. I know.'

'You do?'

'Perhaps you should join a dating agency.'

'Mother!'

'Or take out a small ad. Get yourself out there.'

This time DI Holden is speechless.

'It would make me happy. If you would just find someone. Then I would die happy.'

'Die happy? We're meant to be having a nice evening out....'

'And I would live happy too, for however much longer I've got.'

'God!' Holden picks up her glass and lifts it to her mouth, but there is only a dribble of white wine left.

The waitress appears at the side of the table, bearing coffee and chocolates. They relapse into silence until she is out of earshot, and then Mrs Holden tactfully changes the subject.

'So what do you think will happen to Bella?'

This is more comfortable ground for her daughter – violent death. 'I expect she will plead involuntary manslaughter. Throw herself on the mercy of the judge. Play the mother card – how David will need her now that Jim is dead and Maureen is likely to be in prison for a long stretch.'

'Poor Maureen. She was only protecting her family.'

'She killed two people. And she knew what she was doing.'

'But who will look after David and Vickie?'

'Christ, Mother. I'm a detective, not a social worker. I'm paid to solve crimes, not save the world.'

'I know. But I can't help feeling—'

'Feeling?' The word explodes across the room. Several pairs of eyes turn involuntarily, and then turn away as Susan

Holden sweeps the room with a ferocious scowl. Then she focuses her baleful gaze on her mother. 'Feeling is a luxury I can't afford. Not as long as I'm doing this job.'

Mrs Holden says nothing for half a minute. She has too much experience in dealing with emotional fury. Not just recently from her daughter, but long before that, from her husband. Eventually, she speaks softly, so softly that her daughter is barely able hear what she says. 'To feel is to be alive.'

Detective Inspector Susan Holden is briefly tempted to make a dismissive remark about people who read too many fortune cookies, but instead she looks across at her mother and bursts into tears.